BRIANNA

SOME CALL IT MAGIC,
SHE CALLS IT LOVE

INTERNATIONAL BESTSELLING AUTHOR
T N TRAYNOR

T. N. Traynor
Publishing

Book cover designed by Maria Pagtalunan
mariachristinepagtalunan@gmail.com

First Printed Edition, England March 2022

ISBN: 9798432028426

Contents

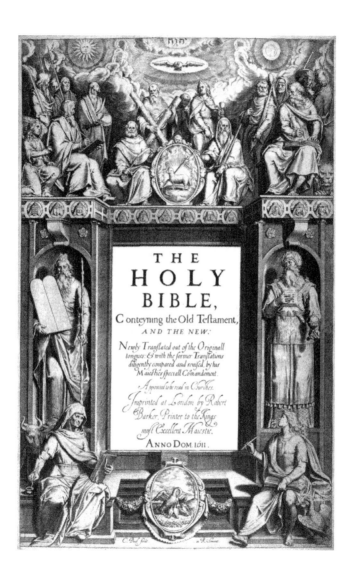

THE
HOLY
BIBLE,

Conteyning the Old Testament,
AND THE NEW:

Newly Translated out of the Originall
tongues: & with the former Translations
diligently compared and reuised, by his
Maiesties speciall Cõmandement.

Appointed to be read in Churches.

Imprinted at London by Robert
Barker, Printer to the Kings
most Excellent Maiestie.

ANNO DOM. 1611.

Dedication

This story is dedicated to El Shaddai, my Strong Tower.

Brianna's story was inspired by Romans 8:28

And we know that all things work together for good to them that love God, to them who are the called according to His purpose.

I would like to thank the following people:

Nigel, thank you so much for all your hard work and invaluable advice during the editing process, I don't know what I'd do without you.

Julie, thank you so much for being my first BETA reader and for your amazing feedback and encouragement.

Maria, thank you for your wonderful book cover, and your unending patience with all my amends.

Andrew, what can I say? You are my rock.

Story Setting

THE RESTORATION 1660 - 1666

Charles Stuart (later Charles II) arrived back in London on his 30th birthday, after already living an eventful life. During the English Civil War, at the age of fifteen, he fled England to live with his mother's cousin, Louis XIV King of France. After Oliver Cromwell's death, he offered all he could, to whoever he could, to ensure his placement on the Throne of England. He offered a pardon to everyone involved with his father Charles I's, execution, except for the fifty-nine men who signed his father's death warrant. Tolerant forgiveness stretches only so far after all.

At first, the people rejoiced, for life under the harsh whip of Oliver Cromwell had seen poverty and unrest rise due his strict religious policies.

Cromwell, a Puritan, believed that everyone should lead their lives according to what was written in the Bible, convinced that if you worked hard you got to Heaven. Cromwell closed theaters believing them to be pointless enjoyment. He also closed many inns, pushing people to lose their only income. If boys played football on Sundays, they risked being whipped. Women caught doing unnecessary work on the Holy Day would be put in stocks. If caught swearing you received a fine, if you repeated the offense you were sent to prison. Even going for a walk on Sundays carried a hefty fine. Cromwell believed women should dress in a particular manner and makeup was completely banned. But he is probably best remembered for being the man who banned Christmas. In June 1647, Parliament passed an ordinance banning Christmas, Easter and Whitsun festivities, services and celebrations, including festivities in the home, with fines for non-compliance. Soldiers, under orders, went around the streets and took by force any food being cooked for Christmas celebrations. It is fair to say, that by the time of his death in 1658, he was truly hated by the people. Not yet sixty, his life was cut short when he caught a fever. His war strategies, beliefs and determination left a stamp on English history that split many a family. Had he been tyrant or savior?

So when Charles II was put on the throne the people rejoiced!

However, their joy was relatively short-lived, for although he had been raised a Catholic, Charles II gaily enjoyed his days encouraging fornication and general depravity, everything that Cromwell had fought so hard to eradicate. Such extravagance cost money, and soon new taxes rained down upon people who could ill-afford them. And so England continued to fall into dark days of oppression. The end of the Civil War might have stopped the killing, but it left behind a bitter land. Soldiers, who survived, returned to their homes to poverty and hardship, the war having depleted both money and spirit from good, honest, God-fearing folk.

Amongst other things, the new king had promised that a tolerant religious settlement would be sought. Despite Charles's promise to accept Presbyterians into the Anglican fold, as detailed in the Worcester House Declaration, enthusiasts from both left and right wrecked every compromise.

The bishops returned to Parliament, a new prayer book was authorized, and repressive acts passed to compel conformity. Town governors were put out of their places, and nearly one-fifth of all clergymen became deprived of their livings. Authority in the localities was now firmly in the hands of the gentry.

The Conventicle Act (1664), barred Nonconformists

(Dissenters) from holding separate church services, and the Five Mile Act, prohibited dispossessed ministers from even visiting their former congregations.

The Great Plague of London (1664–66), and the Great Fire of London (1666), were interpreted as divine judgments against a sinful king and nation.

Hardship brings either the worst or the best out of people. Many looked to God to deliver them, while others forged ahead determined to create their own fortunes. From 1640 Britain was the most dominant slave trader, transporting Africans to America. Forging ahead with foreign enterprises Britain reaped in wealth from other countries. These seekers of wealth and fame did not care for the sorrow they created, nor did they share the wealth when they returned. Instead, the gap between the rich and the poor deepened, as did resentment and the wide-spread belief that England was slipping further and further away from God.

Weaving its way through civil war, religious fanatics and decadent kings was an abhorrent evil that was driving terror into everyday folk, the upsurge of witch hunters. In 1604, King James I made an amendment to the Witchcraft Act, to include anyone who made a pact with Satan. This meant the first half of the 17th century became a time filled with fear of the unknown, and the possibility that someone misunderstanding you or what you did, may lead you to the ducking chair or burning stake, whether innocent or not. The rich made merry, while oppression crushed the poor and drove them to fear everyone and everything.

Into this dark time of sorrows and ungodly acts, two women walked, bringing with them the Word of God and hope. Their names were Rhiannon and Brianna.

Prologue

ONCE UPON A TIME, LONG, LONG AGO in a land called Cymru there lived the most beautiful woman the world had ever seen – Rhiannon, daughter of Simeon the Fair and his beloved wife Estella. Some, who lived in fear and far from God, called her mother Estella a witch, for rumors of her magic had spread throughout the valleys.

Rhiannon's life started full of blessings and rich comfort. Married at sixteen to Aeron O'Byrne the Valiant, Rhiannon traveled to his kingdom across the seas to Éire, where they lived for several years in love and peace. In the year of our Lord 1644, to add to their joy, a daughter was given. They named her Brianna the Gracilis, due to her tiny size. All was well with life, until one fateful day when Aeron was thrown from his horse and fell down a cliff to meet his most untimely and bloody death.

The people of Éire immediately turned upon Rhiannon, claiming her witchcraft had caused the horse to rear. For legend claims that Rhiannon had inherited her mother's blessing, but those who saw her miracles accused her of weaving magic. Around the manor walls crowds ranted that God had judged her practices evil, and wrought His anger upon their young lord causing his death.

One true friend to Aeron, who knew his lord had loved his lady true, whisked both mother and child away before the villagers could tie them to the stake they hastened to build. In a day full of eerie fog and salty tears, he bore them safely across the water, rowing them back to her homeland of Cymru.

Once her foot touched the shore, the friend wished her well and abandoned them to their fate, his duty to his former lord

11

complete, his conscience now clear. For unbeknown to any but him, the man was sure it was his sudden shout that had driven his lord's horse to startle by cliff's edge.

Rhiannon thought to return to her parents' manor, but upon the path home she learned the place was no more. King's men from England had heard rumors of Estella's magic, and had burned both folk and buildings to the ground. Witch Hunter's, appointed by mysterious envoys, reputed to be the hand of first King James I, and then later King Charles I, flooded the land like cockroaches, scurrying into every nook and cranny searching out anyone who potentially might be called witch or Devil worshiper. Their austere black attire alone was enough to strike fear wherever they ventured. Riding upon massive black stallions (reputedly funded by the king's purse) the men raced from town to village with killing intent, their hounds ever before them. All eagerly seeking the heavy purse each town's magistrate would pay them, for finding, torturing and ultimately killing anyone considered to be a witch.

And so a game of hide-and-seek began... which mother and daughter would have to master well to avoid the hangman's noose, ducking chair or worst of all – the burning stake. For though the names of witch hunters changed over time; their fervor of killing witches remained. Careful not to show their power to any but true believers, they trod the lesser used paths and spent most of their time in solitude, bar the animals that often flocked to them.

Years passed and the baby girl grew into a fine beauty in the image of her mother. Despite their nomadic lifestyle and lack of permanent friends both so-called 'witches' were content and happy. Yet the land was full of grief, from Civil War widows and misplaced and forgotten soldiers, to the purging of Catholics and the closure of theaters, Oliver Cromwell had created a contention amongst the people that was slow to fade.

And what did the people *genuinely* think about King Charles II? Now on the throne, most commoners, (who had rejoiced at his coronation) muttered under their breath and spat when his name was mentioned, their savior he was not!

———————————————

In the year of our Lord 1664, Brianna acknowledged her twentieth year not with merriment, but with grave earnestness.

For in the last full moon just gone, they had run across a path the current witch hunters followed. Now all had changed. Urgency crawled under their skin. Their feet became blistered and swollen from running. It was a time that marked change, for they acutely perceived that death chased at their heels, for the *Black Wolf* was on their trail.

Chapter 1

AUTUMN, FLUSHED WITH a mix of warm and brisk winds, beckoned to Brianna's soul. Winter was cruel, but for now vibrant colors sprayed the land with beauty and the gay abandonment of one last party, before closing up against the freeze of wintertime.

Turbulence bubbled within her chest as she raced across the bracken-filled moorlands that separated Hawkes End and Coventre. Contradictory emotions and thoughts made the pulse in her temple beat with painful thuds. To run without clogs or sack-bound feet nurtured a feeling of freedom, while all the time the chains of confusion manifested thorns within her soul. Her muscles, used to daily labor and periods of long walking, were strong and carried her swiftly. Free! Her life before her was full of promise and dreams, was that not true? Mama was wrong! God would surely not take her mother's life before the following spring!

It must be said that Mama's previous visions had all come true, but she must have misunderstood *this* message from God. *He wouldn't allow wicked men to slay His faithful child... would he?*

The remnants of joy subsided. Brianna's steps slowed. Above, dark clouds gathered, heavy and menacing, pregnant with rain. She hitched up her heavy skirts, and danced across the stepping-stones of the shallow river. The stones' cold seeped through her soles, chilling her body, distressing her mind.

"It can't be true!" she cried to the skies, as she reached the other side.

She waited for an answer, none came.

Tears of frustration poured from the corners of her eyes, she wiped them away with angry swipes, knocking back her long, raven black hair. Without pins or hat her velvety tresses tumbled freely around her heart-shaped face.

"We are your servants, Lord. Please, do not hand us over to evildoers."

The rustle of wind racing through bracken was her only answer.

In a rare moment of self-pity, Brianna gave in to tears and sorrow. Crouched on the ground, she hugged her knees tight to her body and wept. It went against everything she believed, everything she had been taught, but the *thought* of living without Mama was too painful, too raw.

Words from the Holy Book floated through her muddled mind.

> *Yea, though I walk through the valley of the shadow of death, I will fear no evil: for thou art with me; thy rod and thy staff they comfort me.* (1)

Fast followed by…

> *Let your conversation be without covetousness; and be content with such things as ye have: for He hath said, I will never leave thee, nor forsake thee.* (2)

Comfort, as tangible as an embrace of affection, penetrated Brianna's distress. The Lord would never leave nor forsake her *or* Mama, for His word is yea and amen!

Mama told her often… fear is the doorway through which Satan walks in. Fear is the stealer of peace, and that crippling hindrance which births doubt.　She would *not* succumb. Through *His* strength, she would overcome.

Brianna rose, stood straight and reached for the heavens with outspread arms and countenance emanating hope.　Rain, slow only for a moment before passing into downpour, splashed against her upturned face.

Heartbeat thuds, skips and misses – as if her life had paused.

With the shock and jolt of a heavily beaten drum, hatred for the Black Wolf knocked upon her heart's door demanding entrance, as it was prone to do these days with increasing frequency.　She had to fight harder than ever before to block its entrance.

Chapter 2

BENEDICT EVERLEIGH, son of Benjamin and Mary Everleigh, wrought fear in every place he visited. He knew it well, carried it in his countenance closer than his shirt. Fear was advantageous. It forced people to loosen their tongues and turn traitor on their neighbors and friends.

As was their custom, since they'd started on this crusade five years ago, Benedict rode up front; his brothers, abreast of each other, flanked his horse. A black arrow-head of righteousness they formed, piercing the way forward, seeking out darkness, delivering the Light of the Lord wherever they went. Caleb and Levi, brave and loyal bloodhounds, ran ahead of Benedict, ever watchful.

As they entered the city through one of the remaining gateways, all three brothers placed their black, beak-shaped leather masks over their faces. They had skirted London on their last visit, for news of the plague had reached them. Although the capital lay three days behind them, they would take no chances with the Black Death.

Once, Coventre had been a booming walled city, industry and riches had overflowed, but with the demise of favor a lackluster had slipped amongst the ancient cobbled streets, its grand buildings and churches. The demolished wall, which once had offered safety and shelter to the Parliamentarians, was now a symbol of loss and vulnerability – a submission to a king they never wanted. Loyalists themselves, the brothers observed no pity for the defiant city.

Benedict had been thirty-three when he'd received this calling from God, the age of Christ when he ended his human life upon the cross. He had noted that fact and buried it in his spirit as one of the many signs that he'd received confirmation from God. Benedict's ambition of following his father into church ministry died five years ago, his life now forfeit to serving God in this most righteous way. God had given him a new directive, making him drop his earthly dreams of having his own parish and comely wife: find and destroy every witch in the great kingdom of England. *'Cleanse the land of evil doers'* commanded the Lord, *'restore to me a place in which I can dwell.'*

Matthew and Nathaniel never heard directly from God, but so faith-filled were his brothers, that they would follow their eldest brother into the depths of Hell if he told them that's where they needed to go.

Benedict saw a merchant raise his hand to cover his lips (as if a hand would hide his gossiping from the Lord), the merchant leaned closer and whispered to the man by his side. Benedict caught the end of his comment and upon hearing the name *Black Wolf* his lips did twitch, causing a smile that some might describe as a sneer. Their reputation preceded them, this was propitious. Things would run smoothly here, as they searched out possible witches and Devil worshipers.

Two witches in particular he determined to interrogate. Mother and daughter named Rhiannon and Brianna; he'd been catching whispers of them for the last two years. Almost a full-moon ago, in Winchefter, the people had called these two vagabonds 'Miracle Women,' he had listened well, and filled many vellum pages of his commonplace book regarding their so-called miracles. They never even pretended to pray before healing the sick! Heretics both! Not to worry, he would have them soon; he could feel it in his bones.

Chapter 3

THEY'D LEFT THE CITY of Coventre way before the rooster's crow. Their secretive departure aided by the fact that the city's surrounding wall had been demolished, by order of Charles II only two years earlier – in revenge against the city that had forbidden entrance to his father, and had given the Parliamentarians a stronghold during the Civil War. A few of the gate-towers still remained and a guard within, but with the knocking down of the wall, they were able to pass along narrow alleyways and make their way unnoticed out into the grasslands beyond. With many a furtive glance they were sure that they had left unnoticed. Yesterday, they had spoken several times, quite loudly, that they planned to head to Nottingham. To reinforce this falsehood they had crept out of the northern part of the city, and only when they had gone a fair distance did they turn and head south.

It said much to their lifestyle that they were used to navigating the pathways by moon's gentle glimmer. Normally, Brianna would pass a word or two of complaint against the early hour, or the heaviness of their worldly belongings. But not today! She had been up and dressed before Rhiannon stirred. If she could have her way, they would out-run her mother's prophecy.

"Slow down child, for we will surely step into a rut and turn an ankle if you keep up this pace."

Brianna slowed, but her mother caught sound of her heavy sigh.

"They travel the highways and byways on stallions. Do you really think we can outrun them? Come child, you know 'tis only the cloak of God's mercy that has shielded us from them thus far. We walked right passed them in the city of Winchefter, our faces clearly visible to them, and theirs to us. If our lives were not in God's hands, they would have bound us then."

"I just do not understand why *He* would allow them to take you away from me!"

"Come, you speak with the tongue of a petulant child, you know better than that. The Lord giveth and the Lord taketh away. Besides, I am filled with delight that I will once more be in the arms of your father. Glory be to God."

"And me? What about me?"

"Shush child! Hush! *Self* is such a crippling disease, know you this well."

"I don't want to be on my own." Brianna's heart was heavy, her mind full of things upon which she had never pondered before. Like sharp stones under bare feet, the thoughts brought her great discomfort.

Rhiannon reached out and took hold of her daughter's arm. Despite being in her fortieth year, her face still held the beauty of a woman in her prime: eyes that sparkled like stars, lips ruby red and skin, despite long days in the sun, as smooth and pale as milk. With thick, long, coal-black hair and eyes as blue as dark cornflowers her appearance caused many a man's head to turn. But it was the warmth of love pouring from her soul that Brianna saw.

They put their loads down and embraced. Mother rocked child, causing them to sway like long grass in a breeze.

"Your father and I will watch over you from a window in Paradise, and we will continually plead your welfare to our Father in Heaven. You won't be alone, child." Rhiannon gently held Brianna away from her. "I know…" she tapped first her head and then her left chest, meaning she knew not only in her mind but in her heart, "that your husband awaits your arrival in the valley where the Nightjars sing. You will not be alone for long."

Brianna wished she could believe it, but having lived twenty long years, she was yet to meet any man who quickened her heart or sparked her mind. Deep inside her she believed that she was destined for a spinster's life.

"*Believe* me," Rhiannon said, cupping Brianna's chin in her hand.

"As you say, Mama."

Rhiannon sighed deeply, as she bent down to pick up her sackcloth bag which she slung over her back, before placing the holding strap across her forehead and adjusting her wide-brimmed straw hat. Brianna picked up her large wicker back-basket and did the same.

Except for the clacking of clogs and the rustle of their skirts along the dry earth, they walked together in silence until the sun was high in the sky. Most unusually, for a well-beaten path, they came upon no other travelers.

Autumn meant shorter days, and what should have taken two days had rolled over to a third, and still they were not there. For her entire life, Brianna had slept in the open during the warm seasons, but winter was in a hurry this year and the north wind blew bitter. The thought of another night upon the byways filled her with displeasure. Not only did she yearn for the warmth of a fire, but for the shelter that would hide them from prying eyes, for unease had settled upon her spirit like a mantle of thorns.

She was pulled back from her journey of negative thoughts by the sudden awareness her mother had stopped walking.

"What is it?" Anxiously, she spun left and right searching along the beaten mud track, seeking that which had caused Mama to stop.

Rhiannon swung her bag down off her back and dropped it by Brianna's feet. "Stay here," she commanded before striding across the field.

As she followed the way her mother walked, Brianna spied workers in yonder field. Midday sun played upon golden-yellow wheat, which swayed rhythmically in the light breeze. Glad for the respite she shrugged out of her back basket and dropped it on the ground.

"Hail good farmer," Rhiannon called out as she waved and smiled. A smile, she had found, was a better key than coin or clever words.

"Good day traveler well met. Whence do 'ee rove?"

The farmer and two other workers stopped their reaping and rested their scythes to their sides, for women in traveling cloth rarely dallied to pass the time of day with them.

"Daughter and I head to Bedyford, in search of work. We hear the Port Master has been granted numerous ships to partake of Newfoundland fishing. He will need all manner of workers, and we are skilled in netting and seek winter employment."

"True 'ee speak, for my second cousin Darvon has himself set off to turn his hand to hook making with the blacksmith, another cousin of mine."

"May God bless the works of his hands," Rhiannon said softly with a tentative smile.

"Indeed, indeed, God bless him and all his endeavors."

No one saw, but Rhiannon gave a slight sigh of relief. Having great discernment, she saw a man who used the Lord's name without hesitation and with genuine sincerity – unlike some people who said the words with a quick response and no conviction, putting forth words merely to comply with expectations and remain safe. In these turbulent times, everyone knew Catholics and Presbyterians were more like rabbits than men, hiding in priest holes throughout the land, waiting for God to restore them to their callings. Her smile broadened, they should be safe here for a while.

"What say you to two extra hands to bring in the field?" Rhiannon swept her arm wide to indicate the field half harvested, and to another beyond the hedgerow not yet begun.

"Many hands make light work, but truth be told I have no copper to spare."

"We do not need coin, merely a dry place to sleep and an evening meal if you should have enough?"

"Aye, we can always spread a meal to bless a traveler or two, and there is the barn that is drafty but mostly dry. Ye are welcome to bed for the night there."

Her smile was sincere and full of gratitude. "May the Lord bless you and keep you. I am sure my daughter will be as grateful as I."

"Will 'ee stay three days to see the full harvest?"

"Yes, I believe that will be acceptable and appreciated, good farmer."

"Name's Billy Coombes, these here are my sons Peter and John."

"Tis truly a pleasure to meet you," Rhiannon said.

Peter and John gave short nods in response, neither sure that such a fine-talking woman, even though lowly dressed, should be sleeping in their barn or bringing in the harvest with them. But they held their tongues, picked up their scythes once more and began swinging with powerful sweeps. Their winter survival depended on getting the wheat into sheaves and safely into the barn before storm or hail could damage them, and with a lazy sun this summer, the spring-planted crops had been slow to ripen, leaving harvest on the verge of being too late. Their strenuous sweeps at the wheat stalks made their bodies swing with precision and caused their off-light white smocks to dance over their heavy farming clothes.

Billy nodded towards a not too distant building. "We break for a bite to eat soon. Make your way to the house, meet wife and explain. Go 'ee straight across the fields for the paths do wind and bend and take many more steps. She'll show 'ee to the barn, and then when we've all eaten you can return with us to the field, where we will reap till the sun sets."

Rhiannon thanked him again, and then hastened to fetch Brianna. They were both in need of something to eat and the prospect of sleeping under a roof rather than a hedge brought much cheer.

Their midday meal of bread and cheese, and a beaker of cider, was filling and flavorsome. Humble but wholesome, it was one of the best meals Brianna had partaken of in a long time.

"That was a blessing, thank you kindly," Brianna said with hearty gratitude. "The cheese was so full of flavor, you could present that to the king and he would not find fault. And it was a delight to taste wheat bread again, so light and delicate, a rare treat compared to rye and barley bread."

"You are most welcome," replied the farmer's wife, Mary. "Our Susan bakes the bread each morning; she has a flair for it, that's for sure. And our Betty here, she churns the cheese and throws in all manner of herbs to tempt our appetites, don't you petal."

"It's the maturing that adds such depth," added Betty, her smile brightening her whole face. "This one has been drying for five months, and the herbs are chives and sage. The warm flavor comes from the watercress that grows in the stream."

"You truly have a talent," beamed Rhiannon.

"Bread and cheese both be way too fine for that merry monarch and his mistresses," bellowed Peter.

"Speak you the truth, brother, truly spoken," added John with a hefty thump upon the wooden table-top that caused their beakers to wobble.

"Shush!" screeched Mary, looking at Rhiannon and Brianna in alarm.

Rhiannon reached out her hand and laid it upon Mary's tightly clenched fist. "We never disclose any conversation that is exchanged within our hearing. You need not fear."

Mary would ponder upon the gentle touch for many a year to come, for peace had blossomed in her heart, and although she could not explain how, she knew they were safe to speak their minds. She looked at her husband, her smile and slight nod were all he needed to know his sons were safe.

"Tis the hearth tax that came out two years past that has become our cross to bear. We have bricked up all but the kitchen hearth, so we only have to pay one shilling twice a year. We used to have four fires burning during winter to warm the old building," Billy waved his arm around to encompass the entire farmhouse. "In winter, we all sleep in the kitchen now to keep warm. And all to pay for his dalliances, promiscuity and masquerade balls! 'Tis shameful! We do not miss the austerities inflicted upon us by Old Ironsides, but Lord above is there no middle ground?"

As a lady with fine heritage, Rhiannon took his words for her grand opening, not of lofty views, but of humble faith. "Thank the Lord that all our woes are temporal, for when we see Him face-to-face, we will be restored to peace and love, and we will suffer no more once we reach Heaven."

"Be you Catholic?" croaked Billy, fear freezing his features, for Catholics were still not in favor and to harbor them could bring nothing but misfortune.

Rhiannon's smile was soft and somewhat sad as she shook her head. "No, we do not call ourselves Catholic."

"Presbyterian?" snapped John.

"Do you really believe we must have a label if we have faith?" Rhiannon asked.

"Tis not about what we believe; 'tis about what will befall us if we harbor undesirables!" growled Billy.

For a moment both mother and daughter closed their eyes as they raised their hosts to the Lord within their thoughts. The sound of logs crackling under a heavy cauldron, in which simmered their evening meal, was the only sound for a long moment. The family exchanged confused looks, but no one spoke for they all felt the presence of something *different* in the room.

Naturally, and simultaneously the family bowed their heads.

"Our father which art in Heaven…" began Rhiannon.

Everyone joined in; even the youngest of the nine siblings aged only three.

"Amen," echoed around the table as the Lord's Prayer ended.

"We are all children of God," said Rhiannon. "Brianna and I do not give ourselves any other label than ones our Lord Jesus gave us. We take the Bible as the very words of God, and we believe. Therefore, if you want to attach a name to us, then call us children of God, or branches of the vine. We think of ourselves as friends of Jesus and our bodies as temples of the Holy Spirit. Catholic, Presbyterian, Puritan, Anglican – none of these names describe us, and yet we are a blend of all, for in truth all denominations have Christ at their center."

"Are you witches?" asked the farmer's second youngest daughter Phoebe.

"We are not, yet to our sorrow that name has followed us wherever we roam, for people always fear that which they do not understand," answered Rhiannon.

"You sound like a witch!" piped up Sarah with a croak, another daughter who was now sidling up to Mary for comfort.

"Might be best ye move on with first light," said Billy with a most vigorous, brook-no-nonsense type of nod.

The one remaining adult at the table, who had thus far kept her thoughts within her head, was Grandma Rebecca. Wisps of pure white hair escaped the bun at the back of her head, and floated around her face like a halo. Her skin was as dry and cracked as bark and the whites of her eyes a dull yellow. With missing teeth and unpleasant breath, she was undoubtedly old and approaching her last days.

"You speak with such confidence," Rebecca croaked. "From where does your knowledge come?"

Rhiannon gave Brianna a slight nod, and so Brianna answered the frail old woman. "My grandmamma Estella was given a gift of faith from the Lord when she received her very own copy of the Holy Bible. Being a lady of high birth she could read, and the words of the beautiful book caught her heart and spirit. She read it every sunrise and every sunset up until she passed the precious book to Mama on her wedding day. With the passing of the book, so too faith was given, and the miracles that followed grandmamma began to follow Mama."

"What kind of miracles?" asked Sarah, now firmly wedged on her mother's knee.

"Mostly healings," answered Brianna.

"Like Jesus kind of healings?" asked Mary, with a mixture of awe and fear.

"Yes, just like those," smiled Brianna.

"Well then, if you fancy turning water into wine, we'd not take offense," laughed Peter nudging his brother in the arm. John didn't respond, his countenance stern, his furrowed brow ridged with deep lines.

"If you really can create miracles, why are you still poor?" asked Phoebe, "if I could wield magic, I'd create a pot of gold."

"In our spirits, we know that we cannot abuse the power of God that dwells within us, therefore we never pray for ourselves, only for others," said Rhiannon. Brianna blushed, for lately she had been asking rather a lot for herself, well for Mama really, no, if she was honest it was for herself.

"And besides," Rhiannon continued, "we are not witches, and we do not partake of magic."

"Oh," said Phoebe sounding slightly disappointed.

"I will not see the end of another winter," said Rebecca, "tell me more of this place that has no more suffering? I grow weary of the preacher's sermons describing our sinful fall into hell. Your beliefs are filling me with hope, and I have had precious little of that for as long as I can remember."

Rhiannon knew the three men were itching to return to work, she could tell by the way they fidgeted in their seats. "Good farmer, I know you have asked us to leave, but what say you to exchanging two meals and one night in your barn, for which I will reap with you, and Brianna will stay here and continue fellowship with your family as well as helping Mary as need be? We will leave with first light, as you wish."

John sort of grunted, an obvious 'no, be gone now,' kind of sound. However, Billy looked at his mother-in-law who was sitting up in her chair with more vigor in her body than he'd seen in years. He glanced at his wife; her eyes were questioning but also pleading.

"Far exchange," Billy said. "But ye need to be gone by first light."

Chapter 4

MAN'S DESIRES DO NOT ALWAYS fall in line with God's plans. The farmers might have longed for the two strange women to be gone, but the Lord wanted them to remain a little while longer.

True to their word, Rhiannon and Brianna were up and dressed with first light and about to head on their way. It was as they were coming out of the barn that a scream pierced the chill morning air. Instantly, dropping their belongings, they hitched up their skirts and raced across the farm yard in the direction of the scream. As they ran, the farmhouse door flew open and both John and Peter came charging out. All four raced towards the field that was now three-quarters harvested.

In the dim morning glow, as one, the four stood at the hedgerow and frantically searched the field. It was a moment before John spotted his father's boot sticking out from the wheat mass. "There!" he yelled, and they charged towards the fallen farmer who was lying on his side.

"Pa!" cried John, falling to his knees by his father's head.

"His leg!" hissed Peter, pointing to a gaping wound and a pool of blood.

"Pa, Pa, what happened?" asked John grasping his father's head with both hands to try and get Billy to look at him.

"I was swinging, somehow I tripped, and then the scythe swung awkwardly and caught the back of my leg. How bad is it son?"

John's eyes filled with tears. What could he say? They all knew that wounds like this invariably resulted in infection and death, and that *only* if the wounded person survived the loss of blood. His sorrow-filled eyes said it all.

Billy sobbed. "You'll look after your mother and sisters the pair of you, promise me!"

Peter dropped down beside John. "We promise," they said together.

"Will you let us lay hands on you, Billy?" asked Rhiannon.

"No witch will touch him!" barked John turning to them with hatred in his eyes. "This is your fault. Witches the pair of you, he asked you to leave and you spoke ill words against him."

They had been accused of this so often that they were used to it, but the pain of people not understanding always hurt and cut to the core.

"If that is so, John, why are we still here? Let us help, for you know as well as us that a wound that size will result in death. Why don't you have a little faith?"

John jumped up, his fists clenched. Anger radiated off him like steam from a bog. Before he could rant, Peter grabbed his trousers and yanked at him. "Be still, John." His voice soft, resigned. John took a step back, not trusting himself.

"Go ahead," said Peter.

"Billy, what say you?" asked Rhiannon.

Billy muffled a "Yes." Rhiannon and Brianna sank to the bloodied earth and laid their hands over the wound, blood gushed through their fingers.

"Laceration, close," said Rhiannon.

"Close," said Brianna.

They stayed with their hands covering the cut until they beheld the skin beginning to bond and knit itself together.

"There," said Brianna, leaning forward and smiling down at Billy's face. "Can you feel that?"

"Yes," said Billy in awed shock.

"What?" asked Peter, turning to look down at his father's leg.

The women removed their bloodied hands and revealed an ugly scar marring his calf, the wound completely closed.

John hissed and took two steps back.

"How?" said Peter in awe.

"We are children of God, and God made us in His image. He spoke and the world was created, we speak and His will comes forth."

"Heretics!" hissed John.

"John!" said Billy, pushing himself up and twisting his hips so he could look at this leg. "It's a miracle. You truly are women of God. God bless you, God bless you both," and then he broke into sobs. Shock and relief mingled equally in his grateful salty tears.

The brothers insisted on carrying Billy back to the farmhouse despite his protests, being jostled in the cradle of their arms, and the relief of knowing he wasn't going to die, filled the farmer with a merry bubble that exploded into full belly laughter by the time they reached the house.

"What is it? What happened?" Mary was trying to shove her hair into her mop cap as they brought her husband in. "What's wrong with him?" Mary looked to her sons, fearing her husband was suddenly 'touched' in his mind.

The brothers each told the event with a different attitude, Peter one of awe and John full of anger, for they had unwittingly allowed witches into their home.

When Billy's laughter had finally subsided he grabbed Mary by the waist and pulled her down, planting his lips firmly over hers. He kissed her like he hadn't done since John had come into their lives. She was flushed and blushing when she was finally able to pry herself out of his arms.

"Husband! What condition has seized your mind?"

Her look of shocked indignation seemed to set fire to his bubble of joy and he roared with laughter until tears raced down his thin cheeks. It took only a moment before the children, one by one, but excluding John, caught his infectious laughter. Seeing her children collapsing with laughter soon worked its way into Mary's spirit until she too was laughing. Her body rocked back and forth as she held her sides, for Phoebe's honk of a laugh was just too amusing.

"You've all gone mad!" snarled John, before turning on his heels and leaving them to it.

That seemed to make them all laugh all the more.

"Oh! Poor old John, he never did have a sense of humor," laughed Mary, trying her hardest to pull herself together.

Rhiannon and Brianna smiled at each and quietly stepped towards the door. Despite the gift of a miracle, they would keep their word and leave.

"Wait!" yelled Billy.

They stopped and turned around.

"Tell me… tell us, about your faith," Billy said and although his eyes were still full of sparkles, his laughter was dissolving.

"First," said Rebecca, wiping tears off her wrinkled face, while sitting in the rocking chair. Everyone looked at her. "First, the harvest must be brought in. My bones are aching and I know rain is close by, there is not much time. Delay your

33

parting, stay, bring in the harvest in the day and tell us about your faith by night."

Everyone turned their heads to look at Billy. He stood up and walked towards the two strangers. For the miracle of healing wasn't in part, it was complete, whole, and there was no pain or stiffness in his leg. Indeed, if it wasn't for the scar which remained, he would have said he dreamed the whole thing.

"My mother-in-law speaks with the wisdom of age. Will ye stay until the end of harvest as we previously agreed?"

Rhiannon smiled, "If it pleases you, we will."

"Yeah!" yelled Sarah, "will you make us laugh like that again? It was so much fun!"

"We did not make you laugh," Brianna chuckled, "tis the joy of the Lord that brings such gaiety."

"Well please ask Him to bring it again," laughed Sarah.

The two days of harvesting saw much merriment. Billy, not blessed with an angelic voice, would not stop singing, day and night! Everyone was offered the choice of joining in or covering their ears, for he told them… "I have no intention of stopping."

Even John's bristles became less visible, he was often caught with a smile on his face, and to everyone's relief – for his singing voice was mighty fine, he started joining in with his father's songs. The whole farm was alive and laughter seemed to break out for no obvious cause. Their border collie bounced on four legs, demonstrating his excitement, which only made the children laugh more.

The first night after the miracle, their evening nourishment was quickly devoured and chairs pulled around the fire, giving Rhiannon and Brianna center stage to talk. John sulked at the back of the room the first night, but claimed the chair next to Brianna on the second.

On the first night Rhiannon did most of the talking. She shared their understanding of the Holy Bible, which they took literally to mean what it said. She explained how they accepted the truth that they were all made in God's image, and therefore the power of God lived within them.

"For God *spoke*, and it was so…" said Rhiannon. "This means words are carriers of power. So when we speak, we too release power, that's why miracles happen, because we speak with faith."

"You didn't ask God to heal Pa," said Peter, "you surely border on heretics if you think of yourself as gods."

"We are not gods," answered Brianna, "but we carry His Holy Spirit within us. We believe we release the Spirit whenever we speak."

"But we are taught to pray and to ask God to do things. We are not told it is possible for us to do these things ourselves, it feels wrong, like you are going against everything we have been told from the pulpit," said John. He wasn't accusing them exactly, but his lack of understanding was clear.

"I once met a man," said Rhiannon, "who everyone said looked exactly like his father. He also talked and even walked like him. The villagers said he was his double, like a twin in looks and character. I asked his mother why this so awed the villagers. She smiled and told me that the thing was… her son had never once met his father, who had left the village before he was born." Rhiannon looked at the family who were glued to her words.

"This is what the Holy Bible says... Philip saith unto him, Lord, show us the Father, and it sufficeth us. Jesus saith unto him, have I been so long time with you, and yet hast thou not known me, Philip? He that hath seen me hath seen the Father; and how sayest thou then, Show us the Father? (3)

Rhiannon looked at their faces which showed no dawning of understanding. So she continued, serenely and simply, her spirit of love pouring through the words from the gospel of John.

"Believest thou not that I am in the Father, and the Father in me? The words that I speak unto you I speak not of myself: but the Father that dwelleth in me, he doeth the works. Believe me that I am in the Father, and the Father in me: or else believe me for the very works' sake." (4)

Tears made her eyes sparkle like stars; the emotions this verse wrought, always stirred her heart and filled her with humility.

"So..." began Peter, who had straightened in his seat and was becoming alive with understanding. "If we are made in His image, and if Jesus is in the Father and the Father is in him, then that means that the Father is in us, and we are in Him."

John scraped back his chair and left the room. It was too much for him to understand and take in.

On the second night Rhiannon carried into the kitchen her most prized possession, the Holy Bible her mother had given her twenty-two years ago.

Sitting in her chair by the fire, with the family gathered around, she carefully unwrapped the leather covering, folding back four corners to reveal a Bible. The room was filled with the sounds of gasps.

The book measured one-foot high, and half-a-foot wide. The leather binding was black and soft to touch. The four corners were laid with golden triangle plates. In the center was a diamond-shaped gold plate. All of them were stamped with patterns, even the golden buckle that kept the book closed. It spoke of riches and mysteries. To the family's knowledge, only clergymen and kings would hold a Holy Book such as this.

"My father," continued Rhiannon "was an acquaintance of Robert Baker, who was a printer to King James. When my father learned of a new version of the Holy Bible being printed he immediately rode to London to commission a copy for my mother. Mr. Baker was much in debt and the printing of this edition had taken the printers to near bankruptcy. Apparently, he was more than grateful to my father, who offered to pay a substantial amount to have a personal copy for my mother. A bound copy normally sold for twelve shillings; my father paid three times that to help support a fellow scholar and to gift his wife a unique present."

'Oohs' and 'aahs' floated around them, as Rhiannon opened the cover to reveal an illustration by Cornelis Boel. The image of the apostles surrounding the title page text was breathtakingly beautiful. They got off their chairs and gathered around Rhiannon to gaze upon the illustration.

"We read the word of God every day. We fill our minds with scriptures until the words are all we live and breathe."

"We can't read," whispered Sarah filled with awe.

"Would you like me to read to you?"

The answer was a resounding "Yes" from everyone. Rhiannon went straight to the gospel of John, the book she considered to be the one that most reflects that Jesus is God's son. She also personally took strength from the fact that John knew Jesus loved him, so much so, that he could lay his head against him. This tender image portrayed to her that Jesus was accessible, and therefore so was God.

By the time she finished reading the gospel, the two youngest girls were asleep, but everyone else was awake and full of questions.

Chapter 5

THE HARVEST WAS IN and Mary and her daughters had been baking all day to celebrate and offer thanks to God, for the wheat was in the barn and the rain still not come. There was plenty enough to sell to the miller in exchange for sacks of flour and some extra coin too.

Although they had originally planned to leave this day, Rhiannon and Brianna had been happy to stay one last night at the pleading of everyone, well except for John who had become quiet but was no longer hostile.

A ham had been roasted, fresh bread baked, and several cheeses and pickled vegetables adorned the table. In the center of the table, in a place where tiny fingers couldn't reach, was an enormous apple pie. It was a feast fit for a king, although not King Charles of course, no… he could go whistle the men all muttered. Everyone gathered in the kitchen talking over plans for the winter, except the three youngest children who played outside with the dog. The kitchen was warm, the atmosphere merry. Billy was still singing, and every now and again would grab Mary around the waist and demand a jolly step or two around the large wooden table. She knocked him and mocked him, but she always played along and danced with him.

Abruptly, the door flew open and banged against wall, causing most to jump.

"Pa!" yelled Teresa.

"What is it lass?" said Billy, instantly releasing Mary and striding towards his daughter.

"Strangers come, three of them on black horses."

Billy swung around to look at Rhiannon and Brianna. "How well did you cover your tracks?"

There was no need to ask how he knew it might be witch hunters approaching.

"We implied to everyone we spoke to that we were heading north," answered Rhiannon.

Billy looked at them for a moment, and then made a quick decision. "Come," he snapped, "tis best to be safe than sorry." They didn't hesitate but with haste followed Billy out of the farmhouse.

He strode across the cobbled yard towards the chicken coop. Looking towards Teresa he asked, "How far?"

"They had turned off the main path, and had just gone past the first bend on our track when I spotted them."

"Go back in the house, wash yourself clean. Help your mother stay calm."

"Yes, Pa," she said before rushing to the farmhouse.

"You're hiding us with the chickens?" asked Brianna.

Rhiannon put her hand on Billy's arm to slow him. "If it is *them*, and they think we are here, they will search every inch of the farm, this will not hide us. We should run, if they catch us we can say we were hiding in your barn without your knowledge."

"Your things! Peter, John!"

"Here Pa," said Peter who had already thought of their Bible and wares stored in the barn. "I'll take care of it."

They entered the large coop that housed about forty chickens. Billy strode to the back of the chicken house and pulled the wooden roosting shelves into the center. With the shelves' removal a small opening appeared.

40

"It will be uncomfortable and smelly, I'm afraid. But I think you'll be safe."

Neither woman hesitated. They dropped to their knees and crawled inside.

"I'll come back for ye when they're gone, until then, for the love of God, be silent."

They nodded, and Billy set to pushing the roosting shelves back into place. They could hear him shuffling, and realized he was resurfacing the ground with fresh hay. Outside he immediately set to helping John pitchfork heaps of rotten grass and manure around the farm yard, and extra heaps along the side of the coop in which the women hid.

Despite being twenty years old, Brianna moved as close to her mother as she could, so Rhiannon could wrap her arm around her. She felt like she was five years old again, small, insignificant and powerless. Her mother's prophecy was ringing in her mind louder than a cathedral's bell, churning her stomach and making her dizzy.

Rhiannon was still, calm. 'Maybe she thinks today is the day,' thought Brianna. That prospect sent chills down her back.

She wanted to ask God to delay His plans; just for a little longer… she opened her mouth to speak, and then snapped it shut quickly, as the clip-clop sound of several horses and the barking of dogs reached their ears.

Rhiannon's arm tightened its grip around Brianna, for she might be ready to meet her own calling to Heaven, but she wished for her daughter a little longer on Earth. For this planet – this life – was merely a school, and Brianna had not finished her education yet. She was still to be honed in the fire, of this Rhiannon was sure.

Over time their bodies began to ache more and more. With no room to stand they were cramped. They wiggled their toes and fingers, and by the minute grew ever colder.

They heard much of the discussion held in the farm yard once the dogs had been ordered to silence, and sighed when the voices faded, obviously entering the house.

As the last of the sun's light paled, cold seeped from the ground and bit their flesh. Both mother and daughter blew into their cupped fingers trying to bring warmth to their hands. A few times they stiffened when they caught sound of the dogs sniffing around the hen house. But God's hand kept them safe, for today was not the day they dreaded. After a gruesome amount of time their bodies were near frozen and pain-filled.

Why were they taking so long with the family? They rested their foreheads against each other after Rhiannon whispered, "Pray" into Brianna's ear.

Silently, they lifted the family, and beseeched the Lord for help and to keep them safe. Long minutes ticked by, the horses tethered to the fence occasionally neighed, a reminder the hunters still remained.

Brianna realized she must have slipped into sleep as she prayed, for she startled awake at the loud voice of the man she knew as Black Wolf.

"We'll just take a look around and then be on our way," he declared. His voice was deep, mellow, not what you think a hunter might sound like. Brianna thought if that voice was attached to any fellow but him, she might be attracted to it. Its husky rasp was a mix of education and rawness. She found it appealing, like a mystery to be unwrapped. Not for the first time, she wondered why he was so intent upon their murder. She shivered then froze as the chicken coop door opened.

Rhiannon lifted her hands and placed them on Brianna's face and pulled her close. She cradled Brianna's head in her arms as if to hide her from the terror that walked just a few steps away from them.

"You've a healthy flock, I see, God blesses you."

Brianna's heart was beating so wildly she feared Black Wolf himself would sniff her out, let alone the dogs whose sniffs were becoming more frightening than a storm full of thunder and lightning.

"Aye, we are grateful to God and His mercies, He has been good to us," acknowledged Billy.

"Crops, livestock and a large family, you truly are blessed."

Something in his tone made Brianna raise her eyebrows, *Was he jesting with Billy?* she wondered.

"I'd be more blessed if He would grant me more sons in place of daughters," laughed Billy.

Black Wolf chuckled, rich and from deep within, as if he understood clearly the farmer's predicament.

"And you say, 'tis only a short ride to the next farm?" The witch hunter's voice was fading; they were clearly going back into the yard.

"Yes, indeed, William is but a short ride down the road and he has room aplenty to house you overnight."

"Very well, thank you for the meal, God bless you and yours."

Brianna had a sudden urge to call out to the man who hunted them like animals, she wanted to demand what right he had to do so. Rhiannon must have perceived something stir in her daughter's spirit for she tightened her arms around her.

Not long after, the other men confirm they had found nothing to suggest anyone else was on the farm. With relief, they listened as the men mounted and left.

Billy didn't come for them straight away, and the women were glad. They had been in this situation before, and knew that the hunters had a habit of sending one of them back to check things were the same as when they left.

The farmhouse door closed, and they sighed, relieved that Billy hadn't come straight for them.

Rhiannon was rubbing Brianna's arms trying to warm her when the clip-clop of one horse returning drifted through the wooden slats. The rider made his horse circle the house and barns and outbuildings, before standing still in the yard. The stallion neighed and stomped one hoof upon the cobbles several times, he seemed restless and angry; exactly how Brianna pictured Black Wolf.

Brianna's eardrums hurt from the vigorous pounding coming from her heart. Each echo of hoof against the yard's cobbles sent chills down her.

Hatred, that most horrid emotion, hammered upon the door of Brianna's heart like a mason shaping a stone. 'Go away,' her soul cried to the emotion as well as the witch hunter, 'go away.'

A measure of time passed after the rider left, before Billy came back. He opened the coop door, rushed to pull back the shelves and helped them out. Their bodies complained mightily as they crawled out. Their muscles cramped and contracted painfully, causing both women to moan.

"Tis sorry I am, mighty sorry. It's just when they arrived I wanted to appear normal, so I invited them to join us in our meal. It just seemed the safest thing to do. I never realized they would stay so long. They asked to sleep in the barn, but Phoebe, God bless her soul, yelped *she* wouldn't sleep with the rats and that was that."

"God bless her," said Rhiannon trying to straighten her poor, pained body.

44

"Come on inside, we have plenty of food for ye both, and Mary says you're to sleep in the house tonight."

"You are too kind, but we must leave as soon as possible, we will not put you at any more risk," replied Rhiannon.

"Nonsense, I will not hear of such a thing. Come, come, everyone is waiting for ye."

Mary and her daughters hovered around them like bees around flowers; they helped undress and redress them, and washed them with care using warm water to bring life back into their cold flesh.

"I will wash these now," said Maggie, the eldest daughter.

"I'll help," said Teresa, holding up the dresses splattered with chicken muck stains from crawling on the floor.

"We can do that," said Rhiannon.

"Indeed you will not!" said Rebecca shuffling over to them. Rebecca took hold of Rhiannon's hand and led her to the rocking chair in pride of place by the large hearth. "Sit you down, and warm your toes," she commanded. Rhiannon laughed and did as she was bid.

John picked up a chair from beside the table and brought it over to the fire. He nodded at Brianna. She smiled and sat down next to her mother.

"Tell me Billy, for I am curious," said Rhiannon, "how come you have such a hidey-hole as the one in the coop?"

Billy dragged his chair closer to the fire and sat down on it backwards, so he could rest his arms along the top. He declared with a measure of pride, "My father built it, to hide me in during the war. I was a strapping lad with hard muscles and good health, prime pickings for conscription. I was the youngest of four sons. My older brothers all went to war, none of them returned. My father refused to lose all of us, and so he told everyone I had gone to war with my brothers, and hid me when anyone came near the farm."

Mary came and dropped her arm around her husband as he leaned forward in the chair. "I would have done the same, although maybe I would have hid both my sons and allowed neither to go."

"They were shooting men who refused to join," said Billy. "And deserters had better hope not to get caught, for their death was slow and painful."

Mary kissed his head. "Pray to God we never have another war."

"Amen, to that," said Billy.

Peter fetched hearty plates of food for mother and daughter to eat by the fire.

"Thank you," said Brianna. Before eating, she gave thanks to God for the food, when she finished Rhiannon joined her saying amen.

Billy had got up and started pacing up and down in the kitchen.

Rhiannon followed him with her eyes, as he muttered to himself and strode across the stone floor. "We won't stay Billy. We will leave as soon as we've eaten. We are putting your family in jeopardy just by being here."

Billy spun around to face her. "I've been trying to work out how you can pass the hunters on the road to Bedyford without being seen. If they're heading there too, do you really want to go? Why not head back north?"

"We often stay on the moors, or in the woods, until we know they have been and gone," said Brianna.

"But the weather's bitter, and if I'm not mistaken the rain will be here before we slumber this night," said Peter.

"We have a leather roll that keeps us dry, well mostly," smiled Brianna, before taking a large bite of her pickled cucumber.

"Pa!" said Peter, his face poured forth his concern.

"I've been thinking that we can hide ye within the wheat sheaves and take ye to miller Joseph. From there it is but an hour's walk into town. If we pass the hunters returning north along the way ye will know ye are safe, and if not then I will ask Joseph to hide ye overnight."

"Can we trust him, Pa?" asked John, who had moved close to the conversation.

"Aye, sure as eggs is eggs, Joseph is an honest God-fearing man."

"So was Albert the tanner, but he turned that Royalist soldier over to God's Army when they passed through!"

"Let's not glorify these fighting men with the name 'God's Army,' the New Model Army followed Cromwell into both battle and church. They might have been well-trained and disciplined, even filled with religious fervor, they were not, however, *God's Army.*"

Everyone looked at Rhiannon whose face was stern as she spoke.

"The Holy Bible tells us, that those who believe in the Lord Jesus Christ become soldiers of God and enter His army. Not by picking up the physical weapons, but by wielding the spiritual weapons. For it says…

"Finally, be strong in the Lord and in the strength of his might. Put on the whole armor of God, that you may be able to stand against the schemes of the Devil. For we do not wrestle against flesh and blood, but against the rulers, against the authorities, against the cosmic powers over this present darkness, against the spiritual forces of evil in the heavenly places. Therefore, take up the whole armor of God, that you may be able to withstand in the evil day, and having done all, to stand firm. Stand therefore, having fastened on the belt of truth, and having put on the breastplate of righteousness, and, as shoes for your feet, having put on the readiness given by the gospel of peace. In all circumstances take up the shield of faith, with which you can extinguish all the flaming darts of the evil one; and take the helmet of salvation, and the sword of the Spirit, which is the word of God, praying at all times in the Spirit, with all prayer and supplication." (5)

The room was charged with emotion, and utterly silent. Rhiannon had stood up at the beginning of the passage from Ephesians. Her countenance had become regal, her chin high, her arms slowly rising at her sides. She was almost angelic, powerful and full of majesty.

Goosebumps ran along everyone's arms. Billy made the sign of the cross over his face and sank to his knees. John and Peter immediately did the same. The younger girls huddled together not knowing what to do. Mary fetched Maggie and Teresa in from the outhouse. Once again she felt the presence once again of something impossible to describe, she grabbed Maggie and Teresa by their hands and rushed them all into the kitchen. She took one look at her men on their knees and fell down beside them.

Tears spilled down her cheeks. She looked up from the floor towards Rhiannon, and placing her hands together in prayerfully, she beseeched her. "Tell us what we must do to ensure we are saved!"

"Acts 16:31 tells us... And they said, Believe on the Lord Jesus Christ, and thou shalt be saved, and thy house."

"We believe," said Billy, "we all believe."

"We do," confirmed Mary, Peter and John.

Rhiannon continued reciting Acts: "And they spake unto him the word of the Lord, and to all that were in his house. And he took them the same hour of the night, and washed their stripes; and was baptized, he and all his, straightway. And when he had brought them into his house, he set meat before them, and rejoiced, believing in God with all his house." (6)

"We were all baptized as babies," said John.

"The baptism of the Holy Spirit is a different thing. It is a gift directly from God. Luke 3:16 tells us... John answered, saying unto them all, I indeed baptize you with water; but one mightier than I cometh, the latchet of whose shoes I am not worthy to unloose: he shall baptize you with the Holy Ghost and with fire."

"I don't want to be set on fire," sobbed Maggie.

"Only those who seek and wish to receive will be granted the Holy Spirit," said Rhiannon softly.

"I seek," said Billy, his voice croaking with emotion.

"Aye, me too," said Peter.

"And I," said John, Mary and three of the girls.

Rebecca was sobbing, her frail body shivering with emotions, it was a croak but everyone heard her whisper, "And I."

"The Lord is already here. He created you; He already lives in your spirit. He promises to never leave nor forsake you. He

49

longs to give good gifts to you, and the best one of all is His Holy Spirit. Now, you who are thirsty, drink… for the Lord your God loves you!"

Rhiannon moved around the family, touching their heads, passing on the gift she had freely received years ago from her mother… faith.

Rebecca wailed, sobbing like a baby, she rocked her body back and forth as the love of God flooded through her. "I'm sorry Lord," she cried, "so sorry." The rest of family also cried with the wonder of receiving such love, all except John.

John experienced a jolt in his body, as if someone had run a sword through him. It was without pain, rather it was filling him with… what was it filling him with? He sought around striving to find a description for what he experienced.

Joy!

He laughed. Like a bark, short and loud. His body rocked forward when he laughed again. The rest of the family began wiping their tears and looked to him. Before anyone could have counted to ten… they were all laughing. John rolled onto the floor and rocked back and forth and laughed for all his worth.

Tears of gratefulness to God slipped down both Rhiannon and Brianna's faces.

"The joy of the Lord is your strength," said Rhiannon. "Long may His joy reside within you."

Chapter 6

THE JOURNEY IN THE CART had been bumpy and uncomfortable, but it had carried them swiftly and safely to the mill. Much embracing and many encouraging words had been exchanged between them and the farming family before they left that morning. It was sad to part company, but they knew their calling in life was to bring back hope to as many as possible, and that meant moving on. Hope had faded in a people oppressed and downtrodden, who lacked a personal relationship with Jesus, not because they didn't believe, but because they had never been told they could have one. Bibles were purchased only by Churches and the wealthy. The rich mostly let their Bibles gather dust, while men of the cloth selected passages to read to keep the people exactly where they wanted them: giving offerings and tithes to the Church coffers and abiding by their teaching.

Quoting Philippians 2:14 – 'Do all things without murmurings and disputings,' so-called men of God hastened to reinforce paying homage to the land owners and magistrates. After all, the lords and ladies of the fine manors paid their salaries and ensured their comfort. The Puritans had sought to bring both the Bible and Jesus alive to the people, wanting to reverse what they perceived as the slide into sin that Henry VIII had birthed in the country, by wanting to have more authority than the Pope.

It was hard for normal folk to discern what was religiously correct. Religion fired men with such fervor that they would willingly kill family members in the name of their faith. Rhiannon and Brianna didn't care for religion. They loved Christ, and wanted Him glorified, nothing else mattered.

"We're here," called Peter, bringing the massive old Shire horse to a halt.

Peter and Billy pulled back some wheat stacks and helped Brianna and Rhiannon out of the cart. Peter took a piece of grass out of Brianna's hair with a grin.

The water mill was tiny compared to others they'd seen on their travels. Surrounded by a waist-high dry-stone wall, and shadowed by three towering oaks, the mill appeared quaint, petite, seeming more like a house than a mill. The overbearing thatch roof cascaded down to just above the top of the door. Two tall brick-built chimneys stood side-by-side to the left, and to the right the solid wooden wheel was being melodically turned by the flow of the stream.

They knew the moment they laid eyes upon Joseph that he was a man of God, his heart was good, even if somewhat jaded and confused.

"Well met," said Joseph with a wave.

"Good day, Joseph," beamed Billy. "We bring a bountiful harvest for exchange, and two friends who pass by on their way to Bedyford."

A man of many thoughts and few words, Joseph nodded in their direction knowing who they were, for the three black riders had stopped at the mill only a short time earlier.

"How many wreaths do you bring?" asked Joseph.

"Twelve and five," replied Peter, "shall I put them in the normal place?"

"Aye, then take you to store house and fetch out two sacks of flour," said Joseph.

"Only two?" asked Billy.

"I have to start giving a tenth of everything to Church on top of the payment to Lord Wallington. So I have ten shillings to give you atop the flour."

It was plain to see Billy was not impressed. "We've brought you some cheese, Joseph," he said, fetching two large rounds from the back of the cart. "Will you take these in exchange for another sack of flour?"

"I know times are penurious, but I have to keep back some of your wheat. However, farmer William has left me ample honey and two baskets of cabbages which I was to take to market on the morrow, will 'ee take half of his exchange for the cheeses?"

"Aye, fair trade," said Billy, somewhat consoled.

When the stacks were unloaded, Joseph shook Billy and Peter's hands. "Are they for Bedyford now?" he asked, nodding towards Rhiannon and Brianna.

For a moment Billy wondered how much they should say, but before he could answer Rhiannon took a step forward and addressed Joseph. "Yes, good sir, we head there now. Can you tell us the best path to take?"

"There's no beating around the bush, so I'll tell 'ee straight. Three men with king's coin do seek two wandering women, if per chance 'ee be those they seek, I'd not be going there today."

"They are good people Joseph, I will vouch for them. Will ye keep them hidden overnight?"

Joseph was looking Rhiannon directly in the eye; she did not flinch or turn away. "One night I will offer 'ee, no longer."

"Bless you, that is very generous of you," said Rhiannon.

With that settled, farewells were exchanged. They waved Billy and Peter off, and then turned to look at the miller.

"Well, 'ee best come on in, and get off the road," he said, indicating that they should follow him inside the mill. Joseph was a large man, taller than most, with broad shoulders and a rotund pot-belly which rolled up and down when he laughed, which wasn't often these days. Past the best years of his life, his black hair was rippled with white as was his beard.

"You know the witch hunters chase us," said Rhiannon once they were inside.

Both women hovered in the doorway, clutching their belongings and not removing their capes.

"Aye," answered Joseph. "Indeed I do, but you're safe here a while. The brothers passed through earlier, they won't be stopping here again. But even if they should, 'ee can sleep in the cubbyhole behind the fire; they'll not find 'ee there." Joseph placed his hands on his hips and shook his head. "Trust me, or be on your way, but don't be insulting me by standing there doubting."

Rhiannon put her sacking bag down and took off her cape. "So what can we do to help while we are here?"

"Do either of 'ee sew?"

"My needlework is well acclaimed, good miller," said Brianna.

"Well this," he said hitting a pile of clothes on a table in the corner of the room, "is me darning pile. Been piling up since me dear wife died, God bless her soul."

"And when my daughter darns, I shall help you," said Rhiannon.

"I was planning to take the stacks up to the sack floor and empty them into the barrels, so I'm ready for milling on the morrow."

"Then I shall give you a helping hand," confirmed Rhiannon.

Joseph snorted his tsk of annoyance. "Begging your pardon, mistress, but the wreaths are not feather-light!"

"All the more reason to help you," Rhiannon replied merrily.

The best way to show him that she had strong muscles was to get straight to it, so she spun on her heels and went outdoors to start fetching the bundles, one at a time. She heaved one up and rested it on her shoulder with apparent ease, Joseph was speechless.

"Show me the way!" Rhiannon smiled.

Joseph lifted a bundle and headed for the wooden stairs that ran along the exterior of the mill walls.

The steps were narrow and proved to be difficult because of her long skirts, but she managed them. She was grinning when she entered through a tiny doorway into the top floor of the water mill. When all the sheaves were in, Rhiannon helped Joseph to beat them with a flail to winnow and separate the grain from the stems ready for milling. It was dusty work and she tied her scarf around her face to stop herself from coughing.

With a helping hand chores were soon done, and Joseph invited them to share a meal with him. Not surprisingly, his table was a wonderful array of the different foods brought to him by various farmers.

"Help yourself to the biscuits." Joseph sliced off a piece of cheese and placed it on his round, hard biscuit. "Tilly, the baker's wife, made them. She adds a small portion of honey to the flour, water and salt, 'tis that which keeps 'em from becoming too hard to eat." He chuckled and his belly bounced up and down. "If 'ee be looking for work in Bedyford, I am confident the baker will need people. They have been commissioned to make biscuits for the ships that are coming. Although, the West Country Merchant Adventurers are not prepared to cough up fine coin, so no honey will be in the poor sailors' biscuits!" Now he really laughed, but his bark was cut short when he choked on a piece of the dried food so hastily consumed! Brianna jumped up and started heartily thumping him on his back until he coughed up the item of offense.

"Thank 'ee, thank 'ee." Wiping his eyes with the back of his sleeve, Joseph caught his breath, signed and grinned.

Rhiannon finished her food first. As cheese had been in ample supply at the farm, she had partaken of smoked haddock and pickled vegetables. "That meal was much appreciated. Thank you."

Joseph gave her a nod only, for his mouth was once more full of food.

"We will turn our hand to any work," said Rhiannon, "but if we have a choice we will seek employment with the fishermen and turn our hands to mending nets."

Joseph announced he had finished eating with a belch. "Where 'ee planning to stay?"

"We do not know as yet, we will see where the Lord guides us."

"Pah! Good luck with that."

"We do not rely on luck," said Brianna.

"No, I hear witchcraft is what 'ee relies on."

"You're misinformed. We trust in the Lord for all things," retorted Rhiannon.

"As 'ee say."

"You don't have any faith left, Joseph?"

A frown deepened the lines on his face, as he scowled at them. "If there be a God above, he would never have taken me sweet Annie and my four children away from me. What kind of God would do that? Two sons lost to a war we wanted no part of, two sons to influenza, and a sweet, godly wife to childbirth. Bah! 'Ee are right, I have no faith in me, none at all."

His pain emanated off him, waves of loss turned to bitter sorrow.

"Would you let us lay hands on you, Joseph?" asked Rhiannon.

"No, I would *not*."

Freely the women had received their faith, and freely they passed it on, but never to those who declined, so they accepted the miller's word as his decision.

Later, when the miller had retired, they sat close to the smoldering embers and talked with quiet voices.

Brianna tightened her shawl around her and glanced at her mother. "What shall we do for him?"

Rhiannon's lips twisted into a sad smile. "We will give him the greatest gift we can, we will pray for him."

They bowed their heads and clasped their hands together. They praised God for His never-ending mercy and His continued good gifts, and then they lifted the miller up, surrounding him with Bible verses for his health and his protection, but ultimately for the rebirth of his soul and the reuniting of his spirit to his wife and children in the world to come.

When they finished their prayers and praise, Rhiannon wrapped an arm around her daughter and held her close. For a while they sat enjoying the babble of water rushing passed the mill. Soothing and melodic, the burble of the stream washed over them like a tonic to their souls.

"Why would He take you away from me?"

Rhiannon stroked Brianna's hair, her sigh long and low. "I cannot fathom the will of the Lord. I only know His voice and heed it well." She couldn't put into words that she just *knew* that everything would work out for the best. Brianna couldn't see beyond the pain of loss at the moment, maybe she would never understand until they all met again in Heaven. Maybe, it wasn't for her to explain things to her daughter, but her motherly instincts were to shield Brianna from pain, so in her mind she searched the scriptures for comfort.

"Remember Jeremiah 29:11, For I know the thoughts that I think toward you, saith the Lord, thoughts of peace, and not of evil, to give you an expected end. Our God is the same today as He was when Jeremiah walked the Earth, He has not changed. His will for us is the same. His thoughts towards us are of peace and not of evil. No matter what happens to us, we can rest in the knowledge His character never changes."

"So, are we to accept *everything* that is thrown at us, no matter the consequences?"

"Fetch out the Bible, read me Psalm 84."

Brianna leaned over to her mother's sacking bag, and pulled out the Holy Book. After removing the leather covering, she quickly flicked through the chapters in the Old Testament, until she reached Psalm 84.

"How amiable are thy tabernacles, O Lord of hosts! My soul longeth, yea, even fainteth for the courts of the Lord: my heart and my flesh crieth out for the living God. Yea, the sparrow hath found an house, and the swallow a nest for herself, where she may lay her young, even thine altars, O Lord of hosts, my King, and my God. Blessed are they that dwell in thy house: they will be still praising thee. Selah. Blessed is the man whose strength is in thee; in whose heart are the ways of them. Who passing through the valley of Baca make it a well; the rain also filleth the pools. They go from strength to strength, every one of them in Zion appeareth before God. O Lord God of hosts, hear my prayer: give ear, O God of Jacob. Selah. Behold O God our shield, and look upon the face of thine anointed. For a day in thy courts is better than a thousand. I had rather be a doorkeeper in the house of my God, than to dwell in the tents of wickedness. For the Lord God is a sun and shield: the Lord will give grace and glory: no good thing will He withhold from them that walk uprightly. O Lord of hosts, blessed is the man that trustest in thee."

"What do we glean from these words?" Rhiannon asked.

Brianna traced her fingers over the ornate flowers surrounding the H at the beginning of the passage, then her glance rose up the page to the top where on the left was printed 'David's hope.' Knowing the answer her mother expected, Brianna hesitated to respond. What did *she* gather from these precious words? She closed her eyes for a few moments before she answered.

"Your soul is in union with David, you long to dwell in His courts. You know that everyone who lives with God in their hearts will join Him in His house in Heaven. That promise of a future dwelling is more precious than any home on Earth. That one day in Heaven is worth more than a lifetime on Earth, and that men who trust in God will have peace on Earth."

"And you? What do you believe?"

Brianna's bottom lip trembled as emotion washed over her with the force of a crashing wave. Her words stumbled out quiet, hesitant, heartfelt. "I am not content to wait until I reach Heaven before I dwell with the Lord. I know He is here," she tapped her chest, "I believe His dwelling place is our hearts, not a palace in Heaven. I don't look forward to a day of no more suffering; I look for a day when all His people offer their bodies as His dwelling place. I want Heaven on Earth, and I want people to feel His presence now in a mighty and powerful way. Not just words but a *receiving* of knowledge and understanding that surpasses all intelligence."

Clamping her mouth closed with a snap, Brianna took a worried peek at her mother. She had never been so forthright about her feelings before.

Rhiannon was pensive and watched the fire's flickering flames for a long time before she answered. "Interpretation of scripture is in the eyes of the reader, and in the revelation that comes only from the Holy Spirit. If this is what God has shown you, then this is your truth. It is not mine, but that does not mean it is less true than the things I believe scripture tells us. Only when we see God face-to-face will we truly understand. Now we should get some sleep, for tomorrow we shall head for Bedyford and see what God has in store for us there. Sleep well, precious daughter of mine."

"Sleep well, Mama."

Whistling woke them in the morning. They yawned and stretched and quickly rose to greet the miller.

"Good morrow, good morrow," he called as he stoked the fire with fresh wood.

"Blessed day, Joseph, I trust you slept well?" said Rhiannon with a smile, for it was clear to see he was in good spirits.

"Indeed, it is a good day! Now have you some bread and honey before 'ee depart. And you young lady," he tilted his head towards Brianna as he placed wooden plates on the table, "look 'ee at this!" He raised both arms high in the air. When he received nothing but puzzled expressions, he burst out laughing. "No holes," he declared pointing to his armpit. "I'm almost fit to venture to chapel on Sunday!"

He was laughing, but the women looked at each other with hope brimming in their eyes, had God answered their prayers so quickly?

"You seem in mighty fine spirits today," said Rhiannon.

Joseph sat down on a stool at the table. "Come on, hurry up. A man must work to earn a living, but first he must eat!"

They quickly sat down at the table with him.

"I had a dream last night." After his short declaration, Joseph smeared honey on a chunk of bread and took an oversized bite. They were on tenterhooks and couldn't eat until he continued.

"Annie came to me last night," he eventually explained.

"She did!" Shivers ran down Brianna's back.

"Told me straight, she did."

"Told you what?" asked Rhiannon.

"That she and the boys won't wait for me unless I let my bitterness go. Can you believe that? She's still bossing me around from Heaven!" Joseph roared with laughter, like he'd told the funniest of tales. "Always pushing that one, she was. Aah, but it did my heart good to hear her chastise my ears so."

"I am glad your dream has brought you comfort, Joseph," said Rhiannon, finally picking up a spoon to spread honey on her bread.

"Comfort and joy, comfort and joy, never thought I would laugh again," he shook his head; still clearly puzzled by the way he was feeling. He lowered his voice to a whisper, and leaned across the table. "I promised her, I'd visit chapel once per month. Isn't that amazing? Me making a promise... in my dream!"

"Will you keep it?" asked Brianna with quiet excitement.

"Well now then, that's the funny thing isn't it? Because that promise feels more real to me today, than the promise I made in church when we got married. And I meant every word I said that day, and I meant every word I said to her in my dream last night. So yes, I will be going, for I am a man of my word."

Rhiannon and Brianna smiled knowingly at each other. Each miracle was different, but each one came with an overflowing of joy and a desire to be closer to God.

Chapter 7

AN EARLY MORNING MIST swirled across the land, its touch icy and damp. Robins, blackbirds and thrushes chirped their birdsong, awaken o world and enjoy thy day for there is ever promise in the rising of the sun!

Joseph had bid them stay a while, to wait and see if the hunters would return, but Rhiannon had an urge in her spirit to move on, and so here they were on the road once more. Their cape hoods pulled low shielded their faces from the damp morning air, and talking was difficult, so they marched with eager step towards Bedyford and a temporary new life in comfortable silence. If Rhiannon had heard from God correctly, she only had a few months left with her daughter. She wanted to find her a home, a nest of security, and please Lord, love. Designing a plan for her daughter's future as they went, her steps were brisk.

Brianna didn't mind the quick pace; she was cold and longed for the warmth of strenuous exercise. She listened to their clogs clacking on the wet path, Lord but she hated walking during the colder months. The overnight downpour, mist and fog had turned the path to a muddy mess and her steps were slowed by the sinking in and pulling out of her clogs. Too many times her feet slipped out of her clogs and into the mire, and it wasn't pleasant. She was concentrating on watching where she stood to try and find the harder parts of the narrow road, when Rhiannon came to a halt, putting out her arm to stop her daughter from walking.

"They're close." She didn't need to say more, Brianna followed her mother's shadow, as they ran off the road and dived through a tiny opening in the hawthorn hedge. Brianna's cape caught on a thorn; she struggled to get it free. The sound of horses approaching grew louder. Brianna's heartbeat quickened. She finally managed to untangle herself and dropped to the ground beside her mother as three men rode by.

Each horseshoe clomp on the ground, echoed the thud in Brianna's chest. She wanted to be sick, her stomach churned. She moaned. The dogs growled. Rhiannon's hand shot out and grabbed her daughter's arm in warning.

Benedict swung around in his saddle to look at his brothers. "Did you hear something?"

"No," they both replied.

The dogs seemed confused. Caleb was racing ahead, sniffing the ground and growling as he went. Levi seemed to follow a scent to the hedge, but then turned and raced back down the path they had come.

Benedict turned around again looking ahead. But something gave him pause. He stopped, pulling on the reins he urged his horse to turn back. With measured pace he returned to the place where Rhiannon and Brianna had pushed through the hedge. Something glistened in the morning light. He swung off his horse and bending one knee, reached down to touch it. He pulled a tiny piece of gray cloth off a branch and twirled it in his fingers. It hadn't been there long, for it was not too wet nor was it soiled. Curious. He looked up as his brothers approached.

"What intrigues you in the hedge, Ben?" asked Nathaniel.

Benedict showed them the cloth.

"Just a passer-by," said David.

Just an arm's length away from the witch hunter, Rhiannon began a silent whisper. "Hide us, O Lord our God, for the time has not yet come."

"Nathaniel, you are the smallest of us. Pass you through the hedge and confirm what is on the other side."

Used to doing everything his brother requested, Nathaniel swung off his huge black stallion, and jumped down. As he approached the hedge, none of the brothers noticed that the hawthorn branches thickened and snarled towards each other.

Nathaniel pushed where he thought he'd seen an opening just a moment before. Thorns tore the flesh of his hand, making him pull back sharply. "Nothing but wildlife could pass through there, Ben."

Benedict felt a shiver run down his back. He was sure there had been an opening just a moment before. He stared at the hedge with furrowed brows for a long time before shaking his head.

"You're right. Come on, let us depart for Coventre. I will interrogate that girl who told us they came south. We should have listened to the others who all said the witches traveled north. I will get the truth from her, and if she is a witch then we will hand her over to the magistrates for hanging!"

"Benedict! She was but a child!" David's face was alarmed. He had faithfully followed his brother these past five years and had lost all the softness of being a kind and good-natured fellow. He'd felt his heart harden with each witch killing, but he was faithful above all else, and believed his brother heard from God. But a child? Hard though he may have become, he didn't believe he could stomach that.

Benedict did not respond. He mounted his horse and continued forward, his back straight, his resolve determined.

Rhiannon and Brianna waited until they were sure the brothers were gone and not returning, and then they held hands and raced across the farmer's field for the relative safety of an oak wood.

Salt-saturated air filled their lungs as they approached the fishing town of Bedyford. The contrast of quiet countryside to bustling town was stark. They hadn't expected to see quite so many people in the streets. They offered a smile to any who glanced their way, and were relieved when their smiles were returned. Not all towns were friendly, especially since the war.

Seagulls cawed and flew in circles above the docks. The River Torridge streaked across the land dividing the town into two halves. As they approached the twenty-four arched stone bridge, they slowed to admire the beautiful craftsmanship.

"Where shall we head?" Brianna asked when they were more than halfway over the bridge.

"I am letting my feet lead us, but the lights over there are calling." Rhiannon pointed towards the far side of the bridge where warehouses lined the river bank.

"You'll not find work in the docks, if that's where yer heading," said a young woman who was approaching from the other side.

"We thought to mend nets for the fishermen," said Brianna.

"Ya too late for the ship industry, men have been flooding in for months now."

Both Rhiannon and Brianna stopped short. They trusted God for all things, but this news was surprising.

"You are kind to guide us," said Rhiannon. "Would you have any suggestions for two travelers hoping for employment and a place to sleep?"

"Umm, I might have done back in the summer, but now I'm not so sure ya'll have any luck."

Brianna moved to tell her that they didn't rely on luck, but Rhiannon stalled her by placing a hand on her arm.

"Does nothing at all spring to mind?"

"Umm, let me see…"

"Maybe, someone who would take us in, even just for a night?"

"Can ya pay?"

Rhiannon shook her head, "Unfortunately not."

"Where ya come from?"

Normally, they would not mention where they had stayed to protect the people that offered them shelter, but Rhiannon felted moved by the Holy Spirit to reveal where they had been. "We've just been staying with Miller Joseph, and before that we bided a while with farmer Coombes and his family."

The young lady's eyes popped wide. "Ya've been staying with Billy and Mary?"

Rhiannon smiled. People may think the world is a small place and believe in coincidences, but she believed in a big God who always went before them. "Yes, that's right. You know them?"

She swished her dress in a very young girl fashion. With a deep sigh, "Yeah, I know them well. We dwell near their cousin the Blacksmith, and several times throughout the year our paths will cross. Tell me, how is John?" She batted her eyelashes and dipped her head allowing an escaped tress of hair to fall over her face covering her expression.

"He fares well," replied Rhiannon, smiling.

Just then, a man cried out from his wide cart. "Mind the way, mind the way!" All three women stepped as close to the stone wall as possible as the cart, laden down with wares, rumbled by.

"It's been so busy here with the commissioning of new ships. On top of that the pottery kilns are firing every day and the town is booming, that's for sure," the girl paused for a moment and scratched at her chin. "Ya know the Blacksmith might take ya in, seein' as you know his cousin an all. Not sure he'll have work for ya, but his premises behind the workshop are big, sure he could squeeze ya in for a night or two if nothing more. Should I show ya the way?"

"That would be very kind of you," smiled Rhiannon.

They turned and walked back along the bridge the way they had already come.

"May I ask your name?" Brianna asked as they turned left after the bridge and made their way along Barnstaple Street. The tide was on its way out, pulling back and displaying dark gray sand. The pungent aroma of fish and seaweed rose to assault their noses. Brianna couldn't help wrinkling her nose.

The young lady laughed. "Ya get used to it after a while, and when the tide is in ya can hardly note it. I'm Audra." She turned so that she was walking backwards for a few steps. Lifting her heavy layered, patch dotted skirt she dipped her knee and performed a small curtsy. "How fare thee ladies?"

Audra's faded, dull-gray and well-repaired clothes, wooden clogs and tattered straw hat, under which a once-white coif covered thin mouse-brown hair, portrayed her poor status.

Their own clothes were also well-worn in, and often repaired. Yet, everywhere they went people instantly deferred to them in such a way as to acknowledge them as higher born. As they put on no airs or graces, this could only be attributed to their genteel accents, the only thing that remained from a history of high-born families, riches and comfort.

"Good day to you Audra, 'tis a pleasure to meet you," said Brianna, who would have returned the short curtsy except for the heavy load on her back. Instead, she dipped her head and smiled broadly.

Audra turned to face forward again, but fell into step in between mother and daughter. "What brings ya to our fair town?"

"We are in need of earning a living that will tide us over winter, and heard Bedyford was the place to be; a booming town, no less."

"Aye, 'tis that indeed, it is."

They hadn't gone much further when Audra turned, and grinning at them pointed. "But hold, for here stands the forge."

The stone building before them stood back off the road a good distance, its blackened brick walls portrayed an industrial tone, and the hammering which pounded their ear drums provided evidence that the Blacksmith was within.

"I'll introduce ya, for Edward, kindhearted soul though he be, is oft ready to bite ya 'ed off rather than give ya the time of day."

Brianna's eyebrows arched high, and upon observing the dismay, Audra dissolved into giggles.

"Come on, Edward be a gentle giant really."

They followed her over the barren land that lay in front of the forge, but waited outside while she ducked through the low load-bearing door frame – the solid door of which was always propped wide-open and back against the wall.

They heard Audra speaking quietly followed by grumbles from the Blacksmith – he didn't sound overly keen on having visitors. Nevertheless, he was tempted to come and greet them by the exceedingly cheerful exhortations of his neighbor's daughter. He had to stoop low to come through the doorway. As he straightened himself upright once more they were able to take in his appearance. Audra had spoken the truth when she'd declared him tall. He was easily one of the tallest men Brianna had ever seen, she barely came up to his chest. He made Audra appear a midget as she stood beside him. His face was largely covered by a black, white-streaked beard and moustache. His eyebrows were also on the bushy side! His nose appeared swollen, his cheeks ruddy, and his black curly hair escaped the confines of a leather cap. His width was great, but he didn't appear overweight. Leather leg-coverings and an apron enveloped his body, while his arms were clad in massive leather gloves. They added to his size, coupled with the mammoth, double-faced hammer that swung from his right hand, he appeared strong and rather frightening.

Rhiannon composed herself, hastily dampening down a sudden flush of admiration. "Well met, good sir. We are acquaintances of your cousin Billy and his family. We are pleased to meet you."

"Humph!" His snort was growl-like and not at all welcoming.

Audra knocked his arm with her elbow. "Ack, come on grumpy."

Edward scowled at her, before turning back to face them. "I've taken on two men to help already; I cannot pay for more workers. Still, I do have a room in which you can sleep, and you are welcome to share my hearth if you will share your meals with me. I am no cook, and although I get by I miss the touch of a woman around the stove. Once you find work you can pay me for your lodgings. Does that sound fair to you?"

Rhiannon sucked in a whoosh of gratefulness, and let out a sigh. "Indeed, Blacksmith that sounds more than fair. 'Tis kind you are to take us in when we have no coin to pay you as yet. I hasten to add, we are both strong workers, and I am sure we will be earning very soon."

"Humph! We'll see I'm sure."

Audra knocked him again, and he pretended to knock her on the top of her head. "Get home girl, there's always work needs doing in your abode so there is."

Audra pulled him down by the sleeve, and kissed his cheek. "Now don't be grumpy, I will fetch me'self back tomorrow eve, and check ya have well-treated them."

"Humph!"

Audra nodded towards them as she set off. "I'll ask around, ya never know, maybe there's still people hiring."

"That's very kind of you," Rhiannon called after her. "We're indebted to you."

"Pah! Don't be daft. Sleep ya well, at least you won't be cold here!"

A good distance away from the heat of the forge's furnace, sat a large wood-built building. The walls weren't perfectly pitched, so the wind slipped through with icy ease between the cracks, meaning the forge might be a hot house, but the blacksmith's dwelling was rather cold.

Over the years, they had slept in woods, caves and on moorlands, so in comparison this rickety home offered great comfort and their thanks were genuine. It took them only two days to find employment. The Chestnut Inn hired Rhiannon as a serving maid and kitchen help, and Brianna found herself a position with a fishing family in need of a general help. The wife of the household had 'umm'ed and 'arr'ed at first, but by the time Brianna had rattled off all her accomplishments the woman had been won over. The fact that Brianna could work with the woman's newborn carried on her back, held fast by a shawl, was the point most appreciated. It seemed the fisher's wife was too busy to attend to an overly demanding child. Brianna loved her new position, and juggled tending the children with her other tasks with skill and angelic patience. She soon became a much-loved member of the Beardwood family.

The days slipped into weeks, and the weeks flew by. With both receiving only every other Sunday as a rest day, it was the middle of December before they were both free on the same day and could attend church together.

This particular Sunday, a bitter icy-bite blew through town. Blue-gray clouds hung low and filled the sky without breaking.

"We'll have snow before the Sunday next," said Edward stoking the fire.

"Won't you change your mind and come to worship with us, Edward? Darvon and family do come." He looked up at Rhiannon as she wrapped her woolen cape around her.

"I'm not for changing, too long in the tooth. You can call me heathen if it pleases, but I'm honest as the day is long when I say… the only good thing to come about from the reign of Charles II is that he did away with the twelve pence fine for not attending church. Now I pay my taxes but not my tithes to the church, and in doing so I'm much closer to building my stone-built home. And *that*… is all I have to say!"

"A simple no would have sufficed, Edward." Rhiannon's words matched her soft smile, and the Blacksmith's eyes twinkled when he looked back at her.

"Aye, probably would, but this grump has a reputation to uphold."

The streets of Bedyford were well-pitched with slats and the stones kept clean. This made walking, even in harsh weather, easy. Mother and daughter, both with cloaks held close and hoods pulled over their heads, went with speedy pace to St Mary's. Icy wind tugged at their capes as they crossed the bridge, and they were glad when they reached the other side. Turning left they made their way to the old Norman chapel. The peel of the chapel bell filled the air. The externally humble two-part building, with its tall bell tower, belied the beauty that lay within. The columns and the Romanesque architecture gave the red-stone built house of worship a grand atmosphere. Of course, it also ensured that the building remained cold in both winter and summer!

They hastened through the ornate doorway, pushing their hoods back and smiling at the ushers. The organ was small compared to many churches they had visited, but as they took their seats, its melodic sounds filled them with comfort. They were squeezed tightly in their pew as the chapel filled to capacity. As the priest made his way to the pulpit, Brianna felt a tingling on the back of her neck and spun around to see if someone watched her. At the very back of the church, near to the door, stood an imposing man of African descent with the darkest of skin she had ever seen. He appeared taller than average and his clothes labeled him as a man of means. His complete attire was black, and for a moment Brianna fancied that his eyes also shone like black onyx. She couldn't help the gasp that came from her lips as a sense of evil washed over her.

"What is it?" asked Rhiannon.

With large eyes Brianna looked at her mother before saying, "Look."

Rhiannon turned her head to look towards the back but could see nothing unusual. "What is it?" she whispered. But when Brianna searched she could no longer see the man that had caused goose bumps to rise on her arms.

"O God the Father, creator of heaven and earth," began the priest.

Rhiannon and Brianna both turned back sharply, and joined in with the congregation.

"Have mercy upon us."

"O God the Son, Redeemer of the world,"

"Have mercy upon us."

"O God the Holy Spirit, Sanctifier of the faithful,"

"Have mercy upon us."

"O holy, blessed, and glorious Trinity, one God,"

"Have mercy upon us."

"Remember not, Lord Christ, our offenses, nor the offenses of our forefathers; neither reward us according to our sins. Spare us, good Lord, spare thy people, whom thou hast redeemed with thy most precious blood, and by thy mercy preserve us, for ever."

"Spare us, good Lord."

"From all evil and wickedness; from sin; from the crafts and assaults of the Devil, and from everlasting damnation..."

"Good Lord, deliver us."

The priest continued to lead them through the new Book of Common Prayer. Although, the words spoke truth over their lives, Brianna couldn't help but wonder where the invitation for God to join them was. There appeared to be rigidity within the page, a 'conforming' that didn't speak of the father-child relationship with the Lord which both women treasured. Two years this new version had been out, and already it felt like chains around their faith.

As Brianna looked around the chapel she saw the reverence with which people followed the service and knew that it comforted them, and for that she rejoiced. So much change had been imposed upon the people of Britain in the 130 years since Henry VIII introduced the Anglican Church, it was no wonder people eagerly adapted to the new Book of Common Prayer.

On their way out of the chapel, Brianna kept searching for the mysterious African man, but didn't catch sight of him.

"*He* was here I tell you!"

The loud statement came from a woman a short distance in front of them. Of middling age and obvious poverty she presented a wretched image. The state of her clothes, both filthy and smelly, was enough to cause the higher-born to pass by in wide circles, taking invisible brooms to brush away the unsightly scene, 'not seeing' enabling them to keep clear consciences and their comfort undisturbed. Within their respectability, education and finery, all Brianna could see was their ignorance and bigotry.

The distressed woman grabbed the arm of a man who was trying to ignore her. "Thomas I tell ee, the man is back. No goodwill does he bring, harm he intends towards you and yours. Listen me well. Keep thy wits about thee for he is the Raven!"

The tall, lanky man knocked her arm and sent her flying to the cobbles. "Get out of town Temperance, and keep thy witching words inside your head. Or it will be the Black Wolf that I send for, and that's the truth."

The congregation in hushed whispers avoided eye contact with the dirty, red-headed woman, and rushed to their warm homes.

"What is so wrong with me expecting Christian charity from my neighbors and betters?" Temperance spat on the floor and cursed under her breath. "I ain't no witch, I'm just a poor and simple widow."

With either pity or a desire to see her gone, a gentleman threw a copper into her lap. Rather than give thanks she cussed at him. "What are yer supposed to do when yer belly is a turning and a churning from lack of food? 'Tis hard to curtsy and grovel I tell 'ee."

"Dirty wench, go back to your hovel," barked an elderly man of high standing. He waved his walking stick at her. "Be gone before someone puts you in the stocks."

As the crowd dispersed Rhiannon and Brianna approached the poor woman. "Come," said Rhiannon, offering the woman her hand. "Come and have a meal with us."

Temperance pushed herself up and stood before them. "Tis not fair, nor true... what they accuse me of. I'm no witch. I'm just a widow whose feet are blue with cold and belly that's not been fed a long while."

"Come a ways with us. Where we bide is plenty of food to fill you today. It will warm you at least."

Temperance looked Rhiannon up and down, she made a movement as if to agree but suddenly froze. Her large green eyes flicked open wide, and her body stiffened in obvious fright. Mother and daughter both turned to see what had upset her so. Standing at the edge of the road was a man in a black cape that flowed in the wind. Beneath the cape his clothes too were black. His face cast in the shadow of his hood was impossible to see.

"Unless 'ee learn your children better, they will repeat the mistakes of the past," Temperance shouted, bringing both their attention back to her.

"What?" asked Brianna, but Temperance had turned and was running down the street.

"Wait!" cried Brianna.

Rhiannon put her hand on her daughter's arm. "Leave her be, it is time to go home."

"But…"

"Now Brianna!" There was sharpness in Rhiannon's tone that Brianna had never heard before, so although she was surprised, she obeyed and walked briskly beside her mother without talking.

Chapter 8

SHROUDED IN DARK SPIRITS the brothers approached Coventre. A bitter north wind blew snowflakes at them with disregard for their comfort or warmth. All around the land was whitening, hiding bleak winter starkness under a deceptive beauty of snow-kissed white.

They had conversed more in the last few days than they had in months. None of it pleasant or amiable! Benedict's steadfastness in his mission, and his inability to hear their arguments had driven a rift between them that appeared too vast to surmount.

"Brother, are you not for changing?" Nathaniel asked as they neared the Greyfriars Gate.

"My mind and purpose are set," Benedict affirmed. There was no need to once more go over their earlier argument regarding the young girl who had told them to go south when last they were here.

"Then this is where I must bid you farewell." Nathaniel pulled his horse to a stop. David and Benedict also drew to a halt, and tugged slightly on their reins, turning their horses around so they could face their young brother.

Nathaniel had grown thin. Benedict was not blind to the ill-health that hung from his brother's every pore, but he had brushed it off, believing God would restore him with vigor and purpose in due course. They planned to return home to fulfill a promise to their mother to be there for Christmas celebrations and prayers. He'd been sure a few weeks of home-cooking and motherly pampering would have restored his brother to vibrant health. Although the snow had eased off somewhat, earlier they had ridden through a blizzard. Nathaniel's black leather, tall capotain hat with its wide rim had kept his head dry, but his cape clung to his body emphasizing his thinness. His eyes, a dull brown, seemed to look at Benedict without seeing. His hollow cheeks gave him a skeletal definition. For the first time, Benedict truly grasped how the hunting and killing of witches had drained the life from his younger brother.

"David should go with you to accompany you upon the road."

Nathaniel shook his head. "God will walk beside me I am sure, David must remain with you."

Benedict tumbled over a plethora of thoughts that flowed in quick succession, ending abruptly on… *so David can keep you on the narrow path.* He turned his glance to David to see which brother he would agree with. Either decision would cause him pain, so he gave a short nod, trying to imply his acquiescence to David's decision whatever it was.

"I shall stay the course, and God willing, see this task to completion." David narrowed his eyes as he stared at Benedict. "These are the last… are they not?"

Benedict's horse took a few steps to the side, growing impatient. Benedict tapped her neck, stalling for time as he summoned the right words. "God has not laid upon me the urge to visit any more towns. I take this to mean that these two witches are the last He has charged us with finding." It wasn't a lie, nor was it fully truthful.

David moved his horse next to Nathaniel's; once there he grabbed his brother's arm. "Go well and in peace. God willing, we will be joining the family for the celebrations of our Savior's birth. Give our parents our thoughts and blessings, and tell them we come as soon as we can. Our long journey draws to an end, praise be to God."

Nathaniel returned his brother's clasp. "God be with you brother."

"And also with you," responded David.

When they let go of each other, Nathaniel walked his horse over to Benedict. Benedict thought he was going to embrace him as he had David. Instead, he removed his hat, and before Benedict could cry out an objection, he ripped the thin leather belt that circled the crown. He turned the belt's silver buckle over in his hand. Benedict had them made by a silversmith when their youngest brother Joshua had died. In the center of each buckle was an angel and over-laying the angel, a cross. It signified that they had become avenging angels for the Lord their God. He handed it to Benedict.

The witch hunter stared at the buckle, but wouldn't take it. "It is yours," he whispered.

Nathaniel kept his arm outstretched. "I never believed in my spirit that I was an avenging angel. I followed you willingly, because I know you to be a great man of God. But this task has been nothing but a bitter taste in my mouth and I can deny no longer that it has sickened me. Take it Ben for I will not carry it, nor my pretense, any longer."

It took a powerful command for Benedict to prevent his hand from shaking, as he accepted the buckle. His shoulders felt a weight he'd only felt once before, and that at the time of Joshua's death. He couldn't speak, so did the only thing he could, a brisk nod of acceptance.

Nathaniel put his hat back on, then without another word set off back down the road that led south and towards home. Caleb and Levi ran a little after his horse and whined, before turning around and coming back with low heads. Benedict was their master, no matter how much they loved his brothers.

David and Benedict regarded one another with sober expression, five years was a long time to have been on the road.

Their mission, although holy, was thoroughly repugnant to all of them. Benedict never wavered and kept his gaze towards the heavens, but both Nathaniel and David had become haunted by the murders of twelve women, especially those the magistrates condemned to die by burning on the stake.

"To Ye Olde Windmill then?" asked David.

"Aye, and pray they have fine rooms available for us."

Although the streets throughout Coventre were ancient, the cobbles had worn with time making a smooth a street as could be found. With paling light most people had returned to their homes and hearths, seeking warmth. Their horses' clip-clops resounded loudly in the quiet alleyways and empty streets. They soon turned a corner into Spon Street, where they approached the inn with much thanksgiving.

"I wish Nathaniel would have spent the night with us and set out with first light," said David.

Benedict grunted. He agreed, but was too hurt by what he perceived as his brother's betrayal to admit his worry over him. They dismounted and led the horses down the side of the inn and into the back courtyard. No one was about, so they tied the horses to the hitching post and entered the building through a rear doorway.

As soon as the door banged closed, the innkeeper came rushing to greet them. The ruddy-faced, stocky man tried his hardest to keep the smile upon his face when he spotted who had entered, for the Black Wolf was bad for business. Looking between them, he asked, "Well met good sirs. Are you one light today?"

"Yes," replied Benedict pulling off his leather gloves. "Please have someone tend the horses immediately; they have traveled far today and need attention."

"As you say, so shall it be. May I inquire; will you be staying a while?"

"We need rooms if that is what you are asking? Do you have free rooms?"

"Yes, yes of course Master Everleigh, travelers are few and far between in winter months."

"Very good. We shall take ale and whatever you are offering by way of a meal by the fire. We are in need of warming our bones."

The Innkeeper nodded, and Benedict and David strode into the front of the inn towards the huge stone fireplace. "Bring something for the dogs," Benedict called over his shoulder.

They seated themselves in high-backed wainscot oak chairs at a small table near the crackling fire, Caleb and Levi settled in on either side of Benedict's legs. Benedict ran his fingers over the embroidered gauntlet on his gloves. His mother had lovingly patterned all their gloves as if they were high-born. The gloves' frivolousness irritated him, while thoughts of home and family brought him comfort.

Five years of tracking down witches had taken a toll on the brothers' camaraderie; the result was a silence that spoke louder than words. After a humble meal and two tankards of ale each, Benedict was about to retire when David decided to speak his mind.

"We have followed you without question."

Benedict lowered his body back into his seat, keeping his gaze firmly on the burning embers within the stone fireplace.

"We have tracked down both witches and Devil worshipers and handed them over to the town magistrates in exchange for heavy purses."

Benedict swung his stare towards his brother. "I do not do this to gain riches!"

"I know why you hunt, Ben."

Benedict returned his gaze to the fire. "I have never mentioned before, and this to the decrement of my character, but I have appreciated and valued both of your company upon this long and arduous journey."

"We traveled with you gladly."

"Past tense, so you too are going to leave."

"Not yet. I said I would remain until these last two witches are caught, I will not retract my word. But I must be honest and say that I do not do it with pride anymore. The toll for this mission is too great, Ben. Do you not have nightmares regarding the women we have had killed?"

"We didn't kill them."

"Strictly speaking that is true. However, if we hadn't hunted them down and handed them over to the authorities, they would still be alive."

A flame of heat spread from Benedict's neck to his cheeks, of which his brother was acutely aware, yet he had more to say.

"Can you honestly say that we have done the right thing?"

"Yes!" The word was spat deceptively quietly. Benedict shifted his weight in his chair and swiveled to face David once more. "You test my integrity!"

David's hand shot across the table and momentarily clasped his brother's arm. "Never! I know you are a man of God and only seek to do His will. All I ask you is... do you not... ever wonder if what we are doing is *right*?"

Benedict pulled back his arm. "If I did, that would mean that I do not trust that I've heard from God, and if that were true I would be lost, for how could I carry on not knowing what is or not God's instructions for me? I don't doubt; I cannot! In all things I believe that God speaks to me. If that were *not* true…"

"You misunderstand me. I do not question if you hear from God, I merely ask how you carry the burden of what we have done in His name."

"I keep my thoughts and prayers focused towards the Lord. I know He would not give me a burden to carry that is too heavy for my shoulders."

"Maybe it is because the Lord gave the task to you and not to us that we struggle so." David paused and looked into the hearth with knitted brows and puzzled eyes. After a while he continued. "In the beginning, after Joshua's death, I was full of fervor to complete this task, but over time I have become empty and have lost sight of the reason for the hunt. You are known as the Black Wolf, and the name suits you well, for indeed you are as black as night and live for the hunt. Not so Nathaniel and I. With each hanging, ducking and burning our faith has been waning. Will you forgive us brother?"

With tear-filled eyes, Benedict looked across at his brother, whom he loved and regarded highly. "There is nothing to forgive, nothing at all. I am just grateful you have stayed the course and are with me to the end." He wanted to add… for I don't think I can finish the course without you, but the words wouldn't come.

"Come lads," Benedict said as he stood up. The dogs stood and stretched and followed their master to their night lodgings.

Benedict's mother – Mary Everleigh couldn't rest. She paced the floor, her hands clasped tight in front of her stomach, which growled as it spun making her feel sick.

"What ails you woman?" asked Benjamin, who had grown impatient by the constant pacing.

"I keep seeing the chapel of Wodestok, and an image of St Christopher with his staff and red cloak. I do not know why but I feel like he is calling me to him. I must go Benjamin. Would you grant me leave and use of the cart?"

"By all that is holy are you gone mad woman? The storm is building; already the snow drifts outside the door. In a few more hours it will be three or four hands deep!"

Mary flew to Benjamin's side where he sat at his desk. She sank to her knees and clutched at his arm. "Please husband, grant me leave, for I'll not be able to settle until I've been to Wodestok and back."

"Mary, love, it is impossible. I have to finish this sermon for the morning service and I can't go gallivanting around the lanes."

"I'll go with Mama," said Anne from the doorway of the study.

"But the storm…" answered Benjamin.

"God will go with us, of this I am sure. Please husband?"

He wanted to decline. If something happened to Mary… well that just wasn't worth thinking about. But how could he refuse when her faith was so strong.

Mary saw, from the sudden slump of his shoulders, that he was about to agree. She jumped up and wrapped her arms around his neck. "Thank you, thank you," she said popping kissing onto his forehead.

"Be off with you," he shooed her away. "Be sure to wear two cloaks each, and take the thickest woolen blanket for your knees. If the going gets too hard for old Nell, well you turn her around and come straight back!"

"As you say my love," Mary heard her husband sigh heavily as he returned to his writing.

The stone marker on the roadside just outside Wodestok had *8.3 miles to Oxford* etched on it, but Nathaniel didn't see it. Moonlight danced and bounced off the snow and it was almost as light as day. Yet he slept, slumped forward over his horse's neck, oblivious to his surroundings. A highwayman's delight, although they would have been disappointed because in his distaste for what he had been a part of, he had never asked for his share of the coffers.

Anyone who saw him might wonder how the horse knew to carry on and more importantly... why he didn't fall.

Nathaniel himself was unaware of the two angels that walked either side of him. Giant warriors both, swords in hand radiating light they protected him from falling as well as the darts from Lucifer's minions. The man was ill, but this was not his time to die, and the angels would accompany him until his mother and sister turned up to take him home.

Chapter 9

RUMORS FILLED THE TOWN about the witch Temperance. People heard her cry out that the Raven was going to kill her if she didn't do as he bid. Most people acknowledged that she was touched in her mind, pitied her and gave her a wide berth. 'Tsk,' others muttered, 'an African man who changes into a raven? The woman is in cahoots with the Devil!' If they had known she would kill three and blind a fourth, they might have paid her cries a little more attention. Indeed, in eighteen years' time at her trial, the good folk of Bedyford would question why the Black Wolf hadn't brought her before the magistrates himself. 'Wasn't it the witch hunter's fault for not listening to the whisperers and dealing with the widow Temperance then? Weren't the deaths of those people upon Benedict Everleigh's head?'

Brianna's heart overflowed with pity for her. She tried several times to comfort the disturbed woman, but her every attempt was vehemently rejected. In the end Brianna settled to praying for Temperance from a distance, though none of her prayers seemed to be answered.

It was very rare that the prayers of mother and daughter weren't answered in an obvious way, but they had long ago given up trying to understand why some people never received their healing touch. Yet there was something about Temperance that caused the lack of a visible answer to prayer to ruffle Brianna's peace.

More and more of late, Brianna battled with fear. She hid it well behind a smile and a composed countenance, but she knew it was growing inside her like an illness, darkening her soul, dragging her away from God. *If* the rumors of Temperance reached the Black Wolf he would surely return, and *if* her mother's prophecy was going to come true they only had months left together. Part of her wanted to subdue the poor woman. Deep within her she knew the motive for such a wish revealed her selfish nature – maybe that's why God seemed distant regarding her prayers for Temperance? Had she become as flesh and no longer worthy of the ear of God? That thought alone drove fear through her body more keenly than an axe splitting wood.

Rhiannon, normally so attuned to her daughter, might have missed the growing distress caused from fear due to the fact that her attention seemed to be held with increasing pleasure upon the dear blacksmith, their growing attraction becoming obvious to all. Both glowed when in each other's company, neither ceased their smiling and often they sat in long conversation in the seats either side of the fireplace.

Knowing her time with Edward was short, Rhiannon was careful not to express her growing affection. Still, it gave such pleasure to converse with someone attracted to her again that she couldn't help spending time with him. Her self-explanation on the amount of attention she paid him was that God-willing, she might be able to lead him to Jesus, and indeed their conversation always artfully pulled towards God and His love.

The night before Christmas, in the year of our Lord 1664, Brianna finished work at the Beardwood's home, and made her way into town to fetch some food to go towards their celebration meal the following day. Snow had been falling for three days and everything was fresh and white. Children threw snowballs at each other and twice Brianna was accidentally-on-purpose hit on the back from a stray ball of snow. Cheerfully, she scraped up some snow and threw it back, much to the children's delight. The smell of roasting chestnuts lured her down Cooper Street. Although she had gathered plenty herself from the woods not far from the forge, she would buy a bag to bless the lad who sold them.

"God bless ya," the boy said as she handed him a copper.

As she took the bag, she felt a compulsion to look up. Across the way, standing in the entrance to a dark alley, stood the mysterious man with ebony skin. She shivered. She wanted to turn and run home, but somehow her gaze was fixed upon his face which kept her standing still. The depths of his eyes, like bottomless pits, compelled her towards him. She took a step. She knew he smiled for there appeared crinkles around his eyes. She took another step, and as she did so she clearly heard the word, "come." He turned, his black cape spinning in the wind, dancing around him like a flock of birds.

Her mind a blank, she followed, two steps, and then two more. A chill descended her spine that heralded a searing heat, and still she followed. Had fear so corrupted her spirit that she held no resistance to villainous danger? The bag of chestnuts slipped from her hand and spilled across the cobbles. He half turned checking she followed, but he needn't have bothered for she complied with his will. Two steps and then two more... then, suddenly, she was knocked from her stupor when a tabby cat jumped from a ledge and scratched her face as he landed on her chest before jumping to the floor and darting down the alley. Brianna yelled out in pain.

"You alright, miss?" asked a stocky man approaching from the main street.

She raised a hand to touch her cheek, and brought away blood-smeared fingers. "A cat scratched me," she replied with a puzzled tone. "What am I doing down here?"

"Well, I don't rightly know, but it seems to me you've had a funny turn." The man quickly made the sign of the cross over his face and chest. "There be strange stuff going on these days, you mark my words, best you be heading home I should think."

"Yes I'll do that. Thank you for your assistance."

"It's a blessing to help others, so it is. You come along now." The man ushered Brianna back onto the main street, before taking himself back on his way.

Bemused for a moment, Brianna tried to work out why she was there, and then she remembered she'd come to fetch delights to enhance their day tomorrow. Smiling in relief she headed towards the market place.

Deep in the shadows of the alley, a man cursed the cat and hit his cane harshly against the wall.

Rhiannon's heart was overflowing with excitement, for Edward had agreed to accompany them to chapel this morning.

His remarkable transformation, due to a cleansed appearance and crisp best clothes, quite put Rhiannon in a flutter.

"You do look rather dashing, Edward," she said as he came into the room. Of course his reply was, "Humph!" But she could tell by the deepening color of his neck that the comment had somewhat pleased him.

On the way, Brianna felt on edge, but could not put her finger on why. It had finally stopped snowing, the clouds had parted, and sunshine poured down on the citizens of Bedyford as they answered the call to chapel and made their way towards the ringing bell of St Mary's.

From youngest to oldest, poorest to richest, everyone wore their best clothes. Young girls displayed giddy attention, swished in best frocks and adorned their hair with ribbon-tied bonnets. Young men never looked so fine, and the ladies' hearts did flutter. The priest, dressed in a pristine black cassock, overlain with a white surplice, completed with a rich-colored embroidered stole, kept his back straight, and his hawked-nose high. He gave the appearance of a rather fine, but overly thin bird fluttering beneath an ethereal dome.

Many embraced and wished a blessing upon each other. The service was overly long, the priest taking the opportunity of everyone's good nature, to remind them all of the pitfalls of not tithing. "Most inappropriate for a celebration of Christ's birth," Edward muttered under his breath.

Thankfully, the Bible readings from the prayer book and the hymns sung were joyous and raised the spirits of all present. An overwhelming peace descended on Brianna as they sang the last Psalm.

'My Shepherd is the Living Lord and He
that doth me feed
How can I then lack anything whereof I
stand in need?'

After the service, Brianna looked for Temperance but couldn't see her anywhere. She hoped the woman was somewhere warm and well-fed.

Joy surrounded the day of remembering Christ's birth. Two men, who worked with Edward including cousin Darvon, complete with wives and numerous children, came to partake in the Christmas day meal with them, which Rhiannon and Brianna had prepared. For once, the table overflowed with tasty food and everyone enjoyed the simple but delightful meal.

Afterwards, Brianna chased the children around trying (not too hard) to catch them and make them laugh. When happily exhausted, they played Tipcats, all of them hitting the smaller pointed piece of wood (the cat) into the air with the larger piece of wood. Trying to see who could keep their cat in the air the longest. Two of the smaller boys had sap-whistles, and it was probably for that reason... that the three sighed in relief when it was finally time for the families to leave.

"I am bereft of energy!" said Brianna sinking into a chair.

"I have not seen you laugh so much in a long time," replied Rhiannon.

Brianna smiled at her mother. It was true, ever since her mother's prophecy, she had been sinking low in her spirit.

"With the Beardwood children and now these... I think I might refrain from getting married, so I don't have to go through all that hard work!"

"I would have loved a large family," said Edward, who quickly lowered his gaze as he put the furniture back in its normal place.

Rhiannon's heart tightened. She couldn't let him get ideas, she would have to set him straight or they would have to move on.

To break the sudden silence Edward said, "We have more company next week, for my cousin Billy and his family will arrive for a visit."

"O, that's sure to please young Audra," laughed Brianna.

"Aye, but maybe not so much young John!" said Edward.

The awkward moment passed, but Rhiannon knew she would have to talk to him soon.

Later that night, after Edward retired, Rhiannon took hold of Brianna's hand and pulled her close for a tight embrace.

"Is everything well?"

Rhiannon stroked her daughter's anxious face, her eyes awash with emotion. "Everything is as it should be, but I would talk with you a while, for our time is running short."

Brianna's heart quickened its pace while her spirit sank like a pebble in water.

They sat on the floor opposite each other, as close to the low-burning embers as they could get, their skirts and under-skirts tucked around their legs.

"Why won't God change His mind?" Tears of frustration slipped from the corners of Brianna's eyes.

"No one knows the ways of God. For myself, I am happy to go to my eternal home, but for you I am concerned you will not see God's will in what is to come."

She took her daughter's hand and began stroking it. "I was born in a very fine manor. My parents were loving and kind, and my father a shrewd landowner and the son of a well-born and highly respected family. I married your father, who was a prince from Éire and a descendant of kings."

"I know, you have told me many times."

"How you used to love stories of your ancestors."

"I used to dream I was a princess, living in a castle far away."

"Did you? I never knew."

"You were always so happy and content; I didn't want to see your smile fade, as I somehow knew it would. I understood you weren't able to make my dreams come true."

"That you couldn't tell me fills me with sadness."

Brianna squeezed her mother's hand. "I am grown now, the dreams are long gone. Carry on with what you must say."

"I thought I was blessed, when you were born I was overwhelmed with gratitude to God for blessing me so much. I took nothing for granted. Then on one momentous day my world fell apart. Before I knew what was happening I had lost my husband, my home and comforts, my parents and my respectability. All security and belongings were stripped from me. I felt bereft, abandoned by God. You were a bundle in my arms, and my worldly possessions a bag on my back. I had, in one day, become a nobody."

Rhiannon's voice was soft and quiet; no bitterness seeped through her tale. Brianna wondered why she was retelling a history she already knew so well.

She took a deep breath and continued. "The first few nights I was beside myself with fear, not for me, but for you. How was I to protect you and keep you well? When you slept, I cried my grievances out to God. At first, I thought he had abandoned me, but now I understand he was giving me time to grieve and adjust. On the third night we were sleeping in an abandoned wreck of a building, its walls were mostly still standing, so we were sheltered from the wind. This night as I called out to Him, He answered. He led me to two places in the Bible, and by the time the sunrise approached my candles were gone but my heart soared."

The fire was nearly out. "Shall I add a few pieces?"

Rhiannon nodded, and Brianna placed a few small pieces of wood on the embers. They crackled and coughed and sank into the deep red.

"Which passages did He guide you to?"

"First… to Job. I read the chapter several times and allowed the lessons within to sink into my soul. As you know Job started off blameless and upright, and then throughout the forty-two verses of his life's story he fell into self-pity. It strengthened me to know that God would forgive me for lamenting against Him,

94

just as He forgave Job. At the end, in verse forty-two I read...
And in all the land were no women found so fair, as the
daughters of Job: and their father gave them inheritance among
their brethren." (9)

Rhiannon's face lit up with love. "I claimed the same
promise for you, that there would be none so fair as you, in face
or deed, and that God would lead you into your inheritance."

Brianna was unsure the Lord would ever answer that prayer,
but not wanting to upset her mother she asked, "What was the
second verse?"

"Romans chapter eight; but specifically verse twenty-eight."

"And we know that all things work together for good to them
that love God, to them who are the called according to his
purpose," quoted Brianna.

"I believe it is the most important verse in the Holy Book.
Everything that happens to us is not only for our own good, but
filtered through the loving hands of God."

"I cannot believe that you being murdered by the Black Wolf
will be for your own good!"

"*Everything!* We don't understand, but we must *trust* and
have faith. Without the promises of God we are as fish out of
water, bashing our souls against the earth until we die. As
waves roll high and crash upon the boat of your life, they speed
you to your destination and safe harbor. Without loss we never
appreciate gain. Without illness we never appreciate health, and
without fear we would *never* appreciate peace. *All* things work
together, not some or a few, all."

The fire of God radiated from Rhiannon with the heat of
passion, and Brianna felt convicted by her mother's words. "I
will try to trust, I promise, I'll try." Tears flowed in a steady
stream, and Rhiannon reached forward and pulled her daughter
into her arms.

"I know you will succeed my fair and beautiful daughter. God has revealed to me the riches that await you. You have nothing to fear, He will be with you every step of the way and His Holy Spirit will light your way."

Chapter 10

FINDING THE YOUNG GIRL, who'd told the witch hunters that the two miracle women had headed south-west, took them three days. By the time they spotted her and chased her to her home, both brothers surged with irritation and frustration. Both longed for the comfort of home and for the ugliness of their calling to be behind them.

Benedict hammered on the rickety door with his gloved fist. The door shook under his anger. David raised one eyebrow at his over-vigorous brother. The look only prompted Benedict to hammer some more.

"Come out, we would talk with you," Benedict commanded.

Other folk in the narrow cobbled street, took one look at the tall, black-clad witch hunters and dived into their doorways, or rushed on through the street as deftly as possible so as not to call attention in their direction. Some, who had hastened indoors, edged their linseed oil-soaked linen cloths back and peeped with bated breath through their window slats. The reputation of the Black Wolf was not exaggerated and they had a right to fear.

"Come out!" Benedict demanded again.

With a creak and agonizing slowness the door opened. A head appeared, but the woman's body remained behind the door, as if that might protect her.

"What do you want? We are true God-fearing folk here, there's nothing that would interest you within." The woman's words shook, and fear emanated from her wide eyes and trembling lips.

David's focus fell upon her few blackened teeth, he shuddered and pity arose in his chest. "Good woman, we would have words with your daughter. You have nothing to fear, 'tis only information we seek."

She cracked the door open a little wider, half emerging into the pale light that struggled into the darkened alley from a cloud-filtered sun. "Which daughter do you seek, for I have eight?"

Benedict couldn't help rolling his eyes, why was it that those who had nothing insisted on breeding with such enthusiasm? Girls as well, praise be to God that she at least had a few sons to soften the blow of burden.

"We know not her name, but she was the last to enter your home before we knocked," said David.

The woman looked behind, and the men followed her glance. A huddle of infants and young girls clustered together behind her.

"Betsy! What you gone and done now?" demanded the woman, letting go of the door and placing both hands upon her hips.

"Nothing! I ain't done nothing. Promise."

"Come forward Betsy," David commanded in a soft tone.

Her chin wobbled and she wrapped her arms tightly around her body. "I ain't done nought, I tell 'ee," half-defiant, half on the brink of tears.

"Come... here... now!" There was no arguing with the Black Wolf, his stentorian tone brooked no argument and the girl stepped forward. In their eagerness for the witch hunters to be gone, her sisters offered their assistance by propelling her forward with tiny pushes.

She barely reached the height of David's waist and he figured she was no more than seven or eight.

"Do you remember us?" asked Benedict.

Betsy nodded.

"Do you remember what you told us of the two women we search for?"

She nodded again.

"WHY DID YOU LIE TO US?!" So loud was his question that she shook as if a great wind had hit her.

She burst into tears, bringing her fists to her eyes.

"Why did you lie to us?" Benedict repeated.

Betsy was shaking. Her mother at last could bear it no longer and quickly stepped to her daughter's side and wrapped her arm around her shoulder. "Betsy love, speak to them quick and true, so that I may close the door and them be gone."

"I didn't lie," she sobbed. "I don't wanna go to the pits of hell. I know better than to lie, I do, I do."

The mother looked up at Benedict, lifting her chin in slight defiance. "My Betsy has never been known to lie before. I don't know why you think she has started now, but I tell you, your thinking is wrong."

David took a step backwards indicating his desire to leave. "The girl made an honest mistake Benedict, let us be on our way."

Benedict's attention was firmly on the girl's hands that remained at her face. Each finger displayed warts, one of the true signs of evil. He reached forward, knocked the woman aside and grabbed the girl by her shoulders. He shook her. "You Devil's spawn! You lied to protect them. Admit it, admit that you never saw them head towards the road to Gloucester! We know you lie, for we have searched every town and village that way and no one has seen them."

Betsy started screaming hysterically. The girls behind all started sobbing. The mother regained her stance and lunged at Benedict and started bashing him with her fists, all the while screaming, "Get off her. Get off her!"

"Benedict!" David yanked his brother by his cape and pulled him backwards.

Benedict let go of Betsy and turned to snarl at David. "Unhand me!" His glare alarmed David, and he let go of Benedict's cloak as if he'd been slapped.

"Woman you can hand your daughter over to me to take to the magistrates, or you can admit your guilt in her witchcraft and I will fetch you to the gaol as well. Which is it to be?"

The woman tightened her grip around Betsy, while at the same time glancing at her other daughters behind her. She started crying. "My Betsy's a good girl I tell you. She don't lie, and she's no witch. You're wrong; as God is my witness you are wrong!"

"She is but a child," urged David.

Benedict did not move.

"She's no witch," wailed the mother.

"This is a poor home, it is not a place of Devil worship or witchcraft. Look around you Benedict; do you see any signs of witchcraft?"

As if pulled from his stupor Benedict began to cast his gaze around the room. It was true, no herbs hung from the ceiling, no straw dolls lay about, in fact there was a distinct lack of anything in the place bar the bare essentials. He slowly turned his gaze back to Betsy's face.

"Why did you tell us they went south?"

Betsy gulped, but she looked up at him. For the first time Benedict noticed the clarity of her blue eyes, not green like most witches. "I promise you, I was coming back from the south-side well when I saw them creeping down the alleyways. I followed because I was curious as to them being up so early. They climbed over the broken wall so as not to pass through the gate then they headed up to the river, like they were going to go north. But I saw them turn on their path and head south. I swear to you I did."

"Maybe it was some other women she saw?" said David.

"Nah, I know it was them."

"How can you be so sure if you weren't in cahoots with them?" Benedict's voice was a hiss.

"I know it was them, cos I'd been looking out for them every day, ever since they healed Millie."

"Who is Millie?" asked Benedict.

"She is the daughter of the farrier, down Hill Street," replied the mother.

"What healing did she gain?" asked Benedict.

"They don't rightly know what was wrong with her. Only she'd been in her bed for ten days and had a fever. Knocking on death's door she was, when the women went to visit."

"The girl survived then?" asked David.

"Apparently, she got right out of bed right there and then and was restored to full health. It was a miracle. Many returned to Sunday prayers because of her, and that's the truth."

Benedict narrowed his eyes and his tightened lips urged the woman to close her mouth and utter no more.

"Many a person has done good deeds to hide their wickedness from the eyes of man. Being responsible for someone's healing doesn't mean that God is with them. Even

Satan himself is an angel of great beauty, you would not recognize him if he stood before you!"

"Shall we go and pay the farrier a visit?" David interrupted, while praying that God would send a bucket of Holy Water to drench his brother.

Benedict knew David was trying to usher him away from Betsy, but his skin crawled with a thousand spider-touches because he wanted to arrest her.

"It's not far from here, won't take you long," said the mother guiding Betsy to stand behind her back.

Benedict wavered. His instincts told him the girl was a witch, yet he had told David and Nathaniel that Rhiannon and Brianna would be the last witches they would arrest. Torn, he didn't know what to do. Then he spotted a spark in David's eyes and knew he must let the girl go if he didn't want to lose his family.

Without a word, Benedict spun on his heels and left.

"Take care to rub milk from the Dandelion's stem on her fingers, it will dissolve her warts, and ensure she washes her hands continually to prevent the spread." With that advice David gave a curt nod and strode down the alley after his brother. He caught the sound of the relief-sobbing that flooded from the woman and her daughters. He made the sign of the cross over his forehead and chest for the girl had just had a lucky escape and he knew it well.

The farrier was a giant of a man and not easily intimidated, yet he knew well that these brothers were instruments of evil and many a woman had lost her life because of them. In truth, the rumors of how many women had been killed as witches by the Black Wolf had been greatly exaggerated over time, but Benedict did little to contradict them. The farrier was a God-fearing man and didn't want to defer to witch hunters, but he also wanted to protect his daughter, and he knew how quickly something as precious as a healing could be turned into something it was not.

"Fare you well," he said removing his apron and inviting them in with a wave of his hand.

"Can we offer you refreshments?" asked his wife.

"Thank you but no," replied David.

"Would you sit?" asked the farrier. David noticed the size of the man's arms, like tree trunks, the strength the man must have would be far more than theirs, and yet he still acknowledged them as his betters.

"We have been told that your daughter Millie received a healing at the hands of two witches that we seek," said Benedict, carefully watching for their faces to give away their knowledge and fear.

The wife instantly paled and twisted her apron in her hands. The husband stood his ground and his expression never changed.

"Rhiannon and Brianna are great women of God; their miraculous gift of healing to our daughter was received with thanks to Jesus," said the farrier.

David threw Benedict a glance. His brother had stiffened and was quenching his rage. 'Righteous rage,' Benedict would call it when he defended his anger, 'borderline sin' David would counter in his mind.

"Tell me," said Benedict, "did they call upon the name of Jesus to heal your daughter, or did they simply *tell* Millie she was healed?" Benedict knew from countless tales that the women didn't call upon Jesus to come and do the healing, but he wanted to see if these were honest folk.

"No sire, they did not. They laid their hands upon our Millie's forehead and commanded the fever to leave," said the farrier.

"Only someone who is intimate with the evil of sickness would be able to command it what to do. This proves, yet again, that these women are thoroughly wicked and must be brought to trial for witchcraft!" Benedict snarled.

"Sire, we are simple folk and we do not profess to understand the workings of either God or the Devil. But this we know, our daughter was dying and now she is not. For that we thank and praise God every day."

"Did they tell you where they were going when they left Coventre?"

"No, they did not."

Benedict couldn't help the disappointment that flooded his body. He wanted this over and done with.

"What did the priest say of your daughter's healing?" he asked.

"He said God works in mysterious ways, and who was he to question God's will, for strangers healing when he could not."

Most of the priests they'd met over the years had answered the same way. It seemed that things were easier to understand when as one nation all worshiped God through the Catholic Church. What calamity Henry VIII brought down upon the people when he invented a new way to worship... so he could commit sin. The purity of worship, the innocence of man, the integrity of all things was falling into the pits of hell. Benedict was tired of trying to turn the tide.

"Shall we go?" asked David.

Benedict took a deep breath, "Yes, let us be gone." He looked at the couple before him; there was nothing to be gained here. "Thank you for your time."

As they made their way once more to the inn, David felt relief. "Do we return home for yuletide?"

"Yes, let us go to the one place we know to be full of righteous people," replied Benedict.

David was not in the mood to argue with his straight-backed brother, but he knew that all Benedict need do was to look with open eyes, for all around him, every day, were righteous men and women.

A bitter winter kept the brothers at their parents' home for much longer than Benedict had wanted. January slipped into February and he grew restless. He cried out to God daily to be able to complete his mission before spring.

Then callers and missives started arriving, and Benedict grew excited in his spirit.

Rumors about a witch called Temperance reached them.

It was said that the woman talked to the Devil who came to her in the appearance of a black man, and that after talking to her he would transform into a raven. Her tabby cat was said to carry poison in a glass vial around its neck, and people who spoke ill against her became sick. It was whispered with shock that she openly confessed that she turned herself into the tabby cat to carry out her curses. He'd met her once, when they'd searched Bedyford for the two heretics. He'd thought her more mad than witch, and had ignored the rumors about her then. However, the growing accusations were becoming too forceful to ignore, which is why they set off once more to return to Bedyford. Holes reported in the leg of one woman were a clear indication she must be using a doll to pierce the woman's body!

Nathaniel couldn't be persuaded to join them on this last crusade.

He didn't mention to David that they headed south once more to claim the purse for Temperance's arrest. Instead, he inferred that God was directing them towards Rhiannon and her daughter. Unbeknown to Benedict, that was exactly what the Lord was doing.

Chapter 11

FEBRUARY 1665 BROUGHT THE COLDEST weather England had ever seen. The town of Bedyford did not escape the harsh weather front that froze rivers and sank ships without remorse.

Only by wearing all of their clothes could they keep the bitter chill from their bones, and every day they gave up thanks that God had provided them a home with a roof for these white-tarnished months.

Each day the town's folk searched the skies hoping for an early spring. They looked in vain. Though the snow had stopped falling, frost had never been so busy and everything was eternally white. At first thought fun, even beautiful, now the snow-turned-ice represented death and hunger. The days harsh, the nights harsher, and the grave diggers kept busy.

Most days the sun did not manage to pierce the gray blanket that hung over their heads, a gloomy portent of winter's brutal claws. It wasn't a time to stop and gossip in the streets, it was a time to venture away from the hearth as little as possible. Yet all must eat, and not all could store up a full season's food supply, and so venture out they must. They scurried passed people they would normally stop and share a word or two with, now a nod was all the time they would give. Tempers grew high, and flesh became thin.

"You will be swift?" asked Rhiannon.

Brianna nodded as she pulled her cape around her shoulders.

"Where do you venture?" inquired Edward.

"To the forest to forage for some Wood-Ear, we will add it to the potage to thicken it some," replied Brianna.

"You'll not find any. Nothing can grow out there," said Edward. "Remain here in the warmth. We have enough, if we are careful, to last a few more weeks."

"You are kind to worry, but I must also walk for a while." She couldn't tell him without appearing ungrateful, that she was going crazy looking at the walls. The comfortable home had become a prison in the last few weeks since Mrs. Beardwood had let her go due to business being so quiet. She could stand it no more. Mama was lucky, for the tavern still had customers and she still ventured to work each afternoon. As for Edward, business was slow, so he filled his time by turning his hand to making things to sell in the spring markets, such as cauldrons and ladles, such work kept him busy.

Brianna kept their fire constantly lit, and stirred the potage all day long. In between she sewed, cleaned and mended... but she was still going crazy with the confinement. This excursion was overdue. She had been waiting twelve days now for the clouds to break so she could go with the sun to keep her warm. Now, it felt like that day was never coming, and she could wait no longer.

The first step outside the door was the hardest. Her every nerve tingled with cold and urged her to return to the hearth, but she was determined and off she set. Her pace was brisk, as she willed her movement to warm her limbs. The road out of town was deserted. She walked down the center of it, praying she would not slip on the ice. Once beyond the town's perimeter she cut across the wasteland and made her way to the forest. Although her skin tingled with the air's icy touch, her soul soared at the freedom. Soon she was singing and praising God in tongues. No sign of spring burst through the snow and ice with sprits of green, yet nature was nature, and although it might be delayed it would come soon.

The first trees she came to had no sign of tree mushrooms, and she began to think Edward had been right in his prediction.

Thinking the trees more protected from the wind might grow the Wood-Ear she ventured into the dense wood. Immediately, everything darkened as even the dim light of the hidden sun couldn't pierce beneath the branches of ancient trees. To her delight, she didn't have to venture too far before she came upon a tree whose branch joints spurted raised arcs of bark, out of which grew the desired mushrooms.

"Ha-ha, tonight our potage with be thick!" she declared to no one but the trees. She placed her wicker basket on the ground and walked around the tree trying to calculate how best to climb it.

"What'ya doin'?"

Brianna nearly jumped out of her skin. Spinning around she found a young lad of maybe eight or nine watching her from behind a tree.

"Are ya a witch?"

"No, why would you think such a thing?"

The lad stepped out from behind the tree and walked a little towards her. "You walked around that yew three times, thought maybe ya were casting spells or such like."

Brianna placed her hands on her hips. "Did you hear me chanting spells?" she tartly replied.

"No, but ya did sing on the way here, and though it did sound angelic-like I thought maybe ya were summoning the Devil – for I cud'nee understand a word!"

"Hush your mouth young man! Those are terrible words to speak over a person. I reject your dangerous mutterings and inform you I am a Christian and love no other than the Lord Jesus Christ!"

The boy crossed himself and muttered under his breath, "Father, Son and Holy Spirit."

"Do you do that because you are religious or superstitious?"

The boy opened his mouth, but before he could speak Brianna pointed at him. "Careful what you say and speak you the truth, for Jesus listens to everything."

"Course I believe, go to chapel every first Sunday in the month, don't I."

"Very well then, I shall believe you. Tell me... are you good at climbing trees?"

"The best there ever was."

She studied his painfully thin frame and made up her mind. "Then what say you to a deal? You climb the tree for me and pick those mushrooms, and in exchange I will give you a full bowl of hot potage for your troubles."

His eyes lit up, and Brianna smiled. "What's your name?"

"Named Oliver, and well met," he bowed with a flourish which caused Brianna to laugh.

"Brianna at your service," she answered giving a curtsy. "Now come, let us pick these mushrooms and return before we freeze." She bent her knee and clasped her hands together.

Oliver grinned as he took a leap, stepped on her hands and jumped up to the lowest branch. He picked the first mushroom. "Ya ready?"

"I am indeed."

He dropped the mushroom and Brianna caught it and dropped it into her basket. He shuffled along the branch and reached up to the next one. Soon twelve mushrooms lay in the wicker.

"I think we have enough now young Oliver, they don't last long and must be eaten within three days, come on down now."

"The next branch has huge ones, I'll just fetch them."

A gnawing of anxiety suddenly burst in Brianna's insides. "No, we have enough, come down now."

"Nearly there." Oliver pulled himself up onto the next branch, which creaked under his weight. "Here ya go," he said, dropping down three mushrooms which had grown in a tight cluster.

Just as Brianna lowered her gaze to drop the mushrooms into the basket, Oliver screamed. She looked up immediately to find Oliver falling. She ran forward to catch him, and just in time broke his fall. They landed harshly on gnarled roots poking through the ground.

Oliver was screaming hysterically, and for a moment Brianna didn't understand. She pushed herself up and turned to the boy who had rolled off her and landed an arm's length away.

A black raven was hovering over his face and fiercely pecking at the boy's eyes. For a moment she was stunned into a stupor, and then anger flowed through her spirit.

"Be gone you minion of the enemy!" As she pointed at it, a tornado of air hit the bird and sent it flying. It crashed with a thud into a tree and dropped to the ground, lifeless.

Oliver's screaming had turned into pitiful sobbing. Brianna brought her attention back to him. His hands were clasped over his eyes, from beneath which flowed an enormous amount of blood. A moment's panic rose within her, then she crushed it.

"Greater is He who lives in me, than he who lives in the world."(10) She put her hands over Oliver's. "Whatever damage there be, I command thee to be undone. Eyes and flesh be restored to full health."

111

With the passing of heat through her hands, Brianna knew the healing had been imparted, yet Oliver continued to sob.

"Oliver," she whispered.

He didn't respond.

"Oliver." She stroked his hair, but his crying did not cease.

"Oliver, hear me. You are fine, now stop your crying."

His sobs became sniffles, occasional gasps for air expanded his chest, but still he kept his hands over his face.

"Let me see you."

"No…" he sobbed.

"Oliver, remove your hands. I promise you, all is well."

Slowly, he pulled his hands down from his face, but kept his eyes shut tight.

Brianna picked up the hem of her dress, which was wet from the snow, and began to wipe away the blood. When his face was as clean as she could get it without actual water she stopped and stroked his face. "Open your eyes."

"He stole my eyes – he stole my eyes – he stole my eyes!" He started sobbing again, his frail body shaking.

"He did not. Trust me, you still have them. Open your eyes, and you will see me."

Once again Oliver made an effort to stop his sobbing, when he had nearly accomplished being calm he opened his lids. "O miss," he cried when he realized he could see just fine. His relief was so overwhelming that he flung his arms around her waist and started crying again.

After a short while, Brianna stopped stroking his hair. "It is time for us to go before we freeze. Come, hot potage awaits us back at the blacksmith's house."

They stood up, knocked dirt and snow from their clothes and looked at each other.

"Are you alright?" Brianna asked as she picked up the basket.

"Why did he try to take my eyes? Is it because I am wicked?"

"The desolate look on his face made compassion flood through her." She took his hand. "We should walk to warm ourselves. And no, it is not because you are wicked."

"But I lied, and ya told me not to. I didn't mean to, will ya tell God I didn't mean to? I believe now, honest to God I do."

Oliver was shaking something terrible, and she feared that shock was setting in. Brianna upped their pace as they left the forest and rushed them homewards. "You must tell God yourself."

"I don't know how."

"Of course you do. You just talk to him, like you're talking to me right now. There's no difference except you can see me with your eyes, but you can feel God in your heart. Just start with 'dear Jesus' and end your chat with 'amen.'

Oliver was quiet as she part-dragged him across the wasteland, then her heart was warmed as he prayed his first prayer.

"Dear Jesus, I is mighty sorry I am, for being so wicked. Thank you that misses here could do a miracle on me even though I didn't deserve it. Amen." His words warmed her heart for their innocence was like a jeweled crown upon his head.

A short time later, they sat beside the hearth and tucked into potage made thicker by mushrooms. Long after they had finished eating they sat together in silence, she thought maybe he had fallen asleep for he had curled into a ball by the fire.

She spent the time conversing with God in the silence of her mind. One moment she praised Him for the wonder of healing, the next she questioned why a raven would attack a boy so. And lastly, guilt arose in her like a tide because for a moment she had hesitated to heal him.

"I best be getting back," said Oliver pushing himself up.

"I'll walk with you." She felt a need to ensure he remained safe.

"Nah, thank 'ee but no ta. I'll run like the clappers, be home in no time."

She walked him to the door. "Are you sure?"

He surprised her by throwing his arms around her waist. "Thank you," he said, his words choked with emotion. Then he opened the door and was gone, running around the smithy and out of sight.

"God bless him and keep him safe."

That night her guilt strangled her dreams. She dreamed the raven had returned to peck out her eyes, and no amount of commanding him to leave worked. Just as she thought he would win, the bird flew back a little and transformed into a man. The man's laughter woke her to find her nightdress wet with perspiration.

It was the start of the end, she knew it. For three weeks the people had steered clear of Brianna, crossing to the other side of the street if she approached them, making the sign of the cross for protection. The atmosphere in the town was building, and it was mighty negative.

"Why didn't you tell me?" Rhiannon asked her for the tenth time.

"It was nothing; I thought it would go unnoticed."

"Giving a boy back his sight is not *'nothing'*."

Brianna sighed and sank on her knees in front of the fire. Her thoughts had always been open to share with her Mama, up until five months ago when Mama had shared her vision with her. Since then such negative thoughts had been bombarding her mind that she had begun to close up and keep them to herself. Surely, if she did not speak them out loud they would carry no weight?

"We do not know if he lost his sight, because he didn't open his eyes until I told him to do so."

Rhiannon stopped pacing and sank into the chair in front of her daughter. "I have a question for you."

Brianna groaned.

"Why is this, the first healing you have done in Bedyford?"

Brianna switched from kneeling to sitting, and pulled her knees close to her chest.

Rhiannon sat back in her chair and waited.

"For the last six seasons, Black Wolf has followed us from place to place. And how? Because rumors of our healings reached his ears and drew him ever closer. I did not want to start those rumors or draw him close. I never want him to find us. I don't want you to leave me." She dropped her head onto her knees to hide the fact that she was crying.

After a while when Rhiannon still remained silent, Brianna lifted her head and glared at her mother. "Why do you want to leave me?"

"You know that I don't."

115

"Then why are you happy to go along with God's plan? Why? Why?"

"Because I know that God is always just and fair, His ways are always good, His plans are divine, and nothing happens to us that doesn't come through His fingers of love. If this is what He wants, then He knows what He is doing. I trust Him. I believe Him when He says that He will never leave nor forsake me... or you."

"Agh!" Brianna buried her head back in her knees.

"I know you don't understand, but please trust."

For a moment nothing but the crackling fire could be heard. Rhiannon willed her daughter to see, and truly understand. Before they could discuss the matter any further, they became aware of a ruckus outside. Voices, lots of them, shouting and obviously coming their way. They both stood and stared at the door. Had the Black Wolf found them already?

Someone hammered on the door. Rhiannon moved and put her arm around her daughter.

"What are you doing here, Wilkins?" They recognized the question to have come from Edward. Rhiannon tightened her grip on Brianna.

"We've come to get your guests. Don't stand in our way, else we'll know you're in cahoots with them and for the gaol you'll be too!"

They didn't recognize the person talking. Cheering went up after he finished. *Is this it?* Brianna thought.

"Come out, or we'll knock the door down and come in and get you!"

Rhiannon prayed as she crossed the floor and opened the door. The crowd fell silent, and took a step backwards. She wanted to laugh at their superstitious ways as they all began crossing themselves.

Edward came forward and stood next to her. She slipped her hand into his, and she thanked God for him, even though she knew it was only God who could get them out of this situation.

"They need to come with us, Edward," said a man that Brianna instantly recognized as the shipyard owner.

"And pray tell... why is that?" Rhiannon asked.

"She is a witch!" bellowed the man pointing at Brianna. "And if she be one then her mother must be one too."

"We are not witches," said Rhiannon quietly.

"You lie! She caused the raven to peck out his eyes, and then she put them back in, and we have a witness!"

"If she was the cause of removing them, why would she put them back?" asked Edward. "You speak no sense Wilkins, forget this folly and return to your hearths before you catch a chill."

"Do you threaten us? Are you in cahoots with the witches?" barked someone from the back of the angry mob.

"Yeah, are ya?" someone else shouted.

Brianna placed her hand in her mother's free hand. They exchanged glances; it was time to start praying.

"Who accuses them?" demanded Edward.

"I do," came a deep voice from the back. The crowd opened up and the black-clad African moved forward.

Brianna's heart skipped a beat. Fear tickled her back.

"She ain't no witch, she's an angel," cried Oliver as he pushed his way forward past the man who spoke. He came to the front and stood in front of her as if to protect her.

"It's alright Oliver, go home," said Brianna giving him a gentle push.

"No miss, I will not. What they're saying, it's wrong."

"You said she sang with strange words and danced around trees, did you not?" asked a buxom woman with a harsh expression.

Oliver couldn't speak, for indeed he had told his mother that very thing, but he never dreamed she would tell the town of it.

"Huh! The wench is a witch I tell you! We should build a fire and see if she burns!" cried the woman when Oliver did not respond.

Brianna searched the crowd for anyone who could see the truth. She found no sympathetic looks. She did lock eyes with Mrs. Beardwood though, who dropped her gaze instantly; she looked more sorrowful than angry or hateful. Continuing her search, her eyes eventually fell upon her accuser, and found him smiling at her. The whites of the man's eyes gleamed against his dark skin. She wanted to speak faith-filled words and condemn him to the underworld, but Rhiannon tightened her grip on her daughter's fingers urging her to withhold from speaking words of power.

"What is your name?" Rhiannon asked nodding towards the African man.

"I am known by many names."

I bet you are, thought Rhiannon.

"This is Mr. Nğoy," said Wilkins. "He is the owner of Ventigo Shipping, a most respected man from the Americas. If he says he saw you in an act of witchcraft we believe him!"

"Why Mr. Wilkins, should we all take each other at our word?" asked Rhiannon, who then paused for a second as the word of the Lord flooded her mind. "If that be so, then tell me,

118

should we believe your wife when she tells her neighbor how you hit her so?"

The man reared back as if slapped, he did not know his wife spoke of their private affairs.

Rhiannon glanced beyond the flummoxed man and searched. When her gaze fell upon the tall skinny figure of the butcher, she nodded towards him. "And what of you Mr. Brown, should we believe the farmers who say you over inflate the prices, demanding to pay little but charge too much?" The man went red in the face.

"Mrs. Rosewood." Before Rhiannon could continue, the tiny woman from the large farm north of the river suddenly turned and fled. Whatever it was, she did not want people to know.

"John!" A large man to their left jumped at the sound of his name. "Should we believe you took money from the inn-keeper's till while his back was turned?"

"Who accuses me of such? I demand to know." The man's words were belied by his reddened neck and shaking hands.

"Shall we all play judge?" asked Rhiannon.

Much whispering went through the crowd; many people hastened away just in case their name might be called, many muttering under their breath about true witchcraft.

When only ten accusers remained outside the door, Rhiannon turned her attention back to Mr. Ngoy. He seemed to tower above everyone else, although in fact he didn't. Such was his presence.

With deliberate slowness, and calling upon everything she believed, Rhiannon spoke words of power over him. "Mr. Ngoy, you will speak only the truth... did you see my daughter commit witchcraft?"

Silence built as the remaining people awaited his answer. He tried to lie, but when he opened his lips nothing would come. Anger flashed over his face. How could this little woman override his lord? He stuttered for a moment, and then the truth burst forth against his will. "No, I did not!"

A gasp flew from the lips of the bystanders. Some of them turned and fled, ashamed to have been caught up in something so wicked. Mr. Ngoy spun on his shiny black boots and strode away without another word. The last few stepped forward, hastily offered their apologies and then raced away.

Oliver tugged at her arm, tears filled his eyes. "I'm right sorry, Miss. I did tell my ma, but I did'nee know she would blabber to the town!"

Brianna stroked the lanky hair off his face. "It is fine Oliver, see, they have all gone. Go home now and worry not, all is well."

He gave her a quick hug around her waist and then ran off.

Mother and daughter looked at each other. As much as they hated the idea, it was time to move on. They set about packing their meager belongings. In the morning they would go.

Chapter 12

THE LORD CALLED AND RHIANNON ROSE. Throwing her cape around her shoulders she hastened from the Blacksmith's abode and rushed into the cold of night.

"Here I am Lord." She looked all around and could see nothing but dark shadows, for the night's moon was hidden behind dark clouds.

"Here I am Lord," she called again, shivering from the bitter chill of winter's night air. Turning full circle slowly, she searched for God.

A light appeared as a blinding flash, and before her an angel of the Lord appeared.

"Behold, I am Gabriel who stands in the presence of God."

Awe and fear overwhelmed her, and Rhiannon fell to her knees on the hard icy ground, covering her face with her hands.

"Fear not," said the messenger. "Arise, for I am not to be worshiped. I am sent to speak unto thee and confirm what is to come."

He offered her his hand, which glowed like the golden haze of the Sun. She was much afraid and feared to raise her eyes towards him.

"Fear not," he repeated. "Take my hand thou who art highly favored; the Lord is with you. Blessed art thou amongst the children of God."

As she took his hand, warmth flooded through her. She rose but could not bear to raise her glance above the golden cincture that hung around his waist. Gabriel revealed all that was to follow. His words confirmed her dreams and words of knowledge. She was prepared and accepted what was to come.

The angel of the Lord closed his message, "Only the things I have uttered shall thee repeat to the man known as Black Wolf and to your daughter. Bar those things, your mouth will be closed and nothing will thou say to defend thyself. Remember in thy suffering and pain that God will be with thee. He will not leave nor forsake thee, and although thou must bear pain, know that when it is finished thy savior will be waiting at the door of life for thee. He will welcome thee with love and joy. It will be as though thy pain and suffering never occurred. The angelic host is filled with joy, at the prospect of heralding your pathway to Heaven, for thou are much beloved Rhiannon, daughter of Simeon the Fair and Estella the faithful one."

Then he was gone, taking both light and warmth with him, Rhiannon was left once more in the dark and cold. She hastened inside, closing the door as quietly as she could. Dropping her cloak onto the floor, she climbed into bed and lay next to Brianna. With much sadness she pulled her sleeping daughter into her arms. There would be no sleep for her this momentous night, in lieu of rest she watched the crack around the door for light and wished the morning be delayed. Night's hours were spent holding Brianna in a tight embrace, dropping kisses in her hair and whispering in her ear. She drenched Brianna in prayers of love. These last precious hours in the comfort of Edward's home were almost too hard to bear. Yet knowing that God was in control and understanding He had planned this very moment since the beginning of time, kept her from falling apart and granted her acceptance and peace. Man might move with malice and evil intent, but God is infinite goodness, grace and mercy. Therefore, man's evil plans could only proceed through God's fingers of grace and love, of this she was fully sure.

Before she opened her eyes, Brianna knew. The end of hiding in Bedyford was here. All her pleadings with God had been in vain, for very soon He would take her mother from her. Without a word she wrapped her arm around her mother and held on for dear life. Sobbing was swift to follow. There was no stopping the tide of emotion.

When the rolling flow of sorrow began to ease, Rhiannon stroked her daughter's hair, took a deep breath and relayed the message the angel had delivered. She ended with, "Remember well, wrath and vengeance belong only to God."

Brianna didn't respond.

Rhiannon dotted kisses over her daughter's forehead. "My beloved you must remember, you must. Do not let anger and unforgiveness mar your beautiful spirit."

"I will try."

As they dressed it was hard to concentrate. Negative thoughts bombarded Brianna's mind and she became lost in a fog of grief. The town's mob had been harrowing enough, now their path raced towards a crossing with the witch hunter, and *the day* Brianna had been dreading for so long would happen and nothing she could do could stop it.

Rhiannon took the Holy Book and with some formality passed it to Brianna. "As my mother gave to me, so I give to you. Herein lays life, not just eternal life but life for the here and now. Herein lays truth, absolute and life-giving. Herein lays knowledge to guide your steps. And herein lies love to make you whole. Take the Word of God and let it be as a lantern to your feet, so you may always see where you are going." Rhiannon held out the book. Brianna automatically took hold of it with two hands. For a moment they froze in time, locked in a look of unending love. "Keep it safe," Rhiannon choked as she let it go.

Brianna's gaze was blurred as she stared at the much loved book. Into her mind the words from Hebrews 4:12 flowed – *For the word of God is quick, and powerful, and sharper than any two edged sword, piercing even to the dividing asunder of soul and spirit, and of the joints and marrow, and is a discerner of the thoughts and intents of the heart.* She couldn't help but think the words were a warning of the turmoil to come; somehow there was no confidence within her that her thoughts and intentions would remain pure.

Having heard the movements in the early dawn, Edward was waiting for them when they came out of their room. Rhiannon's heart sank as she observed his sorrow.

"Don't fret woman," said Edward, "I knew your time with me was limited. I don't lament on your going, but rejoice only in that you came."

Rhiannon rushed to him and threw her arms around his huge waist. Tentatively he wrapped his massive arms around her, but only for a moment before pushing her back. "You make this too hard," he croaked.

"Oh, forgive me, Edward, I would not cause you pain."

"You should empty the cupboards and take what you need. I will fetch more food from town later today. And as partings are not sweet joy, I will bid you farewell now and be gone."

"Goodbye," Brianna called to his departing back.

"God bless you," Rhiannon whispered.

Then the door banged shut and they were alone. For a moment they looked at each other, with racing thoughts along similar lines – *could God's plan be changed?*

Then the holy presence that Gabriel carried filtered into Rhiannon's consciousness. No, things could be changed, but who knew what sorrow would fall if she left the path ordained for her to take?

There was enough for them to take food to last about seven days, while still leaving ample for the blacksmith.

"You have our wages?" Rhiannon asked.

"Sewn into my hem," Brianna said as she wrapped her cloak around her.

Rhiannon reached up and touched the wooden joint around the door. "Thank you, Father God, for blessing us with the shelter of this home. Continue to bless Edward please dear Lord, and keep him safe from all evil. Should the witch hunters come knocking here, please send them on their way in peace."

Then the two women declared, "Amen."

<hr />

For three days they marched north. They were undoubtedly the worst days of Brianna's life. Not only did fear crush her spirit, but the cold threatened death if they didn't find shelter each night.

They stayed clear of Billy's farm; they did not want any wrath from the witch hunters to arrive at their door. As much as possible they stayed off the road. *The day* was drawing close, but they would not hasten it by being easily found. Rhiannon needed to set her daughter on a path that would keep her safe once she was gone, and her dreams had seen Brianna cherished in Cymru. She felt in her spirit a need to get Rhiannon safely across the Clapton Bridge at Stratford-upon-Avon and set on a path towards the valley where the Nightjars sing; then, and only then, would she be able to accept her own destiny.

When the city of Bristol came into sight, a chill of premonition froze Rhiannon to the spot. "We can't go near the city," she said.

"But the Avon is too wide, we need the bridge," said Brianna with instant panic.

"God will provide for us, come we will veer east where the river is narrower."

They turned and embarked on a walk of sorrow. Neither could talk, both ripped with sadness and moderate despair. The clouds had opened and though their felted woolen capes were able to withstand much of the rain, their skirts soon soaked from the flooding ground. With the path still being partly frozen, the water quickly flooded large areas and flowed with a powerful stream. Brianna would have cried if she had the energy.

A farmer herding cattle to the shed spotted the two almost drowned women, and being compassionate in his nature hastened them into his humble home. His wife took pity and rushed them to change their clothes, the soaked ones worn placed on stands in front of the open fireplace.

They were almost too grateful to talk, and after thanks and offering funds in exchange for shelter (which was refused) they begged to retire. Fresh straw was brought in and makeshift beds created in the corner of the room. Both women so weary did fall into sleep within moments.

The next morning they rose with the cockerel's cry, gave thanks to the kind couple and set off once more. The rain had thankfully stopped, but the ground had turned into mud making walking arduous.

After marching for four hours they finally caught sight of the river Avon in the distance.

"Tis my time to leave you." Rhiannon, regal as any queen and more beautiful than any maiden that had lived thus far, studied her daughter with keen eye and breaking heart.

Brianna's lungs stretched and pulled with the longing to disperse the scream she held within. "Let us move on." She twisted her hands, pulling tight the skin. Pinching; causing pain in hand to disguise pain in heart.

Rhiannon grabbed her daughter's chin and held it tight. Brianna wondered whether to be more scared of the Black Wolf or of her mother's stare. She froze. Her deep-sea blue eyes pleaded with the woman who had taught her everything she knew.

"Today is *the day*, but I must see you across the river first and know you are set upon the right path. If I don't surrender myself, they will track us down and hang us both from lightning tree. God will get you across but I must turn back. You must go forward."

"Where shall I go? There is nowhere safe, better for your daughter to die beside you, than alone and afraid."

Rhiannon let go of Brianna's chin as if it were suddenly as hot as burning coal. "Tsk! You must build your rapport with the one who would save you."

"But He has never spoken to me thus far the way He does to you. Why is your faith in my salvation so great? Everywhere we go people see only magic and strive to destroy that which they do not understand. I would rather go to Heaven with you."

Rhiannon grabbed her daughter and embraced her tightly, but only for the briefest of moments, before shoving her away. "Fickle child, that you should think life so cheap, 'tis a disgrace! You must go forward and seek your future." Her words sounded harsh, but they flowed from her pain and her struggle with what was happening.

Tears streamed down Brianna's face. "Where shall I wander?"

"Head north for three days; then turn towards the setting sun for three more. Then turn left and walk south. I have seen you in my dreams in a place where Nightjars sing."

"How will I cross the river? I should come back with you and cross at the bridge."

"The Lord has promised a crossing for you. Go, go, you break my heart with your dallying, don't make this any harder for me than it already is."

It shocked her to realize that she had only been concentrating on her own sorrow and not her mothers. She threw her arms around her. She never wanted to let go.

Eventually, Rhiannon pushed Brianna away from her. She lifted her chin high though it quivered clear to see. This was hard, but she knew it was the Lord's will. She clung to the remembrance of Gabriel's warmth and all he had told her.

"One last thing…"

Brianna looked at her mother and wondered what she would say.

"You will one day meet the Black Wolf."

Brianna sucked in breath through her nose and felt her stomach spin and cause a sickness to rise.

"When you do, this is what you are to tell him…"

Rhiannon relayed the message that Gabriel had given her for Brianna.

"I cannot imagine ever being able to say those things to him."

"And I never would have imaged your father would die by falling down a cliff. Life can be strange and too difficult to understand. Sometimes it is only when we look back that we are able to see clearly."

As if speaking his name had summoned him, the women suddenly became aware of howling hounds charging across the land. They were instantly wrapped in fear.

"It is too soon," cried Rhiannon, "you are not safe. Go, go child run."

"But the river?"

"Trust God."

"Mother?"

Rhiannon screamed at her daughter, "RUN BRIANNA, for the love of God, RUN!"

"They're almost here," Brianna's whisper was lost, pulled into atmosphere and shredded by wind's spiteful play.

Rhiannon began shoving her, "Remember you well all that I've taught you – promise me this."

Brianna with voice lost, choking in her chest and throat, nodded her understanding.

Dog barks nipped the air like flying stones.

"Confound these wicked men! Would that these were not my last moments, I would seek God to destroy them!"

I should do so! thought Brianna as she backed away from her mother for the last time in her life.

The fleeting thought was clear to see, and Rhiannon lunged forward, grasped her daughter's shoulders and violently shook her. "You must not go against what God wishes, no matter the pain you may feel. To everything there is a season, and a time to every purpose under the Heaven. A time to be born and a time to die. No amount of thwart or struggle against His plans will bear fruit. You waste time, go. Now, I say. GO. GO!"

Clearly came the sound of pounding hooves, heavy, melodic, intent on ill will.

Rhiannon whipped her bag from her back and thrust it at Brianna. "Take my things, and guard the book well, remember 'tis more precious than life itself."

Brianna threw the bag over her shoulder to lie beside the one already there.

A man shouted. Hounds howled. Hooves clopped with murderous echo.

"Go! For all that is holy, RUN!"

And run she did.

Spinning on her heels, she turned and headed for the river. Beyond the river a forest beckoned, dark, quiet, offering a safe-haven. Years of walking had made her lithe and swift. She raced the wind, commanding pain in sodden feet to be gone. Her hood fell back and her long black hair flowed wildly.

"God-speed, light of my life," whispered Rhiannon. She watched her daughter until she was but a spot in the distance, then Rhiannon turned and ran towards approaching death. "Let my sacrifice be enough to keep her safe, Lord. Remember thy mercy and look with favor."

As Rhiannon ran with unnatural speed she stretched out her arms. "Let there be fog to hide her path. Let there be wind to carry her scent away from the dogs. Let there be rain to wash away her footprints." Instantly, the weather summoned obeyed. Fog rose with chilling density, wind howled with furious rage and rain exploded from clouds that a moment ago had seemed spent.

The hounds howled and shrunk back in fear. The horses reared up, neighed and tried to turn back. The witch hunters cursed, but Benedict knew in his bones they were close. Fighting to get his horse under control, he signaled for David to follow him. David raised a horn to his lips and blew. The hounds slunk across the ground and surrounded his horse, but their eyes were wild and their tails were down.

"We press on," roared Benedict, above the sound of wind and storm.

David's horse reared onto its back legs straining its head to turn back. David was tossed to the ground and cursed as he rolled in the mud. Benedict was quick enough to grab the startled horse's reins, and then he leant down offering a hand to raise David up. Before their hands touched, a light lit up the storm. They froze. Despite being hardened men of the road, and devout in their belief that God protected them always; sweat trickled down their backs and dampened their hair to their foreheads.

Rhiannon emerged from the fog like an avenging angel. Light radiated from her skin. The wind blew her long hair and cloak around her body as if she was the eye of the storm itself.

David grabbed the cross that hung around his neck and kissed it fervently. Benedict made the sign of the cross over his heart, and then a slow grin spread across his face, for she was his at last. He reached beneath his flapping cloak and pulled forth his pistol.

"Stop your magic woman, or I will shoot!"

The fire of God burned from the inside out, casting a flame of light about her. David felt more fearful than he'd ever felt in his life. Who was this witch?

With deliberate slowness, Rhiannon lowered her arms. The wind died down somewhat but didn't cease altogether. The rain stopped at the snap of her fingers. The fog began to thin. Never in all her life, had she used the power that lived within her for a purpose other than to heal. The power exhilarated her, making her feel powerful and unstoppable and she knew in that moment why her mother had always urged her only to use her faith to heal people. She knew, without a shadow of a doubt, that she could reach out and stop the beating of both men's hearts, she need only say the words. The shock of her longing to do just that caused her to gasp and to immediately start repenting, and she burst forth in anguished tongues.

Benedict swung down off his horse and approached her, handing both reins to his brother.

"Where is the other witch?"

His voice caused her to stop praying and to look at him in defiance. "She is already across the Avon and well beyond your reach. Be glad witch hunter, for I am the one you want and I have surrendered myself to thee."

"You have not surrendered! God has led me here for your capture."

"And so He has, and sent an angel to forewarn me about this day."

Benedict began to shake. Anger at the witch's words made his blood boil. David, however, was beginning to doubt. Many would have thought the woman's words dark magic, but his spirit had been agitated for his own mother spoke in tongues and the sound was too familiar.

"Where is she?" Benedict screamed at her.

"I have a message for you Benedict Everleigh, son of the faithful Benjamin."

Benedict, shocked that she knew of him, lowered the aim of the gun somewhat.

"If we confess our sins, he is faithful and just and will forgive us our sins and purify us from all unrighteousness."(11)

Just for a moment Benedict was speechless that this witch should quote the Holy Word at him. Then he turned to David. "Go after the daughter, I will have them both!"

David passed the reins of Benedict's horse to him and then jumped upon his own. The hounds barked and ran in circles around the horses.

"No!" yelled Rhiannon.

"Yes," said Benedict. Then David was racing towards the river.

"No!" cried Rhiannon, and fearing that David might catch up with Brianna she raised her hand and was about to command the horse to stop when Benedict straightened his arm and shot her.

Bang!

The crack of the flintlock pistol split the air. The dogs howled and then crouched on their bellies and shuffled towards Rhiannon's body that was splayed across the ground, blood pouring from her back.

David's horse reared, and David yelled, "What have you done?"

"She was about to put a spell on you, God told me this. Go, make sure you catch the daughter. We are near the end brother!"

And that hope, believing the end was imminent, sent David flying towards the Avon.

Brianna, having reached the river bank, heard the shot and froze. She couldn't move; she knew in her soul that her mother had just left this place and gone to one far better. In her peripheral view she became aware of a man on a raft, he waved to her. She couldn't move. Why had she let her mother tell her to go? Maybe it wasn't too late. She turned to go back, immediately seeing a rider in black racing towards her.

"Come here." She turned her attention back to the man who had just called out to her. He seemed calm, somehow full of strength. Not understanding why she was drawn to him, she walked as one asleep to the river's edge where he waited. He raised his arm, she took his hand. All the time the sound of thudding hooves grew louder.

A small lurch and the raft began to move.

"Halt!" cried David, "In the name of God, I tell you halt; you carry a witch away from justice." But did he believe his words anymore? Something vexed his spirit, and this chase didn't sit well with him anymore.

The man waved at him. "Go home David," he called with musical tones, then plunged the paddle into the water and directed the raft forward.

"Stop!" yelled David, fumbling for his pistol, which he brought forth with a shaking hand. "Stop," he cried again.

Brianna turned to look at him from where she sat on the raft. Her hood still lay against her back leaving her tiny heart-shaped face and pale skin to be clearly seen. He lowered his hand, sick to the stomach that he had even contemplated shooting her.

Dense mist swirled over the Avon, and in the blink of an eye both raft and witch were gone.

David turned his horse around and made his way back to a brother he knew would be irate.

Benedict stood over the witch and remained fully focused on her face. As if she might come back from the dead, he waited with bated breath for her to open her eyes.

Lord, but she was a woman of stunning features. Men must have fallen for her charm so easily, for who would not want to kiss those ruby lips? He shuddered and reminded himself that a witch could kill young girls to steal their beauty.

He knew before looking up that David hadn't found the daughter. He tried to be content with having ended the mother's life, but he already knew he would never rest until Brianna had been found.

David slipped from his horse and came to stand by his brother. "What do we do now?"

"We will take the body to the paupers' graveyard and then hasten to catch up with the other one."

"She didn't have a trial, Benedict."

Benedict looked at David's stern face and knew the end of their travels together had arrived.

"I wanted nothing more than to haul her before the magistrates. I feel deprived that the witch did not get the death she deserved. But there is nothing I can do about that now, except to track down the daughter."

"Feel you no remorse?!"

"No brother I do not. This was the task that God set me, and I am near the end of my good fight. I rejoice that one more witch will lie cold in the ground."

"Did you hear her praying in tongues? Did you not see the light of God shining through her? Did you not hear the verse of scripture she spoke to you?" David's voice had been rising with each question. His sense of justice and fairness lay crushed under his feet; he was sickened at being a part of it.

"Satan himself quotes scriptures; do not be so easily deceived."

"There are none so deaf as those who refuse to hear. I love you brother, but I cannot, nor will I, be part of this any longer. You have always been a righteous man. Your prayers diligent, yours studies meticulous. Yet I question – nay I don't ask… I proclaim – you are far from God! Turn for Oxfordshire with me; let us put these atrocities behind us. What say you?"

"I say… safe journey. May God guard your back, and I will see you God-willing in the spring."

David swung back up onto his horse. He was past words. Nothing he could say would dissuade Benedict from the course he was upon.

"Will you not help me with the body before you leave?"

For answer, David turned his horse and galloped away.

Chapter 13

AT FIRST GLANCE the hard-timbered oaks laced with the tiny balls of white mistletoe seemed a thing of beauty. Yet closer inspection revealed the parasitical plant had pierced the trunks with suckers which drained the trees of vitality. Brianna shivered knowing full well that druids would have had a hand in establishing the growth. Furtively she spun left and right, searching for white-cloaked men and women who did not worship her God. With none in sight she breathed more easily.

Fright worked as a wakeup call, and as one rousing from a dream Brianna suddenly became aware by moon's full circumference that she had been walking for almost a month. Her mother's words drifted across her memories, three days times three, she was supposed to be where her mother dreamed of by now.

A stupor had soaked her from the moment she'd heard the gunshot. The recall of the sound still made her jump. Yet, eerily, that sound was all she remembered from that dreadful day. She couldn't have described the raft or the man who took her to safety if her life depended on it. She didn't remember if she had spoken to him, or even muttered her thanks. It was a dream she wished to forget, or better still believe had never happened.

She had walked north, but she didn't know for how long. At some point the setting sun had called to her and she'd turned west, but she couldn't remember how many days ago that was. Nor could she remember when she ran out of food. She'd found eggs in a nest and eaten them one day, picked wild watercress from the river another. Thinking of food caused her stomach to rumble and a wave of sickness washed over her. She'd not find much in this forest; it was time to head south. Maybe she could find this valley of the singing Nightjars? Yes, that's what her mother wanted, that's where she would go the next day.

Brianna stayed away from all paths, preferring to walk across moors and fields. She shied away from people and hid when she spotted anyone. On the edge of an obviously wealthy estate she found a field of carrot tops and making sure no one was around, fell on her knees at the edge and pulled up several purple carrots. She shoved them into her bag, her heart beating wildly in case a farmer should appear. Later, when she found a stream she would wash and eat them. She placed her hand on the ground and thanked God for His provision.

She realized it was the first prayer she had uttered since her mother's murder and blushed in shame. *How could I forget to pray?*

A short time later she found herself crossing a path that led to a place of beauty. She stood on the edge of a gravel sweep, and for a moment pondered on all that had been denied her. Would she have thrived under God's blessing if the roof over her head had been this crimson brick mansion surrounded by dense evergreens? Could such comfort erode faith? Was that why God kept her and her mother on the road?

A man approached leading a horse. At first she could only concentrate on his well-groomed black moustache, which sat over full, soft red lips. *Too plump for a man,* she thought.

"Good day young woman, are you lost?"

She shook her head to focus and glanced fully at his face. His eyes appeared unnaturally large due to the lenses in his small, round, wire-framed glasses. He was a man of means she deduced from his stance and attire, probably the owner of this beautiful lodge. No shortage of food upon his table, his rotund figure nearly popped from under his tight-clad clothes.

"Are you dumb?"

She smiled, though it did not reach her eyes. "No sir, I am not. And no, I am not lost. I stood here only momentarily to admire the beauty of this home."

He preened with swelling chest, and Brianna understood how he could be proud of such a building. She softened towards him, for if he had a hand in creating the beautiful lawns, the shaped Alpine firs and the walls mostly hidden behind deep-green camellias splashed with pink heads, then a part of God obviously dwelled within him, for all good things come from the Lord.

Appraising her to be a pauper, but one of good-standing by the sound of her, he made the decision to be benevolent. "If you go to the side of the house you will find yourself outside the kitchens. Tell cook that Master Stanley sent you for a meal of whatever she has spare. Then once replete, be on your way for I am not amiable to strangers. Indeed, when I think upon it cook is unlikely to believe you for she knows me well. Tell her I said 'now, now, cookie' and then she will know I have sent thee to her domain."

"You are beyond generous, thank you kind sir."

"Toodle-oo, now be gone, before I change my mind!"

Brianna managed a half-curtsy, although not entirely sure if his status warranted one, but then the man was being awfully kind and what harm did it do to show deference to one who showed grace?

He'd been correct about cook, who at first had wanted to run her off the grounds with a sweeping brush, but once imparted with 'now, now, cookie' she did relent.

"You're to stay on the step, I'll not be having that stink in my kitchen and that's for sure."

Brianna took a whiff in the direction of her arm but couldn't smell anything untoward or offensive. Yet, when cook's young assistant did fetch her out with a plate of ham and cheese and bread, Brianna could see the whiff smarted hard and raised a watery eye upon poor maid!

The next river, she promised herself before shoving food into her mouth.

Replete so much her stomach did groan, Brianna stood up and made ready to leave. Before leaving she asked the maid to confirm which way was south, and asked her if she'd ever heard the Nightjars sing.

"Tis that way!" the maid scoffed at the first question, while pointedly ignoring second.

Brianna thanked her and waved with a measure of cheeriness she'd not felt since... She shook her head to clear the sleepy cobwebs that a good sized meal oft induced.

She had walked some way when she heard the tinkle of water. She turned and made her way towards it. Not a gushing river, but a stream large enough to stand in and wash. She contemplated going in fully clothed, but after glancing at the sun that had passed its high point, realized her dress would never dry in time to keep her warm that night. Stripping down to her underskirts, Brianna piled her things together and stuck a toe in the water.

"Aah!" she immediately withdrew it from the icy water's touch. "Maybe I should just wash a little." Searching in her bag she found the cloth that she used to clean herself with, and sunk it into the crystal-clear stream. After she had washed every part of her she could, she lay back upon the grass and stared into the blue velvety dots of sky that emerged between the flowing clouds.

She fell back into reflecting, which caused her some discomfort. For the wanderer's life is not one she would have picked for herself. She plucked a buttercup from between grass blades, something she would never normally do for she hated to watch flowers die. She lay on her back and twirled the flower between her fingers in front of her face. *What fairness dwells in loss? What comfort in pain?* Looking inward instead of upwards caused an avalanche of emotions that spilled so fast they threatened to choke her. *Life is not fair! Indeed no!* The more she raged for lack of her wants being met, the further into the black pit of despair she fell. Once upon a time she might have recognized her folly quickly and put an end to her spiraling thoughts.

But the pinnacle of no-return had been met and passed.

Her inner person crumbled faster than a house built of sand. She crashed into self so quickly she was instantly lost to reason, understanding and faith. Her thoughts, so devastating, smashed upon her soul like bricks from a house that was collapsing. They shattered upon her head, knocking her down, burying her in uncontrollable negativity. She wept angry tears, she screamed until her lungs ached and she smashed her fists upon the blades of softest grass.

Does negativity call to negativity? Brianna would ponder that later, for her screams had roused the attention of two passers-by.

She heard the horses approaching before she saw them. Quick as a flash she jumped up and started scrambling into her dress. Panic rose and threatened to disperse her much-enjoyed lunch. As if ashamed to see her caught not fully clothed, the sun sank behind a dense and dreadful black cloud. The day which started off quite cheery, morphed with lightning speed into deepest oppression. For the life of her, as she shoved her arms into her sleeves, she imagined that all nature stood still with bated breath, for she could no longer hear the birdsong of thrushes which had just a moment previously been in full song.

Two men approached with idle pace, and a premonition off ill-doing sent shivers racing across her skin. Just as they pulled to a stop in front of her, she managed to tie the laces at her corset and sighed that she was at least decent now. Looking left and right she decided if she needed to run, she would head to shelter in yonder woods, most gentry would not enter into such dark places. *Please let them ride by,* she urged the Lord. For more decency from their laughing gaze, she bent down and pulled her cape around her shoulders. Grabbing her bags, she hitched her skirts up for ease of running and made to leave without passing a comment. *Don't follow me,* she urged.

"Where do you roam wench?" The man leapt from his horse in one swift movement. His voice was sharp, thin, prickly. His hand shot out before her escape and grabbed her arm.

With pounding heart she turned to face them. Anger and fear flushed her cheeks. She knocked back the hair that had fallen over her face and tried to be polite.

"Good day to you sirs. I am for Newport. So if you please, I shall be on my way."

They exchanged glances, the still mounted rider held the reins while the man on the ground firmly refused to let her go, despite her attempts to wiggle her arm free. Her captor wore a dark green velveteen jacket, with knee-length cord breeches and a pristine white shirt complete with flouncy ruffle. His attire spoke of standing, but not of dignitary. His pigmented skin and huge mole that grew north of upper lip did little to enhance his appearance. It was hard to look anywhere else but at the hair-spouting offense and Brianna had to school her eyes to focus on his beak-like nose to prevent herself from grimacing.

"What a pretty maid you are. Don't you agree Wilfred?"

The other man remained silent and looked indifferent, as if Brianna was so far beneath him as to not even merit a comment.

"Come now Wilfred, don't you agree?"

He shrugged his overly weighty body. "Comely enough," he answered with disdain.

"How would you like to earn a penny?" the man holding her asked.

She yanked her arm free and took three steps backwards.

He laughed. "Don't be coy... or do be, for I like a little resistance."

Brianna took another two steps backwards, and then found herself near the stream's edge, any further back and she would be in it.

"Come here and join in the fun, Wilfred."

Lord, please, I ask for your intervention.

Wilfred let the reins of their horses drop over a gorse bush and then came to stand by his loathsome friend. The two gentlemen of no integrity flanked her like a caged animal.

"Don't play coy woman. Vagabonds are pleased for a copper or two and you will be no different. Stop playing games and lift your skirt for we would have our fun and be gone, no harm done, and you some money earned. After all, you did entice us here with your cry." His beer-heavy breath offended her senses. Fighting the urge to blast them with a powerful word or two, she called on the Lord for help again, momentarily closing her eyes. She did not want to use her power, for she feared she would use it for wrong.

"Lord, by your grace and mercy, look and rescue me from these evil men."

"Insolent girl!" He back-handed her; leaving a red blotch upon her cheek. "Say another word such as that and I will whip your skin raw." To emphasize his words he raised his riding crop and waggled it in front of her face. Now lie thee down and pull up thy skirt, and be quick or feel my wrath."

"God's wrath upon *you* will leave more than tarnished skin marks you may leave upon me," she snapped.

143

In response to her retaliation he raised his crop high, but as it would come down there appeared a giant's arm that grabbed the crop in hand and held it there still.

"What on earth?" Both men spun around to face the person who dared to interrupt.

"Me thinks, the lady should be on her way," said the stranger.

Brianna looked past the gents' shoulders and peered into the striking white eyes of an African man. Unlike the last she had seen, this man filled her with relief, for God's defense had surely just arrived.

"Be gone my man," yelled the mole-flourishing pompous cad, flapping his arms at him like he would a flock of geese. "Shoo now, go back to whence thou came."

The man shook his head, and with apparently no effort pulled the crop from the man's hand.

"By God, I'll have you whipped and put in stocks for this."

"That may be, but until then I will not let you put a finger on this lady."

"She is no lady you buffoon, she is a vagrant and heading for prison, as you too will now be."

Both gents bristled, but the new arrival did not budge. Alas, they knew they were beaten, for neither was sturdy enough to take on this brute of a man in a fight. With disgusted grunts they mounted their horses, deliberately making the horses stop close to the two tramps. "My crop!" The African man passed him the offensive weapon. Snatching it from his hand the gent did snort, "We'll be straight back with the magistrates, be sure to stay right where you are."

"Harold, I don't really think they will stay put," said Wilfred in hushed tones as they rode away.

"Of course they won't," Harold replied tartly. "But hopefully the fear of it will keep them running far from here, for if I ever set eyes on either of them again I might shoot them with my pistol!"

"Poor horse," said Brianna as they witnessed Harold whip the horse's flank mercilessly. When they were out of sight she glanced up at the huge man. "I am in your debt sir."

"You are free of any debt lady."

Brianna chuckled. "That is kind of you, but I am no lady, please call me Brianna."

He was a mountain of a man, broad and tall with arms like trees, yet his face held a gentle peace. "If I should ever see you again, I shall remember."

"Oh, are you not going my way? Would you not walk with me a while?"

"I do not know which road you take."

"That one," she laughed, pointing to the only one in sight. "I am heading south, to I'm not sure where, but I'm hoping God will lead my steps. What about you? Where do you head?"

"I head east towards the city of London. I have been told the streets are paved with gold there."

"You don't believe that do you?"

He grinned, the whites of his teeth almost filling his face. "I am educated and understand the meaning to be that a man may make his fortune there."

"I believe that may be so. It is a shame, for I would have appreciated your company very much, even if only for a short while." That was no lie, for she feared the two men might return.

Understanding her misgivings of the current road she walked, he grunted. "I am in no rush. I will walk with you a ways."

Her eyes lit up with her smile. "What shall I call you?"

"My name is Zendaya, but you may call me as others do, which is Joseph."

"Zen-day-ya, that is a beautiful name."

"Zend-ayya, it means give thanks to God."

"Oh, that is lovely. I shall definitely call you by your given name."

After a silent pause, Brianna nodded towards the road. "Shall we?"

Zendaya turned out to be just the company Brianna needed. The heavy gloom that had been accompanying her eased a little, and she enjoyed learning about his life.

He came to the end of his story as they sat on either side of a small fire sharing their meager supper of carrots and stale bread which he had within his bag. "And now you know the truth of it, and plainly I speak with you for I feel goodness on you. When the master's ship went down, I swam for my life. I don't know how many survived. Not many I think, but I didn't stop to find out. I ran as fast as I could. Like a gazelle I was," he beamed at her. "You should have seen me! For days I ran until I could run no more. Then good fortune smiled down at me, and put me in the company of good people. They took care of me for a day, gave me some clothes and as much food as they could spare, and set me on the path towards golden streets. Are you shocked, Miss?"

"The only thing that shocks me is that one man can enslave another, it is monstrous and something my mother and I would pray about often since we first heard of it."

"Where is your mother?"

Like a fire drenched in water, all comfort of the day was gone. Pain, raw and needling was back in her stomach and chest.

"Sorry, Miss. You don't gonna tell me, it's alright."

"It's too soon," she whispered with head bent.

"I understand. No more talk now. You go to sleep, I will watch the flames a while."

Brianna said her thanks and took her things to a natural hollow a short way away. It would not only hide most of her, but shield her from the elements. Maybe, it was knowing that someone trustworthy was close by, but Brianna slept that night in a way she had not done since that dreadful day.

The next day they woke with the birdsong, packed their things and went on their way as if they had been friends for years. It was later in the day, when the sun was beginning to dip, that they came across a river and spotted fish.

Zendaya grinned at her, and then quickly stripped down to his undergarments as Brianna looked away. Once he was in the water she turned around again. The river was up to his chest and she saw him suck in his breath from the cold.

He bent his head and concentrated on the water. Like lightning, he drove his hands under the water and pulled out a trout, which he threw over to her. The fish jumped along the grassy bank and Brianna dived at it quickly before it landed back in the water.

Before she knew it, Zendaya had pulled five large trout from the river and was climbing out, shivering but laughing.

"There is too much to eat here," said Brianna, "shall we not throw a couple back in?"

"No, we will cook them all tonight, slowly over a smoky fire, and then we shall have enough food for a few days."

"What a blessing you are to me," said Brianna, very much appreciating the fact that they would have something to eat now besides carrots and stale bread.

When the sun rose the next day Brianna was half-expecting them to part ways. A grateful happiness flooded her when she realized he planned to continue walking with her.

When he found out she had her own Bible, he implored her to read to him each evening until the day's light was gone. From heart, she recited her favorite passages as they walked and so the days went by in comfortable companionship. He said he liked the sound of the words, even though he didn't know Jesus he really enjoyed his teachings. Brianna would normally have shared her faith with a stranger, but she was lost on a road of pain and could not find the energy needed to spread the gospel, though she was more than happy to quote scripture for him.

Brianna cried when she finally opened up and told him what had happened to her mother, but it felt good to talk about her. She explained the reason she headed south was to find the valley where the Nightjars sing, for there she would find her future husband. He nodded, never questioning her unwavering belief in her mother's visions. His own mother had been a visionary and told him many things about his life. One of which was that he would meet a fugitive dressed in a long black dress who would tell Zendaya about a man who would save him. He was still waiting to meet this man, but he knew the day would come when it was time.

Spring was a time of new birth and the promise of life anew.

The healing company of Zendaya soothed her soul and she found herself singing for many hours.

"You shame the birds," Zendaya told her in all earnestness.

With company, the journey seemed easy, and Brianna stopped asking people along the road if they knew where the Nightjars sang, God would lead her there in good time she was sure. For now she enjoyed Zendaya's company. He made a whistle from reeds and played a doleful song that stirred her soul.

"What was that?" she asked when he'd finished.

"A sound of my homeland, when I play I remind my soul that one day I will return."

Though her life had not been easy, she wouldn't have wished to be in Zendaya's shoes.

On a day of no expectations they came upon a place that made Brianna's soul sing. This fair land of Cymru, which the English called Wales, must surely be God's garden, for as they broached the top of a tor the land fell away in front of them displaying a breathtaking tapestry of flowing colors. Cutting the arable land into sections, deep green lines turned fields into boxes. It was so beautiful that tears flowed down Brianna's cheeks as her chest swelled in longing to embrace all she saw.

"My homeland is magnificent, very beautiful. But most of it is brown and dry. I confess in all my life I have never seen such colors as this!"

Brianna wiped her face and smiled at him.

"No fairer place in all the world can there be, than this vale set before us. I feel blessed that God has brought us here."

After a moment of admiration, Zendaya pointed, "What is that building?"

Brianna followed his hand until her eyes fell upon what he had found. The undulating rolls of the hills appeared to push one particular piece of land upwards, jutting out from the rest. Narrow and long and upon its peak a ruined castle proudly sat, heavy as a crown upon a feathered pillow. With bared-faced rock exposed amongst the surrounding lush green tor, the castle seemed almost to have been made by nature, simply pushed up out of earth's core.

Brianna turned to Zendaya with eyes alight with excitement. No words needed, they simply set off to explore what history had left behind, discarded and deserted but clinging to remnants of majesty and boldness. They had to walk around the tor before they found an easy route to take. Starting as a gentle slope it soon turned into a walk that caught their breath. At the top they felt triumphant. The walls of the castle – gray, cold and still standing – rose before them grandly, unashamed of their current dilapidated state.

"I should like to know who built this and why it is now in ruins," sighed Brianna.

"You can see in every direction from up here," remarked Zendaya.

"That is probably why it was built here. I wonder what it's called."

"We should name it Bure."

"Burrr?" asked Brianna.

"Bur-ay," repeated Zendaya. "It means free, and that is what I feel as I stand here."

"Bure it is then," said Brianna, for she agreed, she too felt free up here.

After they had soaked in the view from where they arrived, they moved to the other side of the flat top. Tentatively they approached the edge. Brianna pulled herself backwards quickly. "Can you believe that drop!" she exclaimed, having caught a glimpse of the cliff that fell sharply a great distance to the valley below.

Zendaya laughed. "It is a place where only the birds should go."

She had to agree with him, there was something about heights that frightened her. They set off together into the heart of the ruin, marveling as they went to see how much of the castle still stood.

"I guess in time it will completely crumble," she murmured as she ran her hand along the walls.

"Everything returns to the earth eventually, even big houses!"

As the evening was drawing in, they decided to make camp in a corner of the ruin. Here, although at a great height, they were sheltered from the wind. They gathered dried moss and sticks and their fire was quick to start.

When she awoke the next morning, Zendaya was nowhere to be seen. Curious, she got up and started looking for him. His belongings were still beside the fire so he had not gone on his way yet.

She left the ruins and went to stand on the top of the tor to scour the landscape. Maybe he had gone looking for fresh food?

"Miss!" She turned to find Zendaya striding towards her. "Come, you must see what I have found!"

Even more curious than she'd just been, Brianna followed Zendaya back into the ruins. "Where did you go?" she called to him.

"Come see."

He went towards what from her angle just looked like a pile of stones, but he weaved his way through them and suddenly disappeared. She rushed to follow. To her surprise, Zendaya was standing on the top of a stone staircase. He lit a rush which he'd earlier fashioned into a torch, then with a broad smile, simply repeated, "Come."

She followed him down the steps. They became steep, and she put out her hands to touch the walls. "Are we safe?" she called after him.

"Yes. Come and see what there is inside."

Down into the darkness they went. A cold damp reek quickly surrounded them. At the bottom of the steps they found themselves on a stone floor. But Zendaya led them forward and soon they found their feet upon the softer touch of earth. Down and around and then… the darkness was still there but as Zendaya lifted the torch she could see they'd entered a cave. She walked around the walls touching the flint blues and grays, and the waves of white and gray. The ground was a mixture of exposed rock and earth. Into the right-hand side of the cave wall, someone had long ago carved out long ledges and she pictured soldiers sleeping in there in harsh winters.

She sat on the ledge and grinned at her new friend. "With a small fire you could stay warm in here in the harshest of storms."

They stayed for a moment, and then the torch started to flutter its way out so they made haste for the stone steps that led back into daylight.

"I think you are safe here; there are a few houses around," he did a broad sweep of the vale with his arm, "but not many people to worry you. It is time for me to go on my journey."

Although her heart sank at his news, she'd been expected it. "I am very glad to have met you Zendaya, and I certainly give thanks to God for you. I shall miss your company but I wish you Godspeed and pray His safety be around you as you set off on your adventure."

He took the last smoked trout from his bag, which had been carefully wrapped in leaves the day before. He left it near the fire, gave her a nod and was gone before she could think of anything else to say.

The wind whistled over the vale and howled like a spirit as it pushed its way through the breaks in the stone walls. She looked around her. Could she really make this her home? She left the ruin and stood at the edge where it fell away sharply and looked across the land. Tired of walking, she wanted to bide awhile in one place, and this she supposed was as good as any. Today would be devoted to setting up a dry place to sleep and gathering as much wood as she could to store in the cave, and then tomorrow she would walk to where she could see a row of houses, for surely there she would be able to buy some food.

The next day it rained, and she decided to stay in the cave. Enough light came from small fire at the entrance that she needed to only light one of her precious candles. With nothing else to do but contemplate her life, Brianna tried to engross herself in the Holy Bible. For the first time in her life she struggled. The words didn't seem to be carriers of life and power anymore, they appeared simply as stories and she struggled to concentrate.

The following day it was still raining, its bleak grayness and eternal noise drowned her in depression. She heated some water in her pan and dropped into it the bones of the fish, it would have to do. With it being continually dark outside and even blacker in the cave, Brianna lost track of time. She woke, stretched, walked a little up and down and slept again. After one such doze she woke to find a bright light blinding her. Jumping off the ledge she covered her eyes with the palm of her hand and tried to see who was there.

"Who goes there?" she demanded, though her voice betrayed her fear with its quiver.

"Who indeed," came a voice soft and aged, "are you?"

Panic slipped away as she recognized the voice held no threat.

"I am just a traveler seeking a little shelter."

"And where do you travel stranger?"

She no longer had any idea. The image of the singing birds had slipped into ridiculousness, never more to be mentioned. So she shrugged and in honesty said, "I don't really know."

Chapter 14

THE STRANGER LOWERED HIS LAMP and her eyes were able to focus. He appeared overly melancholy, lost within his skin. Brianna warmed to him instantly, as a surge of motherly-nature made her want to care for him.

He took her silence for fear, and hastened to reassure. "My curiosity was piqued and would not be still until I ventured foot after foot and made my way here, to see who dwelled in castle's old cave. I confess I did not expect to find such a young girl – and alone at that."

"I am a woman, sire. I am one-and-twenty."

"I meant no offense, 'tis just surprised that I am. How came you to these humble parts?"

"By foot."

The man chuckled. "Well that I could well guess. I mean what brings you to this sleepy hamlet?"

"Good man, I sincerely hope the Lord did."

"There are safer places in the world for thee lass, than this dank and uninviting place."

"I hope so, but for now I have run out of energy and need a place to sleep. The cave is surprisingly comfortable and warm when you are used to the open air."

"The North Wind does blow, and we shall have a falling of spring snow. Though it will probably last not very long, what shall you feed yourself with once you are snowed in?"

Brianna's only possible answer was that she would call on the Lord to feed her as He had Elijah, but as her faith was wavering more than a drunken sailor staggering home, she had no real expectation that He would answer her cries and send her food-laden ravens!

Dafydd knew not her thoughts, but her lamentable expression did touch his old heart. He removed his woolen cap and ran his fingers through his bushy gray hair. Once done, he held his cap with both hands took a deep breath, and then offered his comment with true sincerity. "My name is Dafydd. I am a farmer whose wife is with the Lord, and whose only daughter abides in London. My farmhouse is modest but even so I rattle inside it with no one to pass the time of day and help me about my chores. Would you do me the honor of dwelling in my humble abode...? I hasten to add I will expect you to work in exchange for a roof over your head and a share of my meals."

A life alone had never been his dream, and he openly admitted since first the death of his wife, and then the leaving of his only child, he'd become prone to chronic melancholy.

Thank you Lord, I never cease to be amazed at your provisions. "Good man, I gratefully accept your offer. But I must check, are you sure your reputation won't be marred by taking in a waif and stray?"

Dafydd burst out laughing, the sound rumbled around the cave warming it with its merriment. "I should think half the hamlet will be envious, and the other half scolding, but I am willing to take the risk if you are?"

"I am indeed."

They observed each other in friendly silence for a moment.

"Come now, pack what you have and let us return to a proper stove for the potage will spoil if we do not stir it soon. My full name is Dafydd Beavin, and you are?"

"Brianna O'Byrne, and very pleased to meet you I am Mr. Beavin."

"Dafydd will do nicely. Now, I'll fetch water to put out your fire and you put your…" he glanced around the cave and his face saddened, "…your few belongings away."

Brianna couldn't help bristling slightly. "Possessions I may not have. But I have all I need to be rich beyond measure: honor, integrity, pure intentions and faithfulness. I tell you I am as a Queen when it comes to the things that matter. So, you may *see* a nomad, but I *know* who I am." In declaring out loud what had always lined the walls of her heart, clarity sprang forth with a burst of light and the entire world tilted and then re-focused in her sight. She knew who she was! She believed God's Word – she was a child of the Lord Most High. Nothing could separate her from the love of God. Hallelujah!

Brianna's smile lit up the cave, and Dafydd was blown away by her beauty, he staggered and took a step backwards.

"Fare you well?" cried Brianna rushing towards him.

"Stay, stay," said Dafydd raising his hand to stop her. "I am fine, fear not. I am old, but not knocking on Heaven's door just yet."

"Are you sure?"

"If anything is wrong it is that I have lived too many years on my own." In his head he did add… 'and I be too old to fall in love again.'

Dafydd's farmhouse was only a short distance from the foot of the hill; still they were drenched by the time they reached it. The gray stone-built house was long and surrounded by out-houses, all with low-hanging thatched roofs. When he closed the door, Brianna shivered with cold but stood still near it so that the water would fall from her cape far from his furniture.

"Don't stand there lass, you'll catch your death. Go that way, that part of the house has not been used since my daughter left, you'll find her room and change in there."

157

"Thank you." Brianna was touched that yet once more God had led her to a person with a generous heart.

"Tosh, off you go now."

For the rest of the day they sat on either side of the fire and shared their life-stories. He was much moved by what had happened to her mother and had to fetch a cloth to blow his bulbous red nose, which sat at odds with his otherwise skinny body.

At one point he went outside to check on his goats, chickens and hens, but besides that they did not tire of talking to each other.

"So, would you consider me a witch?" She asked at the end of the day.

"I've always believed myself to be a good judge of character. Indeed, I was the only one in the vale that thought young Simon be a rotten egg. Laughed at me folk did. But when he went and got young Sally Blenford in the motherly way, well they changed their tune then didn't they! All admitted I'd seen when none else had. A lot do defer to me still, because of my past wisdom." He nodded, as if to confirm such a statement to himself. "I feel in my old bones that you are as far from being a witch as a stone is from being a loaf of bread. I'm a regular at chapel, have been my whole life. Even on the worst of days will I don my cap and head out to hear the parson's words. But I readily admit I am far from understanding the ways of God. So if He should decree that you and your mother carry power in your words, well who is old Dafydd that he should object?!"

The bed, though it had no clean covers on, was like Heaven. She pulled the feathered pillow tightly to her and poured out thanks to God for providing for her yet again. *How blessed I am*, she thought as she drifted off.

The next morning she was surprised to hear the old man up and about before she'd even opened her eyes. *I must have been tired.* Having slept in her clothes, she yawned and stretched and went to help with the wonderful aroma that was filling the house.

Bacon! What a wonderful smell!

Dafydd turned and waved a cheery good-morrow towards her. "Sit down, sit down. I knew the smell would draw you out, but good-gracious you sleep late!"

"Oh, I'm sorry," she instantly blushed. "I guess I must have been overly tired. I do normally rise with the light."

He grinned at her, the corners of his eyes lined with many creases and she knew he was jesting with her. "Sit!" he demanded, and she sat herself down at the large wooden table in the middle of the room.

Dafydd put a wooden plate in front of her. On it sat two eggs on top of two rashers of bacon and a large wedge of bread beside it. *O thank you God!*

"Pray out loud girl, for we always give thanks in this house for every morsel we eat."

And pray she did, thanksgiving poured from her like a river, she realized she'd prayed well enough when Dafydd burst out laughing. "Amen," he cried, tears running down his age-spotted skin.

"Amen," she finished with a smile.

"Tell me," he said when they'd finished breaking their fast. "Will you abide long with me?"

Misunderstanding him and believing he wanted her gone already; Brianna pushed back her chair and stood up. "I am sorry if I inconvenienced you. I have coin; I can pay you for the meal. I will leave forthwith and not bother you any longer."

"Hush child, hush, and sit you back down." He flapped his hand at her until she obeyed and sat back down.

"I ask only because I am wondering what I should ask of you in return for your board. If you'll be here but a few days, then I would ask you to darn my socks and mend my shirts for my sight is failing, and I can no longer thread the needle. If you are staying longer, then I would ask you to help me outside in the daytime and maybe darn in the evenings only. The amount of time you stay is completely up to you, for I would probably never let you go if it was up to me!"

Tears of gratefulness sprang forth. "Sorry," she said sniffing.

"Don't be sorry lass, be happy. Stay here as long as you are happy, how is that for an agreement? When you are no longer happy here then leave, simple as that."

She agreed, and her new life began.

Chapter 15

IN A STRETCH OF LAND of unending fertile abundance, Trapp nestled secure in its unchanging ways as an ancient oak. It was more a tiny gathering than a village. The hamlet itself boasted only twelve houses, a traveler's lodge and the Cennen-on-the-Brook Tavern. It was busy today only for the fact it was Saturday and the weekly market day. From far and wide the farmers came to the tiny village to trade their wares. The men took the opportunity for a tankard or two of ale as well, whereas, women huddled together and exchanged local gossip and news.

This fresh day in mid-April was a good day to market, for the sun smiled down and the ground hardened, making walking and standing easier than it had been in previous weeks.

Arwen was here, his presence announced by his hearty laugh and jovial exchanges with all. He strode through the tiny cobbled street, swinging his arms as he went. He was assured as any man might be. His confidence, gained from his ability to fight and protect, rolled off his broad shoulders in such a way as to make all the women of Trapp swoon.

He stopped to exchange news with a group of farmers he'd known from birth. His bellowed laughter flowed from his stomach, warm, rich and inclusive. In fact it was rather addictive. Of that you can be sure as people thumped him on the shoulder and told him tales purely to evoke the hearty rumble.

Oblivious to the many fluttering eyelashes, he respectfully skirted around the circles of babbling women and young girls, with a nod – a touch of his cap – a smile – and a cheery greeting of, "Have a good day!" he artfully avoided the longing stares and the mothers who would push their daughters before him. He continued on his way, leaving them with lingering and dreamy eyes. Whether blind to their coyish flirtations, or a very smart man, one is left to guess! Whichever it was, he avoided their attentions with the utmost politeness.

"At six-and-twenty, he is well past the age of marrying, 'tis a crime it is for sure that he's not made attentions towards any of our fine girls." Many heads nod in agreement to the passing comment from Coleen of Overhill Farm. The nodding heads, it should be mentioned, all female of course.

"Well I'll be!" exclaimed Old Man Thomas, tapping his pipe against the tavern wall. The whole street stopped and fixed their attentions upon Arwen with much surprise, as they watched with bated breath his reaction to the approaching stranger. His stroll through the village had come to an abrupt stop. His feet were suddenly glued to the ground, as he observed a vision of beauty saunter towards him. So alien was it for him to be transfixed like this, that the chins of many did drop.

She had come into the village to deliver Dafydd's eggs. Her wicker basket hung from her extended elbow expertly, and kept from knocking into her swaying hip. The morning sun behind, bathed her in reflective light, as if her body was glowing. The golden-corn color of her straw bonnet bounced specters of light in all directions.

Who was this maiden-of-light? For though the village was now well accustomed to her short visits, this was the first Arwen had seen of her.

Her ebony hair, plaited today, fell across her chest and down to her waist. How he longed to see it loose and flowing. He immediately marveled that such a thought had entered his mind!

He saw an angel, and the sight exploded his senses, sending shivers down his back. The audience of astonished villagers gawked as his jaw dropped. Never before had their confident farmer looked so bemused. The would-be-Arwen's-wives put their hands on hips and sent daggers flowing from their eyes at the totally unaware young woman.

Brianna smiled at the handsome man in front of her as she approached. As was her manner of politeness she uttered a cheery, "Good day to you."

Too struck by her piercing eyes and full ruby lips, Arwen failed to respond. This caused a slight frown upon her beautiful brow as she passed him by.

"Good day!" he finally called when at last he found his voice.

She glanced over her shoulder and smiled at him. He was done for. Something mighty powerful had just thumped him in the stomach, and he knew in that very moment she would be his wife.

"Ha!" he laughed out to no one but the sunshine. "Ha!"

His own tasks suddenly forgotten, Arwen turned tail and follow the vision of beauty.

Unaware of all the wagging tongues that had begun, Brianna stepped into Mrs. Tanner's home-come-store to deliver the freshly laid eggs.

A woman well past her child-bearing days glanced up, and upon seeing who had entered rose from her seat by the small fire with a broad smile.

"Hello child," she greeted in a soothing sing-song voice.

Brianna, who had instantly liked this woman the first time she met her, smiled and replied with warmth. "Good morrow to you Mrs. Tanner, 'tis a wonderful day, don't you agree?"

The plump woman portrayed a picture of perfect comeliness. Her swollen cheeks pushed out her wrinkles making them appear less harsh. Her warm-blue eyes danced with life and her step was sprightly still, though many her age now walked with a stoop. Her hair, which long ago lost color and thinned, was hidden beneath a wrap of white cloth.

"How many today?"

"Eight-and-twenty; Dafydd asks for a pat of butter and a full wheel of cheese in exchange today please, using the credit that's been building up, if that be enough?"

"Tell him it's not quite enough and I will need to use the next two deliveries to cover it. But you can take them with you today."

While Mrs. Tanner wrapped a large slab of butter in a dampened linen cloth, Brianna carefully placed the eggs on a specially built wicker stand that the store keeper had made to hold the eggs.

"You'll be saving the old-timer's legs by fetching these in, but you tell him I said 'not to go soft in his old age.' There's nothing like being lazy to go downhill fast, that's for sure."

Quick to defend the man she now considered dear to her heart, "O he's far from idle. He works from sun up to sun down, so he does!"

"I'm sure he does my sweet pea, I simply like to goad him a little, that's all."

"O…"

"Arwen!"

The woman's sudden shout caused Brianna to jump.

"Arwen! what you doing loafing around outside my door?!"

The man she had passed on the street so shortly ago popped his head in the doorway. "Nothing… nothing at all."

"Get yourself in here right this minute and tell me what's afoot."

Reacting more like a six-year-old than a man, Arwen came in with his hands behind his back. He stooped low to enter and could barely stand straight in the small dark room. To cover his real intention for hiding outside her door, Arwen pointed at the eggs newly positioned. "I'll take six," he announced with a certain gusto that made it clear to all that eggs was *all* he was interested in.

"And pray tell... why would you want to buy eggs when you've hens of your own back home?"

Flummoxed, his cheeks deepened in hue, and glad was he for the poor light. Quick to think he blurted, "I did promise Ma Jones a half dozen eggs and oaf that I am, I ran from home without them. To save me legs I thought to take from you, I still have plenty of credit with thee don't I?"

Mrs. Tanner could tell by his furtive glances at a certain young woman that he was combining truths to hide his real intent. She was about to jest and tease some more when Brianna decided to make her exit.

"I'll see you tomorrow Mrs. Tanner, good day to you now." With a nod she made her way out, without even glancing at the man whose eyes would not veer away from her form.

Mrs. Tanner hit Arwen on his arm as he made to move to follow his new love interest.

"What?" he said with mock surprise.

"Don't you chase too hard young man, or she'll run a mile or two and you'll never catch her."

"I... I... I don't want to catch her!" he finally stammered.

"Pffh, stuff and nonsense, I've rarely seen a man lose his senses as much as you have yours. Goodness me if your parents were alive to see this they'd be mighty amused. The 'I can do it all alone' man has finally toppled off his stand of pride and confidence to become but a fool in love."

165

"O Agatha, you do speak too harshly against me," he replied in pretend hurt.

"I'm sure I speak the truth. Now…" she placed six eggs in a tiny wicker box and passed it to him. "Take these to Ma Jones and don't be following Brianna no more."

"Brianna… is that her name. O what sweet sound doth roll off my tongue."

"Get away with you, you big oaf, quiet your speech or the valleys will be laughing at you good and proper."

Arwen took the egg box in his broad calloused hands, nodded his thanks and made to leave. "Brianna…" she heard him murmur as he left.

"Well-well," she said watching him go with some amusement. "Who would have thought that, not I for one."

Some people's acquaintance is transient and half-forgotten before day's end. Not so this raven beauty. She had made a lasting impression and his mind could settle on nothing except the sparkle in her eyes and the enchanting ripple of her laugh. Of course the sway of her hips also replayed in his mind, but he was a modest man and tried his best to keep his thoughts upon her face. He tossed and turned that night in his bed, never in his life had he felt a longing to unite with one as husband and wife as he did now. Some men might stroll leisurely upon their courtship, but he had fallen off a cliff!

"Dear Jesus, she must be mine, she simply must. My heart has been sleeping since the death of all my family. Mother, father, brother and sisters, all taken by the cursed diphtheria these seven years past; since then my heart has not stirred. Not for the sunrise or the beauty of flower or sweet sound of a Nightingale. No advances from hamlet's pretty faces have come anywhere near to awakening my sleeping heart. But harken unto my cry O Lord, for this raven-beauty you have sent to me has roused me from my slumber. I thank you for the rousing, make me worthy of her affection O God and I will never cease to sing your praise!"

***

Arwen found ways to keep putting himself in Brianna's path. She was half-amused and half-frustrated at his overtly romantic overtures. She was soon made aware that his attentions towards her displeased half of the vale. Catching the scowls the women threw her way was an easy task as they hid their displeasure not one bit. She liked Trapp, it had quickly become her home, the last thing she wanted was to jeopardize her standing and have the village turn against her. So, with that thought prominent, she set about to dissuade him from his attentions with all her might.

Today, she walked with quick pace, clearly displaying her annoyance at his persistence to walk beside of her.

"Why will you not lace your arm through mine?"

"You know full well that to walk abroad by the side of a man with no chaperone is cause alone for talk. But more importantly, to link your arms is to declare to all and sundry that you are spoken for and intend to stand before the vicar mighty soon."

"Brianna you are crushing my ardor. Relent you a little and walk with your arm in mine. Let us declare to them all that we are spoken for, for as you know this is my intent."

"Your demonstrations are too forward!"

"Why should we waste time and dally in idle courtship when we could be wed and move on with our days?"

"You assume because you ask I must respond in the affirmative, but I am not docile wife-material Arwen, and if that is what you seek you should look elsewhere. You must slow your advances, or I will shun you ever more."

Not giving him time to respond, she turned and flounced away. Deliberately she engaged Mrs. Tanner (who had moved her table outside due to the warm dry air) in chit-chat and kept her back to her desperate young admirer. Mrs. Tanner returned the talk while keeping a laughing eye upon the sorrowful dolt, who eventually gave up waiting and went on his way.

"You're safe now dear, he has gone about his business."

"Why Mrs. Tanner whatever do you mean?"

Mrs. Tanner rapped her hand against Brianna's arm. "Tsk child, do not play coy with a woman who has seen it all before."

Before she could give her apologies, Mrs. Tanner spun around and went back into her store to fetch herself a drink.

Brianna scuffed her clogs as she kicked pebbles on the way back to the farm. What a quandary she found herself in. How could she explain that a large part of her was still waiting to find the valley where the Nightjars sing, and thence forthwith her true love and husband as envisioned by her darling Mama?

The door not quietly closed, did cause Dafydd to look up from his carving in surprise. He couldn't help but smile when he saw her frowning features. "Arwen?" he asked, although he knew the answer.

"Insufferable! I truly believe he thinks he is God's gift to women!"

"In his defense the ladies have been chasing him as soon as they could walk!"

"Not I!"

"No, not you, but that only makes you more desirable."

168

"Phew…" Brianna expelled a long gush of air and with its departure her ire did disperse. She flopped into the chair opposite Dafydd's.

"The man does woo you as he thinks you must want. Back in my day we simply knocked on the door and asked for the father's consent."

"You didn't court your wife beforehand?"

"Well, if ye consider a coy smile across chapel pews courtship, then we partook most frequently. I didn't have to speak to her, her smile and nod was all I needed to know she welcomed my attention."

"It is not that I don't like him, indeed I like him rather well. It is just niggles that make me draw back."

"I'm in no hurry to be rid of thee lass, so you let them niggles carry on for as long as you like."

The beats of summer resounded hot and slow. Afternoons hung with stillness, becoming a devourer of time. Lush deep-greens faded and became yellow. Brooks ran shallow and birds fled for more tempting pastures. It was a time of huffing and puffing against the stickiness of an early August blast, and Trapp fell into a quiet retreat where people slept in fields at night seeking the cool touch of ground. Everything from flowers to trees and animals to humans wanted nothing more than to sleep the month away.

For the first time in months, Brianna was afraid. Not that her life would be snatched away by the Black Wolf. No, indeed she longed for Heaven and to be reunited not only with her earthly mother and father, but with her Heavenly Father. This creeping, insidious emotion was a fear she'd never faced before.

She didn't want the villagers of Trapp to reject her.

It put her in a quandary, for despite her constant rejections and announcements of her disinterest she found herself anticipating Arwen's next appearance with a growing excitement. His handsome face, with square jaw and deep brown eyes, was becoming ever more attractive to her, but then so too her love for the people of Trapp was also growing.

Wrapping her arms around her knees she mulled over this new emotional fear, trying to dissect it and find its root cause. The current's flow babbled over water-smoothed stepping stones in the slow flowing brook, and the sound mingled with her thoughts, fresh and brimming with life.

Floating, visible, but as yet untouchable, were the thoughts that she wanted to belong. Her heart quickened as clarity began to emerge. Home, she wanted a place to call home, and all that encompassed.

Family.

Connection.

Belonging.

Could these be the reasons for her unsettled gnawings and her growing sense of having spent her life deprived? No, that was an untrue thought, for she was blessed beyond measure. But the reasoning worried her. She delved into her bag to retrieve the Holy Bible which she had fetched along with her on this afternoon's excursion. With a finger of awe, she traced the image of the twelve disciples on the first page.

"How blessed are you men, who sat by our Lord."

The Bible, her constant source of life and love, instantaneously refreshed her spirit. She was being fanciful – it would pass. Deliberately she recalled her mother's teaching on fear, and then began flicking through the pages again looking up her favorite passages. When the heat of the sun began to ebb she realized she was no wiser. Part of her longed to give in to the only suitor she'd ever had. Another part wanted to wait for her mother's vision to come true. And on top of those desires was something she needed that felt stronger than both of them. She wanted a home. Somehow, this singular longing had crowned all her emotions and reigned supreme.

As she stood and stretched and prepared to return, the only thing that was clear was she would have to wait and see what came.

Waiting, she concluded, was somewhat tiresome!

<hr>

In an endeavor to fit in and be accepted, Brianna offered help whenever she could. One activity that she was gladly pulled into was the Trapp Women Sewers. Most of them immediately accepted her, some others (well, Betty's mother Anna, mostly) smiled without their eyes, their words clipped and short reflecting their disapproval of her arrival in their small community.

The others, however, greeted her entrance into the chapel where they sewed due to the good light from the large windows, with eager friendly smiles, which won her over to them in the course of the hours she spent there. She found herself relaxing into the company of these old matriarchal women, who had in all fairness seen it all before. As the Word says... there is nothing new under the sun. Late in their years no competition urged their opinions to be swayed, and thus they accepted the young beauty into their midst with genuine friendliness and curiosity. Their lively spirits were contagious. Only the mothers of daughters who had reached the marrying age struggled to like her.

After attending the weekly group for the first few meetings, the women had urged her to drop her politeness and call them by their first names. Agatha – Mrs. Tanner – the most outspoken on this matter. The older woman seemed to have adopted Brianna and treated her as she might a niece. Within the meetings they talked about everything under the sun, and spent a great deal of time reminiscing, the only taboo topic became Arwen.

It was at the end of one of these sewing sessions in late August, when Brianna left to find Arwen sitting on a tree-trunk-turned-seat outside the chapel. She sighed, for she knew Anna was close behind her and could hear her coming out.

"Go away!" she hissed at him, while walking with head held straight as if she hadn't seen him.

"I cannot," he stated as he fell into step beside her.

She heard Anna "tsk" behind them and cringed.

"O Arwen, you cause me much antagonism amongst the other women."

"O Bri… can I call you that? I fear I must for it comes from my lips as a soft whisper… only for your ears."

She ignored him and so he continued his cause as they strode out of the sleepy hamlet towards home. "Have you not missed me these past few weeks?"

"No," she lied.

"I have been busy." His chest expanded as he displayed his own worth as both a man of means and a provider. He literally brimmed over with masculinity. "I have made for us a bed!"

"Hush your mouth Arwen Evans! What scandalous conversation is this?"

Ignoring her outburst, "You'll be glad of it when you move in. I've been riding the valleys to all farms hereabouts, collecting the best down-feathers available to make you a mattress fit for a queen, for such I believe you deserve."

I'll admit that statement is fair to my ears.

Arwen pointedly looked down at her awaiting her response – she gave none. "The bed I'll admit was my parents, but it is sturdy still and will do for many more years. You'll not mind that will you my sweet Bri? Or should you want me to build you a new one?"

"No wife would be so churlish as to ask you to make her a new frame Arwen."

His grin was broad as he took her words to mean she would be happy to sleep in it.

As if some new agreement between them had been met, Arwen relaxed and whistled as they walked the last part to Dafydd's farm.

At the gate, as was their custom that had come upon them quite by accident, they stayed a while and talked of their day. Where they had been, who they had spoken with, and what they planned for the following day. The familiarity of his presence brought her comfort, and though she wouldn't tell him so, she had missed him dearly the previous two weeks.

He wouldn't tell her that it had been Dafydd's idea to give her distance and to allow her heart to miss him and grow fond.

When all that needed to be said was said she put her hand on the gate hinge. Immediately, he put his hand over it. "Don't go yet my love, stay and whisper your love to me. I have missed you as the day misses the sun until its next appearance. I have dreamed of you in my arms and forever by my side. If birds need joy to sing, so then I need you to smile to stop me falling into the mire."

173

"Will you not speak plainly?" she demanded, looking at him askance. "These flowery words have put me in quite a dither!" She could not tell him that her heart beat wildly, nor that she longed for his arms to be around her. But maybe he saw the widening of her pupils and the pink blush that flushed upon her normally pale cheeks, for his heart swelled.

"I would speak from my heart if only my head could understand the feelings that stir within! But these things are new to me and I am as a babe trying to walk. Have pity on me Bri, for I have fallen for you mighty hard."

Her discomfort dispelled like dried dandelions blowing in the wind.

"I like you too, Arwen," she finally admitted.

His spirit did leap within his body which wanted to jump as high as could be, but her turns were flighty and he didn't want to startle her away. So instead, he took her hand to his lips and there placed upon it the gentlest kiss. "Then I shall pray your like turns to love, for mine did a long time past."

She blushed anew at his honest and simple declaration, as warmth spread through her body.

"A little more time," she whispered before turning and rushing into the farm yard.

Quietly, and only for his ears, Arwen proclaimed, "Take your time my fair maid. I shall wait for thee. But I know I will not desist until your love for me is full-grown."

Merrily he whistled all the way home.

A certain cockiness commanded his stance and step, which seemed to attract women all the more. Normally, he would respectfully pay young ladies little attention bar a pleasant greeting or two. It was therefore obvious to the good people of Trapp, as plain as plain can be, that he had set his cap at Brianna. The men chuckled and secretly admired his choice. The old maids muttered it was about time. But the poor young lasses took to wailing into their pillows, which they beat with clenched fists, as they harped on about the unfairness of life and love.

Oblivious to the amount of comment he was causing, Arwen didn't understand the old men's jibes nor the young women's red eyes. His mind was so befuddled with a certain raven-haired, ruby-lipped young woman, that all else had become a blur.

"You'd best wed the lass soon before your farm falls into rack and ruin," advised his closest friend Owen with a wink and a hearty laugh. "Thou hast been caught good and proper!"

Arwen wasn't sure he wanted to be caught. Wasn't he the one who should be doing the catching?

"You are wrong, she does not set to ensnare me as you would suggest. In fact, to my misery, she still seems to spurn my attentions. Though I would tell none other, I will confess to you that she is mighty hard to understand. Sometimes I glean that she desires my attentions, and at others she bats me away with cool disdain. I confess, good friend, I am confused!"

Owen laughed long until the amusement of the comment wore down. Wiping his face to knock away laughter's tears with the back of his arm, he set to nodding showing his understanding of the last comment.

"I have been married these three years past, and I still get confused as to what my good wife wants. Now you know Mercy, she is quick to speak her mind, especially when I get things wrong. I told her once 'speak plain woman for I cannot read your mind' but rather than understanding, she set about crying declaring what a bumpkin I was for not understanding the needs of such a simple woman! I tell you... women are very confusing!"

"How did you win her around after such a discussion?"

"It was my father-in-law who set me straight about her wants, and forever in his debt I'll be!"

"Tell me, I urge you, repeat this wisdom so I may use it too!"

"He told me to give her what she wants." Owen nodded confirming the seriousness of his statement.

"But how do you know what she wants?"

"I ask her sisters!"

The two of them burst out laughing.

Later that night, after he'd knelt and said his prayers, Arwen lay on the bed and looked at the ceiling. "Lord, she has no family for me to ask what she wants, what shall I do?"

An image of Agatha immediately came to mind. He smiled and determined the very next day to seek the old woman's guidance.

Chapter 16

THE COMING TOGETHER of the village folk and farmers always resulted in much merriment. That winter had been harsh and the summer dry only increased their determination to enjoy the things they could all the more. So, a new dress was admired with much meticulous study and admiration. A traveler carrying a new song or ditty was urged to repeat and repeat until they had all learned every line off by heart. Yet nothing was celebrated quite as much as the birth of a new arrival into their dreamy, sleepy hamlet.

With no need to plan or organize, the familiarity of a small community built within them knowledge of who would bring what to a newborn's celebration. The good people of Trapp got stuck in, and as was their custom the day after the birth they made their way to the babe's abode, in this case the Durham's farm. Timing so perfect it was as if someone had run down the street ringing a bell crying out, "'tis time, 'tis time,' for one-by-one they left their homes, arms laden down with gifts, and joined the throng of people on its merry way.

Sewers and knitters with hats, booties and tiny jackets; young women with flowers or biscuits or pickled vegetables; old men with beer or chickens and Brianna with her basket of eggs – such was a child's blessing, that even before baptism villagers announced 'we are family' and as such would watch over the latest member of their tiny community.

When Arwen spotted Brianna and Dafydd arrive in Durham's farmyard, his spirits leapt. Surely soon she would agree?

They had danced the steps that lovers throughout time have danced, one moment close another apart. All the time walking through a myriad of emotions – was this meant to be? The old dears of Trapp would chuckle, 'as sure as eggs is eggs' they might have answered if they'd been asked. As streams from mountain peaks join and become one before reaching the ocean, so Arwen and Brianna began to merge, set on a convergence as sure as day follows night.

The growing sense that her mother, had once again, been right in her predictions brought a measure of comfort so soft and warm that Brianna could practically feel her mother's arms around her. That comfort, which was great, did much to heal that dreadful last memory. It reminded her that there were far more pleasant memories on which she could dwell. The Nightjars had not been found, but surely a husband had?

There was also a growing acceptance of their pairing throughout the vale, and this did much to allay her fears of being rejected. Dafydd for one had made it very clear they had his blessing, and in his words… for what it was worth.

After a quick greeting and a sweet smile, Brianna left Arwen and Dafydd to drink an ale or two, and went in search of the newborn. She had to wait her turn to cuddle the tiny girl, who had been named Rose.

"Never could a child have been kissed so much!" laughed Brianna as women constantly leaned down to bestow a kiss of blessing on the little girl's head. With the younger girls eager to hold the baby, Brianna passed her over and went to talk to Agatha who stood with her usual bunch of cronies.

Brianna laughed with the old women, the sound as merry as bells. These last months had seen her bloom and she was as dazzling as any bright star. The sight of her caused Arwen's breath to catch as his eyes followed her every move.

At that very moment in time, the witch hunter was recalling the image of Brianna as best he could. He imagined her movements, believed he could feel her use her magic. Yet no mystery miracles had reached his ears this year, not one. Had she given up her power?

His purse was getting thin, but it would have to stretch for he couldn't go home yet. He raised his arm to summon the innkeeper.

"Another pitcher, and fetch something for the hounds if you will," said Benedict.

"Yes, m' lord," the man bobbed his head and rushed off. The Black Wolf had been residing at his inn for nearly six months now, and whereas normally a long-staying customer would be beneficial, the witch hunter had all but chased off all his other customers, so black was his mood. He had turned up one day in March and except for the odd night, had remained till this day. If he had been anyone but Black Wolf, he would have encouraged him to leave a long time ago.

Benedict sat by the small square window and gazed into the world beyond this musky beer-smelling room that had become his home. He had stayed in Gloucestershire for too long, but couldn't bring himself to return to his parents. After his long stay during the early months of the year, his mother had pleaded with him to give up his hunt for Brianna O'Byrne. Her pleading with him haunted his dreams, yet he could not bring himself to return until this last witch had been killed. He owed Joshua that much.

"This last one," he told himself.

"Excuse me my lord?"

Benedict looked up. He knew he caused this good man much discomfort, but a large part of him simply didn't care.

"Nothing," he answered returning his gaze to the window.

He had sent the word out to the far corners of Britain. One day someone would answer his call and deliver news to the witch's whereabouts; he need only wait a short while longer.

Chapter 17

ON A LAVENDER-INFUSED, cricket-clacking day in mid-September, Brianna embarked on a visit to the village with a spring in her step and a budding joy in her heart.

Trapp had become her home and all manner of emotions came with that realization. As she passed the large spiky bush that welcomed people at Dafydd's gate, she traced her fingers over the rosemary and tickled the sprigs to disperse their sweet woody aroma. She breathed in the healing scent, and on a whim snapped some off to pop into her bonnet.

The time she had spent in this sleepy-dreamy place had been a healing balm to her wounded soul. Dafydd had quickly become as a grandfather to her and her heart swelled with appreciation for him. She worked from morning to night, not only within the farmhouse but also outside. She helped with the chickens and the sheep, and turned her hand to the extensive vegetable plot behind the farmhouse.

Dafydd was more a thinker than a talker, but that suited her well and gave her plenty of time in the late evening to read the Holy Book. Her faith was being strengthened more each day, and for that she was grateful.

Each Sunday they walked together to chapel and after service spent a good deal of time talking with the villagers, as most of them supped an-ale-or-two while standing outside the Cennen-on-the-Brook Tavern directly opposite the chapel.

The women, who had at first been slow to draw Brianna into their conversations, had eventually let their curiosity win them over and they'd begun to welcome her into their lives. The young women still slightly turned their shoulder on her, but the

181

old dears were open and warm. As soon as they found out her sewing was exceedingly good, they had drawn her into their circle and insisted she spent Saturday afternoons with them in the chapel where they created beautiful blankets to sell at the summer fair. The money from which would go to the upkeep of their ancient chapel, which to be fair had seen better days.

She was on her way to join them now. Early that morning, she had made extra bread and boiled some eggs, her contribution to the women's joint meal. She was nearly at the chapel door when Mary and Betty came rushing towards her. She groaned, for she knew these two liked her not at all, even after all this time.

"Good day to you Bri..ann...a," sang Mary in her high-pitched drawl.

"Good day to you too, I hope this day finds you well?"

"As well as can be expected," replied Mary as she pulled up short immediately in front of Brianna, effectively stopping her from entering the building.

It took all of Brianna's will not to roll her eyes. Instead, she waited patiently for whatever jibe was about to be thrown her way. These two young women were both approaching fifteen. The jovial ribbing from family members, that they might remain spinsters all their lives, grated them dearly. They would have to travel to Pontarddulais or Carmarthen in search of a beau, for the only single man in Trapp had eyes for only one woman. That just wasn't right, for Mary had set her mind on Arwen from the age of seven, and Betty soon after. That this vagabond should catch his eye made her blood boil.

"Are you not tired of this place yet?" Mary said through gritted teeth. "I am sure someone *so grand* as yourself would be happier elsewhere."

"We'd certainly be happier if you were somewhere else," muttered Betty, to which Mary gave her a sharp jab with her elbow, and a look that said 'be quiet.' It was one thing to bemoan Brianna in private, but she could not risk that Arwen might find out she was unkind, for how then would she appear before him?

Their flickering of envy marred their features, turning would-be pretties into ugly. Just then Mrs. Tunbridge approached and the two friends wrinkled their noses at Brianna and set off down the path before the old woman could give her penny's worth. Mrs. Tunbridge called after them as they walked away. "Women who like sour words bring about their own bitter ruin." Then she turned to Brianna with a wink, "Shall we go in?"

She could count on the fact now that Arwen would be waiting for her when she came out, and there he was chewing a long piece of grass. He jumped up as soon as she came out.

"Hello my love," he said quietly so others would not overhear.

"Not here, Arwen," she scolded, but when he offered her his arm she surprised the life out of him, when she slipped her own through his.

His grin was broad, his walk a swagger.

"Cat got the cream," laughed Agatha as she watched them walk away.

As they strolled past the tavern, the patrons who were mostly lounging on the grass decided to poke fun and good-humoredly made comments, some of which were probably not meant for her dainty ears, some slightly vulgar comments made her toes curl.

Their good-humored innuendos flushed her face. Embarrassed beyond measure, she withdrew her arm from his and quickened her pace until they were out of earshot.

"I am not the dallying kind and if you seek a kiss ill-gotten as suggested by your friends you must search for it elsewhere!" she snapped at him.

"Please, I urge you, do not deprive me of thy sweet smile. My intentions towards you are yet budding ideas, but I was raised proper and advantage of you I would never take, despite the jests of those who should know better."

Relenting, she turned her steps towards the path home, but threw him a quick smile to encourage him to accompany her along her way.

Arwen offered his arm, which she accepted. Their touch sent shivers of delight racing up and down her spine.

"Thou art fairer than all the flowers in the field."

She giggled. How could she not? This strapping man of sturdy farming stock did not suit well the sweet words he uttered.

Taking her reaction to mean he hadn't done very well, he rummaged around his brain for something more fitting. "Your beauty beckons me like a bee to pollen."

She burst out laughing and unhooked her arm, to playfully swat him with her hand. "Cease your romancing Arwen, or I will put a distance very great between us."

He looked crestfallen and she took pity. "It is not that your words are not pretty, 'tis just I am very much not used to them. Go slowly; let us get to know one another a little more before we take a step further."

He brightened and fell to whistling a merry ditty as they strolled down the lane towards home.

At the farm's gate Arwen asked her, "May I kiss your hand again?"

"No, you may not!" she replied and made a good show of sweeping through the tiny rickety gate and closing it on him. She didn't tell him, but the catcalls from the tavern had made her feel ashamed.

"Can I call on you next Sunday and accompany you to chapel?"

"No Arwen, let us take a step back a while."

He was mortified and stumbled for his words. "Why lass, we are practically wed, I know you love me though you say it not, it is in your eyes clear to see. Please don't let drunken banter remove you from my grasp."

She turned her back on him and headed down the path so he could not see the confusion that filled her face.

Ten long days had Brianna refused to talk to him. He was distressed beyond measure and could not sit for a moment. For the first time in his life, Arwen experienced what he perceived to be unrequited love. With his own pain brimming in his spirit he was able at last to see it reflected on the faces of the young women before him. When he looked upon the faces of Mary and Betty, who he had known all their lives, he clearly saw the pain of longing expressed on their pretty faces. He immediately took pity upon their desires, knowing they would never be sated. He now understood their anguish and wished it upon no one, especially those he considered his friends. So, to break their trance of fixation upon a thing he knew they would never have, he spoke bluntly.

"Dost thou know how I might win Brianna's heart? For I am sworn now to love none other than she."

Two sharp gasps did touch his consciousness. "Come ladies, you are both fair flowers and will soon have the pick of the shire. Tell me how I may win her."

Mary was quick to recover. She took his compliment in earnest, and in a moment became free from her childhood dreams of marrying him. "After all," she told Betty later, "he is rather too old for us, and he is right, for at the fair next week we shall have all the young bucks vying for our attention and we shall take our pick! What fun we shall have!"

Betty, who did not consider him to be too old, would unfortunately hold onto her secret admiration all the days of her life. Even after happily wed and mother of ten, a part of her heart would always lament after her first love. She accepted his eye had been caught by another and determined to muster her pride and never let anyone see how jealous she was.

No more jibes, from that day forth, did ever come Brianna's way from the two young women. Although Brianna would never understand what had happened to alter their opinions of her, she thanked God for it, and took it as a sign the Lord was blessing her union with Arwen.

Despite her recent refusal to talk to him, Dafydd's farm was on his way, and so it was sensible that being one who was driving a cart, he should stop there and collect her for the day's journey. Her tut made the old farmer laugh, as he waved them off from the comfort of his doorway.

"You couldn't persuade Dafydd to come then?"

"Clearly not," she sourly stated.

186

Arwen snorted and burst out laughing. The merry sound rumbled around her ears and tickled her funny bone a small measure. But she was determined not to encourage him, so she simply sat and stared straight ahead. Her pretty bonnet with white fringe covered any amusement that might have appeared in her eyes.

Three farmers brought their long carts into the village. Small haystacks provided seating, and the villagers climbed aboard with much merriment and constant chatter. Wicker baskets full of food, and crates full of wares to sell filled the third cart, while the jolly group filled the other two.

Billy, the tavern owner's son, had brought his fiddle along and they had only gone a short way when cries for his playing began. Happy to oblige, he rested treasured item upon his shoulder, tucked in his neck and pulled his bow.

Everyone was hoarse by the time they arrived two hours later at the Carmarthen fair. Their throats might be dry from singing but the spirits were infectiously high, and men and women both giddy from excitement.

All of them had wares to sell and a Trapp stall was soon set up and laden down. They would take it in turns to sell the goods, and when they were not behind their united stall they set off to explore the fair.

Many a young woman fluttered her eyelashes at the striking looking farmer, but Arwen would not return their looks. At one stage a group of four had forcefully come to stand at his side as he tried to sell their goods. The bright-eyed quartet would dazzle many a young man that day at the fair, but Arwen was oblivious to their feminine efforts and searched beyond them for the only woman that mattered. Brianna rolled her eyes and would not come to his rescue. Agatha, however, took pity on him and did shoo the girls away.

After a while Brianna decided to roam the stalls on her own. She had a mind to buy Dafydd a new pipe, and Agatha a new brush for her hair, for she had heard her moan that the bristles in the one she used had grown harsh.

It was as she ambled between the sellers that she came face-to-face with two men who sent a shiver down her back. Stepping to their side she quickly passed by. But on her way she overhead one of them speak.

"A comely maid indeed, yet there is something about her features that is somewhat familiar to me."

As the men moved on their way she heard their discussion no more. Yet, a shadow of gloom fell across her demeanor and a clear premonition that those men, somehow, would bring a dark day to her door slipped into her consciousness and took root.

Brianna had a mind to make herself a new dress, for hers were very faded due to their many stone-washings. She had reached the draper's stall when Arwen suddenly appeared at her side. As her fingers ran over a very pretty pale blue cotton roll, he leaned over her shoulder and whispered by her ear. "Do you pick something for our wedding day my love?"

He tried resting his chin on her shoulder to see what she was looking at, but she knocked him away. Arwen kept closer to her than a shadow and she could not dissuade him from following her around the stalls.

"Pffh!" All interest in cloth was quickly lost and she went instead to a stall selling all manner of jams. "O, but I do love blackberry jam," she sighed for she did not want to part with any of her few coins for such a sweet luxury. She turned and moved to a part of the field where a man spit-roasting a pig, the smell too tempting, she would spend her coin here. When it was her turn to order some pork stuffed into a hollowed bread roll, Arwen leaned across and ordered two and promptly paid.

"You didn't have to do that," she muttered as they searched for somewhere to sit on grass that was not too turned over by many treading feet.

"Nor this I guess," said he, handing over a jar of blackberry jam.

"Arwen, you shouldn't have!"

"A thank you would do."

"People will think we are courting."

"Good, I want them to."

"Well I don't. So stop, stop right now!" She pushed the jar back into his hands and went stomping across the field to where the older ladies of Trapp sat in a circle.

With this new shadow of possible recognition hanging over her, it was hard to make merry and enjoy all the things of the fair. When she would not join in the dancing in the evening, stating she knew not how, Arwen refused to participate as well, which made several young ladies pout.

By the time they began packing up for home, most of the residents of Trapp were beer-worse-for-wear – though they did make a jolly bunch. Brianna refused to sit upon the driver's box with Arwen on the way home, she sat instead in the back and joined in the drunken singing. Mary and Betty both replaced her with much glee, although their glances towards Arwen always as pretty as pretty can be, their talk turned excitedly to those new young men they had danced with.

When they were not far from home, Anna (Betty's mother) did nudge others out of the way until she could gain Brianna's ear.

"You know I am not a gossip," she started, to which Brianna did think, *well that is debatable.* "But I have a hatred of impurity and this itself does quicken my tongue to speak. For I

189

heard something disturbing today and I feel compelled to tell you of it." Anna paused and searched Brianna's face which reflected moon's soft glow.

"Go on," Brianna urged, for her curiosity was now highly piqued.

"I overheard, I confess once I started my eaves-dropping I couldn't stop for they aroused my inquiring mind somewhat. Anyhow... I was in ear shot, for they spoke not too quietly..."

O please do proceed! Brianna cried in the silence of her tortured mind.

"One claimed he knew you for a witch! Can you believe that? He said he would send a missive to the Black Wolf upon the morrow and no later. Aha, I see from your face and distress there is some truth to his wicked pontifications!"

Brianna hissed through clenched teeth, "There is no truth to it Anna, and I would urge you to repeat to none what you overheard... by accident!"

The slight, though small, smarted and Anna did blush. "I am *not* a snoop," she hissed back. "And whether I keep this to myself or not, well we shall just have to wait and see."

The walls of Brianna's recently built security had just shifted and cracked; fear that they would soon all crash down created a sickness in her innards. Oh, how she wished she had spoken to Anna with more pleasant a tongue!

Chapter 18

DAFYDD'S FARM WAS THE CLOSEST to his own, and therefore Brianna was the last passenger on the cart. A moment of ale-madness descended upon Arwen and instead of dropping her off by the farm gate he carried on ahead.

"Stop the cart!" yelled Brianna when she realized he'd driven past.

"I need to talk with you woman."

Though they rode down a lane of many holes, and the cart shook from side-to-side, Brianna stood and pummeled her fists into his back. "Stop the cart Arwen!"

Eventually, he pulled over and called the horse to a halt. Before she could descend, he jumped down from the driver's box and came around the back to offer her his hands. She looked to refuse him, so he reached forward, grabbed her by her waist and swung her to the ground.

She gathered her bags from the cart and turned around to leave, but he stood in her way blocking her from walking away.

Though nightfall was nigh, a stream of warmed moonlight burst through a break in some puffy gray clouds and anointed the exact spot where Brianna stood, the effect was dramatic and brilliant.

Holy God, she is like a diamond clasped deep within the rock, so magnificent and yet totally unobtainable to me. He turned to the side to let her pass, overwhelmingly crushed with the impression he was not worthy of her. All mannerisms of self-importance sunk from his shoulders to his feet and seeped into the ground. He fully understood for the first time that he was no one special.

"Arwen?"

Her voice reached his ears and heightened his sense of humility.

"Arwen?"

He hadn't realized his stillness until her hand touched his arm.

"You should have your hand and heart sought after by princes and noblemen. I am not worthy of you."

She was done for. All his chasing she could ignore but this honest look of sorrow touched her in a way none of his romantic efforts had done.

Since arriving in Trapp, Brianna had subconsciously slipped into hiding. Her current repressed way of living smothered both her fears and faith. Burying her emotions deep put her life upon a happy equilibrium. Time had drifted by and Brianna had remained still. She talked to God infrequently, and read the Holy Book even less in the last few weeks. Her gift of faith, unused, was crumbling. With her mind wrapped within the peace of repetition and familiarity, she had found calm. The exceeding highs and lows of previous years had been missed not a bit. She reveled in the uneventfulness of life in Trapp. The place and people, unbeknown to them, had become a balm for her battered soul. Though her faith did perish, her body flourished. Weight never seen before hung to her hips and pink-rose-blossom colored her cheeks. With a broad smile and pleasant manner, she had eventually become a treasured darling known for her helpfulness and generosity of time. Within months of being here, it seemed that she had always belonged.

At last, in this very moment where moonlight flickered across his doleful face, she decided it didn't matter why she wanted Arwen. Whether it be true love or the need to have a home and belong, no longer seemed important. The only thing that mattered was that she was causing him pain, and she could do it no more.

"Arwen my love," she whispered and touched his arm.

It took a moment for her words to sink in and then he looked at her in surprise.

"Does this mean what I think it does?" he asked.

She nodded.

He didn't want to touch her. His whole body had started shaking. Instead, he blurted out, "Will you marry me then lass?"

Not quite ready, dubious indecision sat smartly upon her brow, and urged him more ardently to persuade her.

"Let me walk you back," he urged, taking her hand in his and carrying her bag. "Tomorrow you can give me your answer."

Why can't I just say yes now?

"Arwen…"

"Will you not make me smile?"

She raised one eyebrow at him; he obviously thought she was going to say no.

"I can think of nothing but your beauty! You have captured my heart and mind and spellbound me!"

Brianna sighed; it wasn't his easy words that had won her over. She turned to leave. Arwen grabbed her arm and stopped her.

"When you smile, joy abounds in my chest. When you laugh, I want nothing more than to sit at your feet and listen to you all day long."

"And who would farm your land if you did that?"

"I would take you with me. I'd place you on a white horse and let you ride wherever I walked, for I'd never want to be separated from you if you would but say you were mine."

If he hadn't reached in and touched her heart a short while ago, he did now! She was an open book to read, her eyes were smiling, her lips slightly parted. O her lips! Arwen could not repress his delight; he picked her up by the waist and spun her in circles. At first she squealed, then laughed, but he did not put her down until her tiny thumps against his back became more demanding.

"You make my heart sing."

His words were melting the pains of her heart. For as long as she could remember she had dreamed of a man loving her in such a way. She slipped her hand back into his and looked up. In the earthy-hues of his eyes lay everlasting warmth, she sank into them as one caught in a whirlpool. She moved, he moved and suddenly their passion could not be denied.

Chapter 19

HER FIRST EVER KISS set her body trembling. Every inch of her tingled, every fiber of her spirit wanted to belong.

"Whisper your love to me, sweet Bri, make me the happiest man in the valleys."

"You push too hard, Arwen, be content for today and let us meet again tomorrow when the alcohol within your veins has gone."

"What are we waiting for? Let us enjoy the moment. I have seen the look of love within your eyes; your soul does not lie. We do not get any younger. Indeed, my mother at your age had three children upon her hip!"

Now doubt returned, whether genuine or from a feeling they were rushing, she did not know.

She blurted out the first thing that came to her mind. "There are no Nightjars here!"

"What? What does that have to do with anything?"

"O never mind, you wouldn't understand."

"You blow hot and cold. I know not why. I admit I am a simple man. You are too confusing Bri, I leave you to your games... you may play them with another!"

Both bemused and angry, Brianna stomped down the lane on her own, and cried all the way home. Luckily, Dafydd had retired for the night and she was left to cry upon her pillow without explaining. Eventually, she ran out of steam and to calm her nerves started reciting some of her favorite passages.

When the Word did not comfort her she took to chewing her lower lip in concentration.

Her thoughts were a muddle. One moment they seemed to be becoming clear, and then just as she was about to grasp what was going on all became a mess again.

When, like two snakes entwined, your spirit is split between pleasure and pain, to move forward in love is a hazardous thing. Mixed emotions are hard to define and trusting your decisions no easy task – a tip of the scales, left to right, and back again to left, swaying precariously to and fro. Brianna couldn't determine whether her feelings were pure and simply love, or whether her need for stability was goading her to accept Arwen's advances. This internal-eternal debate firmly sat her upon the fence of indecision. Well beyond her years in maturity, she was not playing courting games, she was genuinely confused.

<hr />

Arwen was in a mess. The only thing he wanted was to tell Brianna he was sorry, although he knew not what for, and get her to look at him again with love filled haze. She had been ignoring him since the fair and he was so distraught he found it hard to eat.

His sheep were thinning due to lack of lush grass and the worry about his livelihood as well as his love debacle put him out of sorts.

Arwen stomped into the village with an uncommon rage about him. With no planned intent, his steps took him straight to the Cennen-on-the-Brook Tavern. With his thoughts perplexed he set upon a course of action he would later woefully regret. It started with cider, progressed to stout and ended with mead.

With the hot breath of August, all the patrons of the tavern sat outside, on withered sun-burnt grass beneath the shade of the lofty mature oak trees that grew to the side of the tavern.

The old men chuckled at him. Young men ribbed him. Women passed by and tutted. His world grew blurry, his anger dissipated and doleful wistfulness wrapped its arms around him and egged him on.

"What shall I do?" he cried to none of the drinkers in particular.

Old man Thomas, however, heard and decided to respond. "You must take her a jar of honey."

"Honey," said Arwen, who then burped aloud.

"Yes. As a preliminary to a new entreaty," Old Tom hiccupped, "you should take her a vat of honey. Its honest-to-God sweetness will draw out your maiden's own sweet nature for you to taste, hiccup!"

"Will it work?" cried Arwen trying hard to stand, but feeling the world tilt below his feet. "Whoa," he cried leaning his hand against a convenient oak trunk.

Owen, who had recently joined the merry tribe, waved his beer in the air. "Mrs. Tanner has honey on her shelf, Arwen my friend. She promised me two jars just yesterday. Ask her for one of them and take it with my blessing!"

"Indeed," Arwen wobbled off the tree. "Indeed," he stepped two paces away. "Indeed... I will do that!" And he was gone. Sailing down the road with mighty speed and how he remained upright no one knew.

"I'll wager my best hen she'll turn him down," laughed Old Man Thomas.

"But you told him to take the honey!" said Owen.

"Never worked for me," he laughed. After a moment's pause the group all fell to laughing.

"Why did he have to pick such a fussy maid?" said Graham who lounged against the tavern wall with his cap over his eyes.

"Are you blind man?" cried Owen in shock, and once more they all fell about laughing.

With senses abbreviated and honey clasped tight, Arwen set off for Dafydd's farm. Drinking at festival times was something he did with boyish pleasure, but drinking in the day time of a work day was something he had never done in his life.

"Love sick!" Mrs. Tanner muttered as she watched him stumble away.

Luckily, or maybe not, Dafydd was not at home when Arwen walked through the yard and hammered on the door. Brianna dropped her sewing and flew to answer before he knocked the door off its hinges.

"Whatever be?" she demanded with hands on hips once the door stood open.

"Be my sweetness," he said and shoved the honey towards her.

She screwed her eyes up in puzzlement waiting for him to finish his sentence.

When she did not answer, his shoulders crumbled in defeat. "O my sweet, sweet Bri."

He looked sad beyond words and Brianna took pity. "Come, I shall walk with you towards your farm and see you are set upon the right path."

As the evening was drawing in and she was in a dress which was cotton-thin, she grabbed a woolen shawl and flung it over her arm for the journey home. For looking at him with amused eyes, she figured this walk was going to stretch a fair time.

Arwen mumbled some love-making words and tried to pull her into his arms. She pushed him away playfully, and hooked her arm through his elbow. If he had been sober, he might have recognized the gesture as the fact she had made up her mind to accept his courtship. But his mind was beer-battered and dull and he missed the subtle declaration.

They walked in silence for quite some time, and as they went the evening's cool air began to clear his head somewhat.

"I'm sorry for the bother, Bri," he said at last.

"Tis no bother to accompany you Arwen; in fact I am glad to stretch my legs."

They walked on again, a good distance and still in silence. At last they came to a bend in the path, left to his farm and right towards Llandeilo.

"I shall bid you goodnight here, Arwen. You cannot go wrong now, for 'tis straight to your door."

They stopped there at the crossroads and locked eyes.

"I love thee so much, my fair lass."

She reached up a hand and touched his face.

"Tell me," he demanded passionately, fumbling to grab her hands. "Tell me you are mine. I see love in your eyes I know I do. I do… don't I? I am not mistaken?"

Knowing this was not the time or place, Brianna decided to curb his ardor. "Arwen, I do declare you are quite drunk!" Caught between fear of stepping forward into a new life with him, and laughter at his behavior – knowing full well the drink still had its hold, made her comment more brittle than she meant.

Her words expanded in his mind as a loud and clear refusal. They stung like icy water and meant that in a blink of an eye, he imagined himself free of liquor's hold. Without warning he grabbed her arm and dragged her into the field and out of sight to any stray passersby. He wasn't thinking, only acting on a desire that had been building all summer. Everything in his mind went blank, except for two thoughts, he would have her and then she would have to marry him.

"Arwen! You are hurting me!"

Into the field he dragged her, behind the hedgerow. Then in one foul move, did topple her onto the ground and laid her upon her back. He straddled her, his knees pinned to her sides.

"You belong to me, and I will have you." His head lowered to capture her lips.

"No!" she screamed and batted him with her fists. "Arwen, no!"

He was lost in a torment of want and booze and a blistering summer of desire, so much so that he didn't take in her objections. She tossed and turned her head so his mouth could not find hers.

Frustrated, he grabbed her chin with his hand and made to kiss her. Before his lips could touch hers, she screamed.

"NOOOOOO!"

The hurricane blast that picked up his body and threw him across the field had come on her demand. She jumped to her feet, anger racing through her veins. She raised her hands. She wanted to blast him again.

He moaned where he lay, and in a flash her anger was gone.

"O my Lord, Arwen... are you alright?" She hitched up her skirts and raced across the field to where he lay.

The air from his lungs had left his body causing him to gasp from shock and pain. He rolled onto his side, groaning and not fully understanding what had just happened.

He became aware that Brianna was running towards him. He pushed himself onto his knees, then with a great deal of effort half-stood half-crouched. Fear-tinged humiliation awoke within him, a new experience to Arwen, it did smart his sensitivities and words flooded from his mouth before he could think. Tainted with embarrassment and shame for what he had done, he flung his words at her with more deadly precision than David's stone to Goliath's forehead.

"Stay away from me YOU WITCH!"

"Arwen!" His name came from her throat as a strangled chord. She had stopped running, and reached out a hand to touch him.

He shrank back, shame of his fear making him angry. "I DEFENDED YOU!" he screamed at her, then instantly shrank back lest he had evoked her wrath and she released her magic again.

"Arwen…" tears flowed down her cheeks.

He ground his teeth, and tightly shut his mouth. She was a good actress for she looked distressed, but he would, could… never… forget what she had just done to him.

"When Anna told everyone she'd found out you were a witch I called *her* a liar! And all the time it was *you* who is the liar!"

"Arwen, please let me explain."

"STAY AWAY FROM ME!" Each word he screamed tore at her soul.

He was holding his arm and it was obvious he was in pain. "Let me heal you."

"I swear to all that is holy, you had better stay away from me."

"But Arwen… Arwen…" words failed her. She wrapped her arms around her waist, for it felt like she was being broke in two.

The serpent slithers where sweet flowers grow and Arwen started backing away from her with hatred plastered upon his face.

The injustices that had followed her all her life, suddenly hit home with a rush of anger.

"Your sensibilities are injured, but mine are shattered, for I thought you to be of love and kindness, instead I now see only cold disdain and lack of affection. You wooed me with complimentary words that I now know were empty and without merit. So, who has been fooled the worse? I beg to differ with your accusations and to say that it is YOU who has tricked *me!*"

An immeasurable chasm opened between them – a great divide of trust. Rejection smarts against the heart shrinking it, drawing out love as bleeding, shriveling it. Dried, past recognition; causing irreversible pain that scars the soul forever changing it. Clearly, she was reminded that words are containers of power, and they can destroy as much as they build up.

Before he could respond, for he had raised an arm and taken a step towards her in sudden doubt-filled confusion, she was gone. Racing away from him, his hateful words and crippling rejection.

He bent and picked up her fallen shawl, he scrunched it in his hand and brought it to his nose. Closing his eyes he took a deep breath of her sweet lavender smell.

Of all the rejection she had faced during her life, Arwen's was the worst. It cut to the bone and pierced her body and soul with agony.

Brianna ran and ran and ran.

Thoughts were screaming in her head. Confusion fused with hurt. Was this a test from God to purify her heart? Memories of her mother's teaching rang in her ears. *'When your faith is tested your endurance has a chance to grow, when endurance is fully developed you will be perfect and complete.'*

She wanted none of it! She wanted peace and love, comfort and security. She didn't care if there was purpose in the troubles – she didn't want them!

Her mother's words again… *'God's goal is not to make you happy but to draw you to holiness, for there is an eternity in Heaven filled with happiness, but now on Earth, it is a time to grow and mature.'*

She didn't care! She didn't want to remember. Flinging her hands over her ears did not stop her mother's memory from speaking to her. *'God is more interested in your character than your comfort… God builds your character through a series of tests… your transgressions will reap full justice.'*

Brianna ran and ran and ran.

Chapter 20

"AGHHH," BRIANNA'S SCREAM of frustration sliced across the rolling mist-covered hills. Birds stopped singing their evensongs, rabbits scurried for their holes and a pack of wolves in the distance lifted their heads and howled with empathy for her pain.

Her frustration rolled off her in waves not visible to the eye, yet so powerful the heather-splattered moss beneath her feet withered and died. For the first time in her life she did not feel like a true believer, instead she perceived her faith as witchcraft, for it had brought her nothing but pain. Arms stretched wide she spun around, all the time pulling on her power, and for the first time in her life, cursing it.

"What benefit is it to believe with such simplicity and acceptance if I am doomed to live alone for the rest of my life?"

Like treacle oozing from a spoon, the sun slithered slowly downwards and hid behind the craggy hilltop upon which nestled the ruined castle of Carreg Cennen – as if even the light bearer of the world was afraid of what was to come.

"What good is my belief if I cannot live in peace?" Brianna spun around and around. Her grey silk cloak flowed around her caught in her encompassing whirlwind. Her heart was being ripped and her soul torn, all because of the dual longings within her. She loved God, but she also loved Arwen. Why could she not have them both? Was it really so displeasing to God if she wed and bore children one day – like normal folk? That was *it*, she wanted to be *normal*. No wait, she wanted to cling onto the Book of Life and live her life for God.

"Argh!"

The surrounding wind grew in power. It had a mind of its own. She knew not what it would do once she released it. Fear crawled under her skin. She was on the brink of becoming a witch, she didn't know how, she just knew it was so. At least then she could use her magic for selfish gain. Yes, that's what she would do. Damn both God and Arwen, she would step over that invisible line from good to bad, from light to dark. She would use her power to mold out for herself a life that would be filled with creature comforts. No more running scared, she would knock aside whoever stood in her way!

The last of the light faded. The moon did not rise. Darkness descended upon the land with hushed melodrama. Cold crept through the bracken, inching its way ever closer to the most powerful believer that had ever lived. Soon she would belong to the dark. *They* would use her to advance the 'great disbelieving' that slithered through the souls of men.

She felt powerful, in control. No more running from men. No, they would kneel before her now!

Then, as sharp as an arrow, her soul was pierced with understanding. Her faith was too great, if she used it for evil she was doomed never to meet her mother again.

Was this why so few were given such immense faith? Could it be that if people truly believed they were not only made in the image of God, but that they carried the same power within them, that they would use it for selfish gain?

Her mind, gripped in pain, focused on the only way out she could see, the one way to stop the pain forever. One way to ensure she never used her faith to hurt instead of heal. She turned to face the precipice that dropped down steeply to the land below, the rocks which stuck out like angry fists.

She started running.

Suddenly, something caught in her vision, a blur raced across the land, moving with unnatural speed, she knew it charged straight for her.

"No!" she screamed, she would not be stopped. With powerful pumps of her arms she raced towards the edge.

Then the blur came into focus and was a blur no more but a wolf. He stood in front of her, and she ground to a halt. With arms stretched wide, and frantic eyes she searched for a way around it.

A dire wolf no less; three times the size of a normal wolf, with snow-white fur streaked through with silver. She should have been frightened, but anger coursed through her veins at what she perceived to be the injustices of her life. That belief of being wronged seethed like a living creature within her, blinding her to all the truth she had ever known and understood. A new-found, mysterious hatred was forming at the lifestyle that had been thrust upon her. She'd never asked to be a true believer, life was not fair!

"Let there be a spear," she cried, and into her hand a golden spear appeared. "Let there be death!" She hurled the spear at the dire wolf, but he knocked it away with his paw with the indifference of swatting a fly away.

Her heartbeat stopped for a fraction of a second, and then started again with an assault to rival the crashing of waves in the worst of storms. What was this creature that her magic could not touch it? Too late she thought to run. She charged towards the cliff once more, hoping somehow to swerve the beast. The wolf leaped and crashed onto her back, sending her flying backwards towards the slow slopes of the tor. She rolled and tossed and eventually landed a crumpled heap on the gentler slopes. Her gray skirt ripped in several places. A lump started growing on her forehead and her cheekbone smarted.

She saw the wolf approaching and scrambled to her knees, stood, turned and raced for her life away from the monster. Knocked to the ground again by the impact of his body, she started rolling and spinning uncontrollably down the hill, the beast with her, its jaws tight around her arm. As one they tumbled down until gravity brought them to a stop. Blood poured from her arm. She screamed in pain and wrestled with the beast, hitting and thumping it with her free arm.

The wolf growled but would not let her arm go. Eventually, she ran out of energy and submitted to his greater strength. "I surrender," she whimpered.

He let go of her arm and she froze, more afraid than she had ever been before in her life. He walked about her body where she lay, his breath warming her face with every circle. He seemed nonchalant, like she was of no consequence, then he raised a paw and slammed it on her chest. She stopped breathing. All the running had been in vain. She'd abandoned her mother's treasure without a second thought at Dafydd's farm. She was a failure as a daughter and as a disciple of Jesus. She closed her eyes and whispered, "Sorry."

"For which folly of yours do you apologize?" The breath that carried the crystal-encased-words flowed over her face, trickling cool like the water filled breeze that bounces off a waterfall. Brianna opened her eyes. She blinked before drowning in the jasper amber-flecked eyes that bore into her soul. Everything became still. The wind evaporated, the clouds stood still, until the only thing that existed in the entire world was the color of the wolf's eyes and her heartbeat.

"Is there something wrong with your tongue, Brianna O'Byrne?" Deep and mellow, the wolf's words laughed at her, yet she felt no offense.

"I am sorry for so many things."

The wolf sighed, and not removing his paw from her chest sat down. "Do tell."

"I am sorry for letting my mother down. I am sorry I didn't tell Arwen how much I love him. I am sorry I didn't heal more people. I am sorry I've lived in fear. I am sorry that I am not good enough to be a true believer..." Her words, like her spirit, had fallen to a whisper of what they should have been.

"Whoever told you that you were not good enough?" An edge made his words sting. Shame consumed her.

"I know I have not done anything to bring glory to God." Her whispered words sliced her throat and made her gulp. Her hand automatically flew to her neck. Panic and pain glazed her eyes when she dared once more to face the beast.

"Tis your own lies that hurt you most."

"I don't lie." Razor sharp pricks snipped her throat forcing her to cry out. Tears ran from the corners of her eyes. "Please make it stop," she croaked.

The wolf removed his paw and night's damp air instantly began to creep over her body. The wolf stood, and then before her eyes he began to change. Light danced over his body, making the image of him shimmer. He grew in height and stood on two legs. Brianna had seen the magic of faith-filled words all her life, but the sight of the wolf turning into a man took her breath away.

"Stand," said the man, offering her his hand. She accepted it and he pulled her to her feet. Never before had she seen such a tall man, a giant he must be. Broad shouldered, dark skinned with wavy black hair. He was without doubt the most beautiful man she had ever seen.

"The Father has listened to you, and I have come to deliver his answer."

"I never asked a question?"

"Your heart surely did."

"And what did it say?"

"It asked why this believing had fallen upon your shoulders, why you, and why couldn't you live like everyone else."

She was about to open her mouth and declare that she'd asked no such thing when prickles of pain began in her throat, she closed her mouth.

"I have come to take away your faith."

"NO!" Brianna took two steps back, trembling in fear. Not for the giant who stood before her but for the thought of losing her faith.

"It is too late to change your mind. Your cry has been heard and answered and now I must remove that which belongs to the Holy Spirit." He reached out his hand towards her. Brianna screamed and turned to run. He caught her good arm. She wanted to batter him with her fists, but the torn flesh of the other arm was too painful to raise.

"No, no, no." She kicked him and wiggled, trying to break free.

"Child of faith… remain still."

"No, no, no." She sobbed as she fought against him.

He touched her forehead with the tip of a finger and she could no longer move. Panic-filled pleading eyes begged him to release her. He did not.

He raised his right hand that glowed as gold and pressed it to her chest. Instead of stopping at her flesh his fingers sunk through her blouse and waistcoat, her skin, her muscle, until he reached her heart. Brianna knew she should be dead. Knew she should be in pain. Instead, she felt nothing.

Slowly he withdrew his hand from her heart. "Here it is." He lifted his finger and thumb between which he held something the size of a mustard seed. "Your request is granted, you are free to be who you want to be."

"What have you done?"

"I have done what the Father requested of me."

"What will become of me now?"

"Whatever you desire."

"And if I desire to be a true believer again, will you give me back my faith?"

"No."

Tears rolled down her cheeks. Her hands shook. Already the emptiness of being a vessel that no longer carried the Light of God was consuming her spirit and soul.

"I made a mistake."

"So you did." His words were like a dagger to her heart, and yet they were not spoken with loathing or scathing, nor even pity. They just were.

"Who will carry the truth now?"

"The three dimensions of God will wait until others of faith rise from the dust and seek the gift of faith. To them He will give the gift without measure. Now it is time for me to return."

"Don't go!" Brianna grabbed his robe. "Please, tell me what I should do now, where should I go?"

He removed her hand and slowly turned her around. He wrapped his arms around her and suddenly shot into the night sky with her. She held her breath, but was not afraid. She felt the air rushing passed her as they flew beyond any land she had ever seen. Eventually, a colossal mountain rose before them, and the man flew them to the top of it. She wobbled as he put her down gently on top of the mountain. He stood behind her. Over her head and in front of her he waved his arm. All at once, there appeared before her a multitude of pathways. Each was a different color, creating the image of a fanned rainbow.

"Each person is gifted free will, which means they chose the path they walk upon. Whether you veer to the left or the right or go straight, is up to you. You can become a witch, if that is what you want." She heard the amusement in his voice, and shook her head. That thought had been a moment of madness which she never wanted to repeat.

Brianna looked at the pathways and was at once both filled with wonder and dread.

She turned around to beseech this glowing man who had the ear of God. "Please, undo today. Take me back to yesterday, so that I might make better choices. I want my faith back, please?"

"Nearly everything is forgivable, but blaspheming against God cannot go by without a reaction."

"I would never…"

An echo of her voice drifted along the tor top and danced around her head with silvery sparks… *'Damn both God and Arwen.'*

"O no! I didn't mean it, truly I didn't!"

The stranger had completed the task appointed him, so he turned and began to walk along the mountain's long ridge.

"Wait!" Brianna reached for him, but bizarrely he was a long distance from her. She hitched up her skirts and began chasing him. "Wait!"

His body began to shimmer and fade, and in its place the dire wolf appeared. The wolf looked back at her as she raced with all her strength to catch him up.

"Child of faith chose your path wisely, and remember… your life is the sum of all your decisions." He ran then, swifter than the wind. Her hand stretched out towards him, but he was gone.

Chapter 21

ONE MOMENT SHE HAD BEEN DREAMING, the next she was wide awake. No in between or slow arousing; just a sudden awareness of being alert. Her first thought was that she longed to return to her dream, within which angels had filled her senses with triumphant anthems, sung with such perfect arrangement that her soul had soared with rhapsody.

Swiftly following on from the pain of loss was the realization that something was missing. Remaining spread out upon the dew wet moss beneath a huge oak she patted her body down, searching for she knew not what. And then it hit her. That special dwelling place within her heart for God's faith was empty. Gasping, struggling for breath, she scrunched her body into a ball, her face spilling into damp softness. A wail poured from her mouth. Both hands flew to cover her lips, landing with two hard slaps.

No. No. No!

Her mind was spinning. Gone. How could it be gone?

Then crystal clear, the whisper… 'The desire of your heart has been granted' echoed in the corners of her mind.

"No…!"

Panic was swiftly replaced with acceptance; her body slumped, loosening her tightened muscles. Her fingers splayed across the ground, reaching for the solidity of ground and reality.

This is what she deserved, it was justice for ungratefulness. She was a failure, she'd let everyone down… including God.

Determining that her fate was sealed she relaxed, what will be, will be.

It was only then that she noticed her body was free from pain, more than that, verve electrified her every nerve. She was healthy and energized. As she pushed herself to sit up, her right hand shot forward to clasp her left arm that had been so horrendously mauled the previous night. It was whole, no torn flesh, no blood, no ripped clothes. It was as if her encounter with the wolf had never happened. But to believe that would be to swim in illusion, for Brianna knew without a shadow of a doubt, that her dark night of battle was more real than the breath flowing from her lips.

After standing up, she patted down her dress and cape, amazed to find they were perfectly dry. Not far away from her a dirt path marred the sweeping splash of greens with a brown streak, like an angry meandering scar. She stood tall on her tiptoes, peering left then right trying to gain an idea of her whereabouts. A field, no matter how beautiful, was just a field and she honestly didn't know where she was. The oak behind her, stood tall like a marker perched on the bend of a twisting road. She couldn't see Carreg Cennen Castle towering above the land, so she reasoned she was miles away from Trapp. She glanced left then right again, wondering which way she should go, but before she could make up her mind, she heard a bark and rapid clip-clops of a trotting horse. A sigh, long and low, escaped her accepting lips. The decision was not hers anymore, because before she even saw the rider, she *knew* Black Wolf approached.

Brianna rolled her eyes towards the sky. "You saved me from my cliff top death just to hand me over to the witch hunter? My, what a sense of humor you have." She took a few steps until she stood in the middle of the path, and waited.

The dogs were with her first, a sudden whiff of her scent, howls, and a pounding of paws as they charged.

Hands clasped tight in front of her, Brianna prayed in earnest. She did not like the idea of being ripped apart for a second time.

Saliva, white and frothy, flew from their mouths, their eyes wide and intent on their prey. Fifty feet away, thirty, ten... they ground to a halt and whimpered, shaking their heads. They paced around her with low whines.

"Thank you God," she whispered, heart thumping, knees shaking.

When she was sure they weren't going to attack, she raised her eyes.

She remembered the witch hunter's steed. The black stallion was the largest horse she'd ever seen, a giant of a beast. He flicked his mane and snorted as Benedict Everleigh pulled on the reins. The horse took a step left, and then right.

Benedict absentmindedly reached down and stroked his neck. "Hush my beauty."

When the horse stood still, the dogs settled in the dirt by Brianna's feet. Benedict stared at them, then with piercing intent, raised and locked eyes with the witch.

After the long months of excruciating waiting, Benedict had finally got wind of Brianna's whereabouts. He'd left his temporary home at the tavern, the day before and was on his way to Carmarthen. He shouldn't have been surprised that God had finally delivered his prey to him, but he was. A large part of him had been pondering over the previous years with deep soul-searching. He'd thought he'd reached a place of wanting to return to the family home and start afresh when the news had arrived of her whereabouts. He was now a man full of conflicting emotions.

For a long moment neither of them moved, except for his Adam's apple that worked itself up and down. Was that fear in his eyes?

With a penetrating stare that never faltered, Benedict lowered his right hand and removed his Flintlock from its holster. Slowly, he raised the pistol and pointed it at Brianna. "If you try to run, I will shoot you down."

"I will not run."

There was just a flicker of movement in the gun that betrayed a trembling hand. His eyes bore into her as if trying to read her soul. "If you start a spell of enchantment I will not hesitate to shoot."

"I do not cast spells."

"Liar," he roared. With a swift swing of his leg, he alighted from the horse and came towards her.

She wanted to run.

He must have seen it in her face.

"Run, girl. Then at least this will be over for both of us."

Brianna swallowed. "I will *not* run."

At last the Black Wolf had his prey. She was not what he had expected. There was no fight in her, no spitting or casting of curses. Instead, she looked almost serene; he wanted to knock that composure right out of her.

"You offer no resistance?"

"I will not."

"That is a true declaration of guilt if ever there was one." In one swift movement he had moved behind her, grabbed her arms and tied them with rope. He was nervous, expecting her to fight and claw herself free. Her lack of movement roused his suspicion of her intent, so he dragged her towards his horse and tied her to a rope on the saddle. Then he pulled a cloth from his bag and used it to gag her. There! Now she wouldn't be able to cast spells. She'd been too slow, he had her now. Benedict put a foot in the stirrup and got back upon his horse. He would walk her to exhaustion and no mercy would he show to this blasphemous witch.

For three days they didn't talk. They walked and slept, rose and walked some more. Brianna was strong but she was waning fast, for the witch hunter had barely fed her and the water was not enough to quench her thirst. The sides of her lips cracked and bled from the force of the knot holding the cloth. She was alternatively cold or hot, depending on whether she was sleeping or walking. She could feel a fever come upon her. Sweat began to drip from her forehead at all times, whether hot or cold, her throat burned and her knees began to shake. Needless to say their pace had been slow, and was grinding to a halt.

Too late Benedict realized his folly. Now he would have to stop and allow her to recover, otherwise he would never be able to take her to the magistrates. Curse David for making him promise to hand her over for a fair trial.

For the next two days she mostly slept, and Benedict was forced to care for her. No need for ropes, she was too weak now to walk and he cursed his stupidity often. He spoon-fed her warm broth once a day and prayed it was enough for he was running low on supplies. She looked so normal lying on the bedroll. Delicate like a flower, a black rose, he thought touching the ebony tresses that flowed around her tiny pale face. 'Why does she not heal herself,' he pondered as he sat and watched her raspy breathing.

In the afternoon of the third day her eyelids popped open, just as he was leaning over her. Her clear blue eyes looked straight into his soul jolting him as a bolt of lightning. He shuffled back from her, fearful she was casting a spell upon him even from her illness. Her lids closed without her speaking, and he could tell from the rise and fall of her chest that she had returned to sleep. It was a good sign, he determined, she would be strong enough to continue their journey soon. 'Maybe if I could find a hare, its meat would restore her more quickly.' With that thought, he stood, stretched and reached for his bow and arrow. He wasn't very good at it, preferring the sword as his weapon of choice, but he doubted a hare would stand still long enough to allow him to get close.

A short while later, Brianna woke and knew she was coming out of a sickness. "Thank you Lord," she whispered as she pushed herself upwards.

She searched the area for signs of Benedict but couldn't see him. She could hear a stream somewhere close, the tinkle of water on stones sounded so refreshing she had to go there. She needed to stop in private for a moment, and then when she reached the water she would drink and wash.

The water was freezing and stole her breath, but it was also refreshing and reviving, and she splashed her face with gladness. She wet her hands and wiped them under her arms several times, trying to dispel the smell that rose from them. When she'd finished, she stood on wobbling legs and took a few steps in the direction of the camp. She felt weak and leaned against a tree for a moment to catch her breath. She had just pushed herself off the tree with the intention of returning when she heard the crunch of the witch hunter's boots against the ground as he ran towards her. She lifted her face towards him, and willed her body to be still. Benedict grabbed her by her arms and started shaking her. "Do you think to outmaneuver me? God will not let you go now that I have you." He shook her more violently with each word that fell from his mouth.

Brianna's neck snapped backwards, the pain was blinding, causing tears to flow.

She was like a sparrow in his hands, he suddenly realized, gentle and soft, tiny and meek. He hated that was the image she portrayed. Trickery it must be, he would not succumb. He did, however, stop shaking her, understanding he needn't be so rough to cause her suffering.

He dragged her with him, as he made his way back to their camp.

"Please stop, you are bruising my arm and I feel dizzy from the shaking. Benedict, this is not who you are, please stop and consider your ways. You are good, I know, have mercy and talk with me a while."

"You *sinner*, are for the gallows. London will not have a burning stake for heretics since Edward Wightman, so for that you may at least be thankful. Hanging is a much quicker death. So beneath me are you that I will not tolerate your subjective arguments. You are to be silent!"

"High and lofty disdain is more blinding than loss of sight. You, Benedict, what a potent victor you are in your self-righteous rage! With your injured merit, wounded pride, crippling inability to see beyond own virtuous nose! Were thou a true man of God, thou wouldst bend like a reed and listen to all arguments that surround you. Instead, you stand insufferably stubborn, unwilling to listen."

"Can a stone feed a child? Nay, it cannot. So I say unto you witch, do not hasten to conclude you know me at all. I am as far removed from your understanding as the stars are from the Earth." Words hissed between clenched teeth reveal more than the actual words. Brianna saw in the sentence that they were equally matched in their hatred of each other.

…Yet even as she thought of it, it suddenly became perfectly clear that her hatred had gone. In its stead was a desire to understand and to truly forgive, not for his benefit – well maybe slightly, but for her own salvation. Maybe, if she could wholeheartedly forgive him, God would forgive her and return her faith?

"I forgive you," she blurted without pause for consideration.

"What?" His shock was so great that he stopped their steps and dropped her arm to look at her. "Do not speak of things you cannot understand. You, not only a witch but a *peasant vagabond,* with no standing, no family name or even class – you would offer me something you surely cannot understand; I will not accept your pittance of words. You chose your ending when you decided to follow in wicked and depraved ways. Just for being a vagrant I could have you put into slavery for two years. Your sins are worthy of great punishment. I will hear none of your arguments to the contrary, you are for the gallows. I sit on a higher seat than you can ever dream of. To the London magistrates I will take you, for the most public defamation that has ever been seen. You, girl, are one of the last of your kind. May you all rot in hell!"

Tingles of anger ran across Brianna's neck. She closed her eyes and breathed deeply, she would not let him disturb the peace she knew would soon be hers. Slowly, with deliberate speech she addressed him, raising her stance to be as straight and as tall as she could muster.

"O how loftily you comport yourself, man of darkness, so aptly named Black Wolf! What fine words you use to cover thy nakedness of understanding. I am Brianna O'Byrne, my father was Aeron O'Byrne, lord and overseer and a direct descendant of the King of Leinster. My mother marriage was the daughter of Simeon the Fair and his beloved wife Estella of the household Caddell, with ancestry reaching the throne of England. Your lack of knowledge portrays your ignorant ways. You seek to murder us, though innocent we are, and you do not even know our names! How can you judge us, when you do not even *know us*!"

"I have heard of your works, witch. Your slippery tongue of serpent's devise will not wiggle you to freedom here."

"Arr, but Benedict Everleigh, born of Benjamin and Mary Everleigh of Oxford, I know all about *you.* The Lord is calling you home, your darkened heart belongs to the Black Wolf, but He wants you – his son, Benedict Everleigh, to come home."

Rage boiled clear to see, within Benedict's spirit. If he hadn't made a promise to David, he would string her up right now. Instead, he fetched ropes and a cloth to bind her wicked mouth once more.

Chapter 22

"WHAT DID WE EVER DO to you, that you should revile my mother and I so?"

The fire had burned low, so Benedict leaned forward and fed it with fresh wood. "John Knox said: Men of God are sword bearers in this violent struggle between God and evil as the apocalypse draws near. Where there is sin we must root it out, for to see sin and do nothing is the worst sin of all."

"Firstly, that was a hundred years ago, and the word of God spoken to another vessel. You should be seeking your own guidance."

He turned from the light of the flames, his cheeks reddened, eyes blazing. "You are insolent witch, to presume that God does not speak to me!"

Ignoring his indignation she continued, "Jesus said: He that is without sin among you, let him cast a stone at her. And... I say unto you, that ye resist not evil: but whosoever shall smite thee on thy cheek, turn to him the other also. And if any man will sue thee at the law, and take away thy coat, let him have thy cloak also." (7) + (8)

She studied him, watching for a response. When the features on his face did not move she continued. "When you look at a person and see only their sin, you choose to forget that they too are made in God's image and that the King of Kings loves all men and desires not one to perish but all to have everlasting life."

Benedict snorted. "We are to ignore sin then?"

"We are to be God's tools, and to remember we are made in His image and if truly filled with the Holy Spirit we will reflect His Glory. Therefore, we should humbly love all men. If punishment is required we should first pray and then enforce the law with love and wisdom. Tell me, did you love the women you have put to death?"

For an answer, Benedict retied her hands and gagged her once more.

The next day, Brianna was surprised when Benedict didn't start packing up camp as usual. She observed him from where she sat with her back to a tree. Different expressions flittered across his face and she wondered what he was thinking.

When the potage had been warmed, he approached Brianna, untied her hands and removed the cloth from her mouth. She immediately started coughing and rubbing her wrists which were now black and blue.

"Come and sit by the fire," he said.

She had seen him wince when he saw her bruises and was glad of it, for it meant there was some decency in him yet.

A whisper on the wind carried a memory of a message that she was to deliver. Who had given her the message she couldn't remember.

After eating a little breakfast, she looked at him from behind the hair that had fallen over her face. He was sure to be angry with her questions, yet she had to know the answers.

"Why do you hunt witches?"

At first it seemed he wouldn't respond. He stared into his wooden bowl and continued to eat. She didn't know the part of the land they were currently in, but she thought it must be far from a city as they hadn't passed a traveler in a day or two. Not that she was thinking of escaping, she was resigned to her fate.

223

She had put her life into the hands of God and was no longer worried about what might happen to her.

When Benedict put his bowl down at last, she stopped her wondering thoughts and focused on him. Without looking at her, he began talking.

"My parents have eleven children, I am their fourth born and the eldest son. After my father, the responsibility to protect my family falls to me. I take this position very seriously. You need to understand that." He suddenly looked at her, checking she understood. Brianna nodded several times, but found she could not speak.

"Joshua was the tenth child and the youngest son. He was a rainbow of light, everyone loved him tenderly. He was often sickly and grew with a small and thin frame. But in between bouts of illness he was full of love. You should have seen him," Benedict looked at Brianna and his smile was tender. "He loved life so much; he was always delighted in every little thing. He always gave thanks to God for the tiniest of things. He was a blessing."

Benedict returned to looking into the fire. A red squirrel leapt in the branches overhead and for a moment they both looked up. When it had gone they brought their gaze back to the flames.

"When he was sixteen he fell in love with a young beauty from our village. We teased him about it, but he was so happy he took our jibes in good spirit."

Benedict stopped talking. After a while Brianna could bear it no longer. "What happened?" she asked softly.

"We found him hanging from a tree on the outskirts of the village."

Brianna gasped and put her hands over her mouth.

"He knew that to commit suicide means you can't get into heaven, we all knew he knew that. So, we couldn't believe he had really done it. My two brothers who are just beneath me in age, and I set about questioning everyone to try and find out what happened. Eventually, I overheard three women talking in secret. God led me there that day; I know He did, for I had not intended to visit the cobblers again. But something drew me back. As I approached the house I heard whispers behind it. I made my way quietly to listen to their talk. Sarah Blaine spoke with pride and arrogance of how she and her two friends had cast spells upon Joshua and sent him to meet the Devil.

"The following days became a blur, but eventually all three women were burnt at the stake by the magistrates for witchcraft and Devil worship. After that I could not rest until one night God woke me from my slumber and told me to clear the land of witchcraft."

"I am sorry for what happened to your brother."

"You do not defend the witches?"

"I don't know them. What happened is between them and God."

"And me."

"Yes, and you."

They were silent again for a little while. Brianna could tell by his posture that the fight was leaving him.

"God has given me a message for you, can I give it?"

He looked at her, his expression hard but he didn't say no.

She took a deep breath, sat up straight and began.

"My beloved son, with you I am well-pleased. Lo though I am with you every day you have wandered far and become lost."

Brianna paused before giving the last line; she knew it would evoke a great reaction. She gulped, "Release your pain my son, for Joshua is by my side and is in no need of your vengeance."

Benedict jumped up and knocked the pot over in his haste.

"You dare..." he fought for his breath, "you dare to hint that my brother is in Heaven! I will take your eyes and your tongue for this witch. Heresy, heresy, nothing pours from you but evil and heresy for no man can enter Heaven who hath taken his own life."

Brianna stood up slowly. "The things of God knoweth no man, but the Spirit of God." (12)

"Thou shalt not kill (13) and yet what greater murder can there be than to kill a body that carries the Holy Spirit?"

"For God so loved the world that He gave his only begotten Son, that whosoever believeth in Him should not perish, but have everlasting life." (14)

Benedict was enraged, his face a deep red. With fist clenched he took a step towards her. "Only a witch would twist the Good Word to her own meaning. You will burn, we will turn away from our path to London and go instead to Oxfordshire; there the magistrates will burn you! You will die slowly and in agony as you deserve!"

"Blessed are ye, when men shall revile you, and persecute you, and shall say all manner of evil against you falsely, for my sake." (15)

Benedict grabbed her by the shoulders and shook her. "Luke 12:34 tells us – Think not that I am come to send peace on earth: I came not to send peace, but a sword."

Brianna tried pushing him off her, but he was too strong. Knowing the power of her words had gone, but that meaning and understanding can still be learnt from them, she screamed in his face. "You ignorant man! You cannot take a single bite of the apple and say you are full! To be sated you must devour the whole apple. In 2 Timothy 1:16 it states – Behold, I send you forth as sheep in the midst of wolves: be ye therefore wise as serpents, and harmless as doves. Tell me, avenging angel of God, what harmless dove do you know that would drown, burn and hang women?"

His hands dropped off her as if burnt by fire. He took a step backwards. The pulse in his neck twitched for all to see the anger that controlled his mind.

Brianna's own anger abated. "Horses wear blinders to prevent them from seeing to the side and behind them. It is to keep them focused on the path ahead, to stop them being panicked or distracted. Is it possible Benedict that your pain has blinkered you and kept you on a path of revenge instead of mercy?"

Though his body slackened, his words came through clenched teeth, "You are insufferable."

He let go of her shoulders where bruises were quickly appearing, and strode off into the forest.

Brianna cried; a mix of pain, pity and frustration. *Why O God have you given me this impossible task?*

It was well past sundown before Benedict returned. He had caught a hare and set about skinning it to spit roast it over the flames that Brianna had kept going.

For hours they sat in silence. When they had finished eating he said, "I thought you would be gone."

To which she responded, "So did I."

The next morning they still didn't pack up camp. Instead, Benedict stomped amongst the trees gathering more twigs and branches for the fire.

"Are we staying here a long while then?" she finally asked.

A grunt was his only answer, and whether it was a yes or a no she did not know.

"My mother was a wonderful woman," Brianna looked at Benedict out of the corner of her eye to see if he would react. When no outward sign came that he was listening she proceeded. "From the moment the gift of faith was given to her she wanted for nothing more than to heal people and to share her love of God with them."

If it was possible, Benedict shrunk a little within his clothes.

"I wish very much that I was more like her, but unfortunately I am just me."

"But you can heal… I have been told many times of this."

"Not anymore, my faith has been taken from me."

Benedict hated that she was pulling him in with her soft quiet words, but he couldn't prevent himself, "Why?"

"I rejected it. I don't think I really understood what I had been doing. But since my mother first told me you were going to kill her, I began falling into self-pity. Out of that arose a longing for it all to be over and more importantly for me to be normal."

She raised her arms and shrugged. "So here I am, normal, but no more happy and that's for sure."

The Holy Spirit was sitting with them. He took her simple words and imparted the sadness within them into Benedict's heart. Benedict felt the pain, and his own erupted for he could no longer profess that she was a witch. He had been wrong, so very wrong.

Pain exploded within him. He gripped his chest and moaned. Sinking to his knees, tears streamed; pouring anguish from his soul.

"I hated them." He fell forward, hands landing on the grass as pain contorted his body and soul. Caleb whined and came close on his belly and nuzzled into his master's side. Levi looked up with drooping eyes, and then lowered his head again, preferring to remain at Brianna's feet.

"I hated them for what happened to Joshua." Suddenly, his body jerked backwards and he released his pain heavenwards. Unforgiveness, resentfulness and pride had raged within him. They had done for years, but for the first time he saw them. His body folded inwards again, once more he sank his palms against the earth.

"O Lord, have mercy. Have mercy and forgive my sins. Have mercy, have mercy. I am sorry. O Lord, my God please remove from me all these things."

Brianna left him to talk with God in private. As she walked along the river bank she called out to God to forgive her for her negative thoughts and hatred she'd been harboring against the Black Wolf. When she received a measure of peace she switched her prayers towards Benedict and asked the Holy Spirit to lead and guide him in his prayers and soul-searching. Then in her spirit agreeing with his prayers, she earnestly pleaded that God would grant the witch hunter both forgiveness and peace.

Chapter 23

NO LIGHT YET PIERCED THE DARK NIGHT SKY when later that day Brianna was woken by the Holy Spirit. Before opening her eyes, her love of God flowed through her like a wave. "I love you Lord, here I am." Whisper-echoes of air brushed against her cheeks refreshing her, dispersing all sleep. It took a moment after opening her eyes for them to adjust to the pale moonlight and focus properly. It was difficult pushing herself into a sitting position as she had become stiff from the hard ground. The breath of air traveled around her body and she found herself refreshed and free from pain.

Her gaze rested on the Black Wolf, who lay asleep, just an arm's length away from her. His steady breath showed he hadn't woken.

Air swirled around her face and then moved away.

"I am coming, Lord." Quietly as she could, she stood. On bare feet she tip-toed away with bated breath, every moment she expected Benedict to cry out for her to halt. His voice never murmured.

The Spirit of the Lord led her a good distance away, to a clearing in the forest where a small stream flowed with pure water from the hills. She crouched and drank from cupped hands, and when refreshed she moved into the clearing and knelt.

"Here I am Lord." With eyes closed and hands pressed together in readiness for prayer, she waited upon God. When His voice didn't come she embarked on praise. "How wonderful are thou, O Lord my God, who has made all things and reigns

Most High." With an open heart she is filled with love, it poured into, through and out of her like a mighty tide.

"O how I love thee, Lord Jesus."

Brianna's thanks and praise flow from her with passion and gratitude.

"I am a child of the Lord Most High. I am fearfully and wonderfully made. I believe you, Lord. What you say is good and true and faithful. You are a mighty God. You determine destiny. You are in control. The world and everything in it belongs to you. Thank you, Father that you gave your son, my Lord Jesus Christ, so that whoever believes in him will not perish but have everlasting life. Thank you God, that you granted me faith so that I would believe." On and on Brianna poured out her prayers of thanks and praise. Though her knees began to ache, the only part of her body to move were her lips, whispering, singing, exalting.

Light bloomed behind her eyelids and warmth touched her face, letting her know the sun was on the rise. Her prayers faded, tears fell as precious rain drops soaking the ground.

"Why do you cry?"

Her lids shoot open. *He's like a giant*, she thought. He'd once been menacing, a dark knight; his black cape like raven's wings. It was still too dim for her to see his face clearly and read his emotions, but she wondered how his thoughts towards her had changed.

Brianna had been unaware of the tears that flowed until she raised her hand and touched her wet face. "Many reasons."

"I thought you had run."

"I told you, I will not run."

"Why didn't you?"

She sighed, exhaling in her breath all the frustration she knew was about to come, for now he surely would be more set on her trial and execution. "The Spirit of the Lord bid me stay with you until you are fully free." She braced for his temper and arguments. After what seemed a long time of silence, she rose to her feet and approached him so she could see his face. She stopped an arm's length away from him and looked up at his angular features. His stern, square chin, even though softened with a dimple, made his countenance sever, harsh. The searching of his eyes brought her no answers.

Eventually, he said, "You were unbound, you didn't have to stay."

"God called me to prayer, so that I may be strengthened for all that is to come. If He had told me to flee, believe me I would have heeded His instructions."

"Even though you told me you wouldn't run?" One of his eyebrows shot up his forehead.

"God's word takes precedence over mine."

He sucked in a long breath through his nose.

"You are a conundrum, and I have to admit nothing like what I expected."

"What did you expect?"

"Someone who would hate me for killing her mother, and would claw my eyes out with her nails the first chance she got."

Brianna turned her gaze to the grass. Indeed that image had fluttered through her mind numerous times. How could she explain to this witch hunter, who was the bane of her life, that she was now indifferent to him? He was who he was, and he... well she no longer wished to be anything else but on her way home to Heaven for she had no place else to go.

His next words surprised her, "I don't know what to do with you."

"I thought maybe that is why we have tarried here so long."

"I have no evidence of your witchcraft and therefore cannot present you to the magistrates. You are free to go."

"Go where?"

He looked surprised. "I don't know… wherever you want."

"I have no 'wants' left within me."

"Surely you must?"

She shook her head.

He knew this was his fault; he had killed her mother and taken away her only family. Guilt slashed at him more harshly than any sword could.

"I am truly sorry Brianna."

A flicker of wanting to reject his apologies was quickly batted away by her faith. "As the Lord forgives me, so shall I forgive you."

They made their way back to the camp. Once there he sank to the ground and buried his face in his hands. "What shall I do? I am too ashamed to return to my family."

Where she could see no path for herself, she could envision his clearly. "Benedict it is not by works that we earn forgiveness, which alone comes from the cross. However, much growth is made within when we help other people. I believe you should find a way to live your life helping others. Not as a penance now, do not mistake me. But as a means for you to find joy."

"What form should that take?"

"Ha, I cannot answer that for I don't even know where my own life will lead me from here. You must talk with the Lord, I am sure He will lead you."

"Then I shall return to my parents, there are no people more Godly than them. They will help me on my way I am sure." For the first time in years, Benedict felt light. Suddenly the world seemed full of hope once more.

Chapter 24

NOT WANTING TO LEAVE BRIANNA defenseless, Benedict was teaching her how to fight and to defend herself before he left and set off for home.

Quick to learn, Brianna was soon putting up a good resistance to his attempts to knock her to the floor.

A tiny part of her was sad that this was to be their last day together. The thought made her chuckle because her mother had told her that one day she would hug Benedict goodbye and be sad to see him go. The amazingness of the vision her mother had quite taken her breath away. She'd never imagined she could ever forgive the Black Wolf for hunting and then killing her mother. But maybe that was a part of it, for now she called him Benedict and that alone helped to build a wall between the man he had been and the man he now was.

"I am battered," cried Brianna, "let us stop."

"One more bout. Remember what I have taught you, I expect you to have me on the floor in three moves!"

They crouched and moved in circles; Benedict held his hunting knife in one hand, Brianna a large stick in hers. They shuffled closer together, and then Brianna moved backwards swinging her stick in front of her. She knew from the day's practice that waving the stick was pointless, but it felt good.

He lurched towards her, despite the fact that they had been doing this all afternoon, she still screamed. He grabbed her from behind.

"Fight me girl!" he commanded softly in her ear.

She brought her elbow back and hit his stomach; he bent and moaned a little but didn't release his grip on her.

She was just about to bend and attempt to throw him over her shoulder, when someone came charging towards them.

"Argh!" the person screamed and leapt onto Benedict's back.

Benedict crashed to the ground, taking Brianna with him.

Brianna turned on her back to see a man raise an arm with a knife in his hand. The knife was descending towards Benedict's back.

"Arwen stop!" Brianna screamed.

The tall strapping man that was her heart's desire froze mid-swing.

"Put it down, please, put it down."

He lowered his arm, but his confusion was clear to see.

In that moment, Benedict used his delay to swing around and transfer their situation so now Benedict was over Arwen and holding a knife to his throat.

"Please Benedict, don't, don't. This is a friend, please Benedict." She grabbed his arm and he turned to look at her.

"Are you sure?"

"O Lord yes, please put it down."

Benedict lowered the knife and got up.

Arwen also jumped to his feet, looking first at Brianna and then at Benedict, obviously confused.

"What are you doing here, Arwen?"

"Why, I've come to rescue you." His words stumbled with his puzzlement, for she didn't exactly look like she needed rescuing, nor did she look overly pleased to see him… although *that* he did understand only too well.

236

Benedict moaned and rubbed his head from the bash Arwen had given him when he jumped on him. Arwen took a wide-berth stance and raised his knife again. Brianna placed a hand on the knife and looked into his eyes.

"You really do not need to do that."

He lowered it again and looked on slightly stunned as his love moved towards the witch hunter and placed a hand on his arm.

Her eyes asked him to leave, and he did.

"You're free?"

"I am."

"But how?"

Arwen's somewhat stupefied look caused the awakening of a small laugh inside her. "It is a long story, and I shall tell you all on our journey home, but for now all I can say is that the ways of God far out reach my understanding. God is wonderful though, Arwen. This I do know with every fiber of my being."

He took a step towards her and reached tentatively for her hand. She slipped both her hands in his with no hesitation. Encouraged by this, Arwen began his well-rehearsed declaration of apology – some epic ode to his sincerity.

Yet, "I'm sorry, forgive me," from the composed speech was all that managed to come to fruition.

Brianna pulled her hands free and threw her arms about him. Laughter would hold no more, and bubbles squeaked from her mouth and then erupted with abandon. Nervous release relaxed her into his body, and she laid her head against his chest and listened to his thumping heart. *O how he must wonder what I am about!* His muscles relaxed and he drew his arms around her back and held her close. He didn't fully understand what was happening, but he was grateful for the embrace which surely spoke of her forgiveness.

Tears of joy and relief began to mingle with the fading laughter, until the mirth was spent and gone, and sobbing took its place.

"O Bri, my love." He showered her hair with kisses. "Bri, I am so sorry."

When at last the sobbing ceased, her face was splattered with red-blotches and her breath came in staggering gulps.

Arwen took her tiny face in his gentle, farm-rough hands. "Say you forgive Bri, please, O please say you do! I promise to spend the rest of our lives repenting for how I hurt thee."

"Hush and shush." Brianna placed two fingers against his lips. "I love you Arwen, true I do."

Immense relief and indescribable happiness mixed and blended together an effect that only a full-score of ales could match! Giddiness and an urge to jump, dance, shout and sing hit the pair with equal force. They broke out grinning, lips splitting with length of longest degree. Joy ran through their veins and tingled across their skin, joy in their touch and in their looks. No better way could describe how they felt, except to say they had never been so alive.

Benedict had packed up their small camp by the time they returned, he was just throwing dirt over the fire when they walked up hand-in-hand.

He smiled at them.

"I am mighty sorry for the blow to your head," said Arwen.

"There is no need for apologies; I deserved that and much more besides. Where will you go?"

"Home," answered Arwen automatically, and then quickly looked at Brianna to see that she agreed.

"Trapp is your home, and you are my home, I would go wherever you wanted."

His knees nearly buckled as the words he had so longed to hear were finally said.

"And you?" asked Arwen.

"Home, for a little while at least. I will spend my time on my knees until I know where the Lord wants me to go."

"My horse is tethered back in the woods a distance, so we will say our farewells here."

Benedict came over and offered Arwen his hand.

Arwen took it after a few moments and they nodded at each other. Though Arwen knew it was time to move forward he would probably never feel easy with the witch hunter knowing that he had killed Brianna's mother and almost Brianna as well.

Benedict looked at Brianna, he wanted to embrace her, to express his gratitude but he didn't know if she would welcome it.

She knew his hesitation. Her heart was still dealing with unforgiveness, it wasn't that it had simply been wiped away; she knew it would take work… like a continuing forgiveness, one that would have to be fresh each morning. But it was something she was determined to do, not for Benedict's benefit but for her own. She did what came naturally to her, she threw her arms around him and held on tight.

Benedict sucked in his breath and felt his throat close tight with the emotional rush, and then he clasped his arms around her and held her tight. Eventually, they pulled apart. He couldn't talk, so he gave her a nod, turned, mounted his horse and left.

"Are you alright?" Arwen asked.

"Yes my love." She slipped her hand into his and the two of them set off to find his hidden horse.

Arwen's horse was a massive Shire, its gleaming coat long and silky. She was sturdy more than fast, but neither of them felt in a hurry so all was well as they slowly clip-clopped down the old dirt road.

The sun had passed its height and white clouds raced across a deep-blue sky. Birds sang all around and rabbits played in the hedgerow. It was a picture of peace and tranquility, and therefore it came as a shock when it was interrupted by the galloping of a horse and the cries of what sounded like a madman.

Arwen pulled his horse to a still and they turned in the saddle to look behind them.

Approaching them a black horse upon which sat a blur of black with eagle definitions as the rider's cape flew behind him like wings.

Arwen's arm tightened around Brianna's waist. "What does he want?"

"I don't know."

They waited until he came alongside them.

"Brianna you've got to come, there is someone who needs your help or he will die."

"Who?" she asked, sitting forward over the horse's neck.

"A man, he's hurt. Quick you've got to come."

When they didn't move, Benedict grew frustrated. "He has a family, a wife and children, you need to come, why do you hesitate?"

"I've lost my faith Benedict, I told you that. I can't heal anymore."

"No, no, that's not true. Please you've got to come and help."

"We'll come," said Arwen.

Brianna turned in the saddle to look up at him.

He smiled down at her. "Even if miracles are not at your fingertips anymore we can still see what help we might offer, 'tis the Christian thing to do."

"You're right," she said before turning to Benedict. "We'll come."

They couldn't race with the speed of Benedict's steed but they cantered at a great pace and soon they came upon the traveling family.

Arwen jumped down and then lifted Brianna by the waist and brought her to the ground. She ran up to a man lying on the grass. A woman, who appeared to be his wife, and several children of different ages were all kneeling around him.

"Let us at him," ordered Benedict and the children moved back. The wife stayed holding onto her husband's head.

Brianna knelt beside the man who had a gash in his head that had been bleeding profusely. "What happened?"

"We were attacked by strangers. They took our wagon and horses and they would have left us unharmed, only Stanley couldn't bear to let them take everything we had and leave us destitute, so he charged at one of the three men. The man bludgeoned him on the head and Stanley dropped to the ground. He hasn't moved since, the bleeding has eased but he will not stir." The last words came from the woman as a wail, and she started sobbing.

Brianna was shaking. She knew she no longer had the amount of faith for miracles, but she had to try. She closed her eyes and put her hands on the man's chest. "Be healed," she whispered. No heat or tingling flew down her arms and into her hands. She tried again a little louder. "Be healed." She was aware that tears were flowing only from her right eye, soaking her face. "Be healed," she tried one last time. Stanley did not respond. The wife wailed louder.

"You pray," Brianna urged Benedict.

He shook his head. "A sinner such as me can ask no favors of God."

"You are a forgiven man, Benedict. Now get down here and pray!"

His face was white, but he heeded her words and knelt down opposite her. He clasped his hands tight in front of him and closed his eyes. "Dear Father in Heaven, please hear my prayer. By your love and great mercy, please heal this man. Amen." He remained still with his eyes closed. If God answered his prayer the woman's cries would alert him. When only her sobbing continued, he prayed again, pouring his lifetime of faith into each word. When he said amen, Brianna, Arwen and all the children joined in.

When he opened his eyes it was to see that the man's breathing had become even shallower. Brianna and Benedict locked eyes over the dying man's body. Something passed between them – a measure of understanding, something intangible. She reached out her hands, he took them. They closed their eyes and bowed their heads.

"O Lord, in your mercy hear our prayers and forgive us our sins. We thank you for the cross and for your love. All authority has been given to us from Jesus, so in the name of our Lord Jesus Christ *we* say to you… be healed."

Lightning energy transferred between Brianna and Benedict. Both of them opened their eyes in shock, then instantly looked down at the man *expecting* him to be healed.

Stanley opened his eyes. His wife became hysterical and jumped up screaming, her children gathered around her crying and holding onto her skirts. Arwen went to her side and wrapped his arm around the shocked woman. "Hush now," he whispered, "you are scaring your children."

She immediately became quiet, then after hugging her offspring dropped onto her knees and started thanking God, for her husband was sitting up.

When the excitement of the miracle began to ebb, Arwen put his arm around Brianna. "We should go," he said, "it is getting late."

Stanley and his family couldn't stop giving their thanks, even though directed to give all their thanks to Jesus.

Arwen lifted Brianna and sat her on the horse, then swung up and sat behind her. Benedict, too emotional for another farewell, simply gave them a nod.

"God is good," said Brianna as they set off down the road.

"All the time," answered Arwen.

Chapter 25

THE THREE OF THEM WALKED into the chapel, the air about them brimmed with anticipation. Today the vicar would call the banns for the first time and everyone in the vale would know she had finally said yes! October's sun was warmer than it should have been, and the day was ablaze with light and warmth.

There was a general cry of excited congratulations when the service was over, though when no one was looking Betty would cry a deluge. Arwen received congratulations and had his arm pumped until it ached. Brianna was hugged and kissed on both cheeks too many times to count, and Dafydd was automatically accepted as her family and congratulated just as much as the young couple.

The genuine happiness the news spread warmed Brianna to her bones. She had found a home, a husband-to-be and an extended family all at once. The only sorrow on this cheerful day was that her mother wasn't here to celebrate with her. Though even that was more wistful than woeful, as she knew her mother had seen it all happen in a vision and had already celebrated this day for her.

After a sup or two of ale at the tavern, the three set off for Dafydd's farm to eat dinner together. For celebration, Dafydd had plucked a chicken and today their meal would be fulsome and tasty as it had been left to slow-roast with vegetables on the shelf at the back of fire.

When they were happy and full, the three pulled chairs around the low-burning fire to relax. The fire always burned to keep their potage turning, but during these hot months it was kept as low as possible. Now with the sun's slow drop its heat had waned slightly, making the fire more attractive. All were quiet for a while as Dafydd enjoyed his pipe, Arwen dozed and Brianna continued with the sewing of her new dress.

She had been over the moon with delight, when after they had returned from her 'rescue' Arwen had given her a large fold of the blue material she had wanted to buy at the fair. When he'd picked it up she had no idea. He'd grinned when he gave it to her, telling her that he knew she'd want it for her wedding dress.

Now and then Brianna peeped over her sewing to look at the man she regarded as the grandfather-of-her-heart. He was reclining in his chair, and every so often a sigh as soft as feather-fall fluttered from his lips. His frailty seemed to strike her quite suddenly, as she stitched and regarding him from under her long dark lashes. His aged-spotted hands with their raised blue veins; his overly bushy gray eyebrows that spurted in all manner of directions; his hair, gray from their first meeting, yet now with a lack-luster and a limp disposition – all these things had been on display since their first meeting, yet his daily routine of working all day had never changed and somehow hidden from her the fact his body seemed to be diminishing. She shuddered and determined to pray for him later.

It was a shock to the silence when Dafydd asked Brianna a question. "Will you fetch your Holy Book and read me Psalm 37, verses three to seven?"

Brianna stopped her stitching. "Trust in the Lord and do good; so shalt thou dwell in the land, and verily thou shalt be fed. Delight thyself also in the Lord, and He shall give thee the desires of thine heart. Commit thy way unto the Lord, trust also in him; and He shall bring it to pass. And He shall bring forth thy righteousness as the light, and thy judgment as the noonday. Rest in the Lord, and wait patiently for him; fret not thyself because of him who prospereth in his way, because of the man who bringeth wicked devices to pass."

"Goodness," said Arwen who had woken as soon as Dafydd asked the question, "Do you know the entire book by heart?"

"No, not all, but some verses ring like songs in my heart and memory of them comes easily."

"Why did you ask for that one?" Arwen asked Dafydd.

"I was thinking of the Black Wolf and how hard I would find it to forgive if he had killed one of my own. I was full of admiration for your virtue Brianna, you are a better person than I."

"That is not so," replied Brianna. "I am like James states… one who doubts, like a wave of the sea driven and tossed by the wind. I became torn between two minds and in the process lost a measure of my faith. You are far wiser than I Dafydd, and I envy you your stability of faith."

"Aye, part of you is correct, for Jesus did tell us that a kingdom divided against itself shall not stand.(16) Yet I believe there is more happening than you or I can see or touch.

"Unbelief spreads with insidious clandestine corrosion. A decline in belief in an all-powerful, omnipresent God began with Henry VIII's watering down faith to suit his own needs. His actions allowed discord to ripen among believers. A rift so vast appeared its only option was to keep increasing. This decline into unbelief created a lamentable dolefulness throughout the fair land of Britain; for without God and the promise of Heaven what point has life? We who have held on tight to our faith are the lucky ones. My heart breaks for those who cannot see the destruction being wrought by our faceless enemy – unbelief."

"Your thoughts are heavy today my friend," said Arwen.

"I miss my wife and wish my daughter would have a change of heart and return home, I am afraid my longings dim my spirits."

"Have you news of her recently?" asked Arwen, who had grown up with Beca and considered her a true friend.

"She passed word through the tinker this spring just passed, saying her third child was born and that Aled was providing for them. Nothing more."

They turned their chatter to farming and livestock, and then before the sun was too low, Arwen asked Brianna to come and walk around his farm with him. "I'd like you to see your home, and for me to explain all my plans."

Brianna got up, popped a kiss on Dafydd's forehead and then fetched her shawl.

A short time later, they walked hand-in-hand around Arwen's land, which she was surprised to find was vast.

At the bottom of one long sloping field where his sheep were grazing, he indicated for her to climb over the stile into what looked like unfarmed wild land. With his helping hand she climbed over as daintily as she could, trying not to catch her long skirts on the posts. Arwen leapt over easily and re-took her hand.

As the sun dipped even lower, golden rays rushed across the wild flowers and multitude of ferns, bringing everything to glittering life. Deep red poppies waved in a gentle breeze as they approached a large pond. Arwen led her to where he had carved out a seat in a fallen tree trunk.

"On the other side of the pond the land begins to slope upwards again."

"Do you own that as well?" she asked in surprise.

"I do. I was thinking that in time, we could build our first son a house there. He would have his space but still be close to home. What do you think?"

"I think that is a lovely idea, but first we need to get wed and take each day as it comes. Who knows if the Lord will bless us with children, for as much as I desire them I do not take it for granted that the Lord will bless me with them."

Arwen chuckled. "I do. I have been praying for years for God to bring to me a wife that would bear me many sons, and here you are!"

"We'll have to wait and see won't we."

He wrapped his arm around her and the two of them sat enjoying the sounds of nature, so idyllic as to be compared to Eden.

"The crickets are very noisy down here," Brianna said after a while.

"O, that's not crickets, that's the Nightjars singing."

"What?"

Mistaking her shock, he replied, "I know, it is the least attractive birdsong in all the kingdom is it not?! They come here in May and have normally left by September. I think the warm weather has fooled them into staying over their normal time. I am sure they will leave soon."

The floodgates opened in Brianna's soul, and tears streamed like a river down her cheeks. "O," was all she could say.

"What is it? What has distressed you?"

She shook her head to indicate she couldn't talk, and he waited for her emotional outbreak to ebb.

When she was calm enough, she pulled a handkerchief from her skirt pocket and wiped her face, before turning to look up at Arwen, whose face was full of concern.

"My mother had many visions from God. One of them was that I would find my true love where the Nightjars sing. It was part of the reason I struggled with loving you, for I hadn't found that place yet and so I thought that you couldn't be the one I should wed. And here they are after all!"

"Well bless me!"

They took a minute to soak in this wonderful blessing.

"There," said Arwen pointing. "Can you see, sitting on the low branches of that tree, three of them together?"

"I don't see them," said Brianna leaning forward and squinting against the rays of the setting sun.

"Their gray-brown plumage means they blend in with the land and the bark and twigs of trees. There see, one just flew off!"

She saw them, and her heart soared with joy.

Chapter 26

MRS. TANNER TOOK IT UPON HERSELF to stand in place of missing relatives, especially Brianna's mother. She fussed and fussed and ensured others did too.

When at last Brianna was dressed with her hair piled in soft waves upon her head, Mrs. Tanner took a handkerchief and blew her nose. "O bless you child, your parents would have been so proud of you, of that I am sure."

Her heavy-cotton dress of palest blue was tied at the back with deep-blue velvet ribbon. Her under blouse, made by Mrs. Tanner, was softest-white and frill adorned. All three of the underskirts she wore, to push out the skirt and make it full. She had spent all the nights since she returned embroidering patterns down the bodice, and if anyone looked closely they would have discerned a Nightjar hiding amongst the stitches.

A hard lump formed in Brianna's throat, but she had determined not to cry on this precious day and so shook her head with tiny shakes to disperse the threat of tears.

"Child, I am sure your mother would have prepared for thee a mighty precious and guiding speech for today. I could not even attempt to say what she might have done. But I have lived long and lived well, and so my humble advice I offer.

"Devotion lives hand-in-hand with endurance and long-suffering, don't think you anything else. Love, my dear, is *not* enough to carry you through a life-time. If you want to be happy until the end you must learn to bend with the breeze. You must be able to forgive in a heartbeat, and politeness should be your everyday friend."

"I shall mark your words, and much appreciative of them I am."

With one last look and two brief nods, they turned and made their way to the chapel. At the entrance stood Betty, and Mary who had her hands behind her back.

They took a step to greet her, and Brianna wondered what they would say.

"We have something for you," said Mary. She brought her hands forward, and in them lay a beautiful garland of pink and white flowers. Once again tears threatened to flow for their generosity of spirit did touch her. She closed her eyes to fight back the emotion that this peace-offering represented.

"Here, bow your head and let me place it on," said Betty.

She did as she was bid and lowered her head, for she was a measure taller than both young ladies.

"You look like a princess," Betty said, wiping at the tears that ran down her face.

"Come on now, for everyone is waiting," said Mary, taking hold of Brianna's hand and urging her forward.

"Everyone?" asked Brianna.

"Yes, everyone," grinned Mary.

When she entered the chapel there was a rustle of movement as everyone stood. She was in awe that the building was packed, even with people standing at the back.

"We're your family," whispered Dafydd as he offered her his arm at the entrance. And now there was no stopping them, tears flowed incessantly down her cheeks.

"Don't cry my love," said Arwen when she reached his side. He lifted his arm and wiped her face with his sleeve. "'Tis supposed to be a joyous day!"

"O indeed it is, it is," she smiled.

It was November, and a north wind did blow bringing with it a chilly bite, but Brianna couldn't feel it, because joy flooded her body with the heat of happiness.

When the short service was over and they walked outside they were met with a chorus of 'hurrahs' which made them laugh. Then before they could object, the valley's youths did pick both of them up and carry them with much jolly laughter to the Cennen-on-the-Brook Tavern.

The villagers and the farmers had pooled their resources and the wedding feast was fit for a king. Arwen had given the tavern owner enough money to give everyone at least three drinks.

No sooner had they been carried into the tavern than Billy began to play his fiddle. He was accompanied by Mrs. Walker on the flute, and young Simon who had recently inherited his grandfather's hurdy-gurdy. Instantaneously everyone roared another hurrah and burst into song. As they sang Arwen and Brianna made their way around the group of people shaking hands with everyone.

The fire in the hearth was flamed high, but no one would have got cold should it have gone down, for soon the ale was flowing and the dancing merry.

Much later, Arwen and Brianna set off for his farm. His cart had been adorned with ivy and late flowering roses. Once Brianna was safely perched on the driver's box, he tenderly wrapped around her knees a patchwork blanket just given to them by the Trapp sewing ladies.

They were waved off, and shouts of encouragement given until they passed beyond sight.

"Wait here a moment," Arwen urged as he went to take the horse to the stable and remove her harness. Running back to her as quickly as he could, he found her waiting patiently, the patchwork blanket wrapped around her shoulders. He opened the door, and then turned around and swung her into his arms.

She laughed as he carried her over the threshold.

He put her gently on her feet once they were inside, and turned to close the door. "Wait just a moment more," he said as he rushed to light the candle lantern so they could see.

The glow from the candle flickered across his face, and Brianna gasped as the sight of him momentarily took her breath away. How blessed was she, and so very grateful to God for the partner He had ordained for her.

Chapter 27

BENEDICT FOUND IT HARD TO BELIEVE how much his life had changed within three short months. Constantly, all day long, every day, he gave thanks to God for turning his life around so dramatically.

In a way his new life was due in part to Stanley and his family. When Brianna and Arwen had ridden away, Benedict had been left wondering what would become of the now penniless family. Their plans to set up home in a new town now lost due to not being able to pay rent.

The only thing he could think of was to take them home to Oxfordshire, and to beg his father's blessing to house them while they sought work and accommodation. As they only had Benedict's horse, the going had been slow. The children had taken it in turns to ride while everyone else walked. October had come with a blast of cold air and the going had been miserable to say the least. But finally they had arrived at his father's vicarage, and praise be to God, all had been welcomed in with open arms.

Unbeknown to Benedict at that moment in time, this family had become his first rescuees. But they would be far from the last. It hadn't taken long to find Stanley employment that came with a cottage, and the family professed to be forever in his debt.

There came with their problem-solved a measure of relief to Benedict's guilt. Whether it was that relief, or God's plan all along, he soon found himself addicted to helping others. When his grandfather sadly died at the beginning of February 1666, Benedict found himself in receipt of rather a large inheritance. After much debate with his family as to what constituted a

Godly-living, he went against his father's wishes and built a large tavern by the side of the Fossey Way six miles south of Coventre. It took nearly all his funds to build the long black-and-white timber building, but he had a vision. Before it was even finished he knew he was on God's path.

As he worked alongside the laborers, he was able to share the gospel with them. He helped every person who came his way with a request and was soon nicknamed the White Knight for his constant willingness to rescue people from all manner of calamities. The name made him chuckle daily, but he secretly delighted that the name Black Wolf was no longer his.

To his quiet joy and constant thanksgiving he met and married a young woman from London called Rina. She had walked the road from London, and came upon his tavern on the day the doors opened to patrons for the first time. Exhausted, she had stumbled through his doors and nearly collapsed.

Quick to offer a free meal and lodgings for the night she had gratefully accepted. Once restored with a measure of comfort and relief, she had shared her sorry tale with him. London, from the spring of the previous year had been brought to a halt by the plague. All roads in and out of the city had been closed and thousands had died. Rina lost all her family, including parents and five siblings. She didn't understand why she had been the only one to survive. On her death's-hour, her mother had made her promise to try and find a way out of London if she could. So, once all her family had been carted away and a black X written upon the door, she took to hiding and walking the streets late at night looking for her opportunity. By God's grace she had eventually found a ferryman willing to take her up the Thames and away from the city.

Knowing she could be carrying the sickness she had stayed as far away from people as possible and only ventured near villages when all her food had gone. Slowly, she had made her way north. She didn't know why she picked the paths she did, but she'd come across Benedict's tavern at a time when she hadn't eaten for three days and so had ventured close. It had been five months since she left London, so she felt secure in the fact that she didn't carry the plague with her.

"Work for me," Benedict had declared at the end of her sorrowful tale.

"As a barmaid?"

"Yes indeed, I will need help in the kitchen too, and with cleaning the rooms I have built for travelers."

"I'm not a loose woman, sir. I would work hard, but I won't be dallied with."

Benedict laughed. "How very glad I am to hear it!"

Six weeks later they had wed at his father's church. His parents, having come around to the idea that their son was now an inn-keeper with a mission!

When the signage for the tavern arrived, Benedict hung it from the huge hinge with satisfaction. When he got off the ladder and walked backwards he looked up at an image of a white dove. The Dove Tavern, he hoped and prayed, would become a place of impartation for the Holy Spirit.

Rina put her arm around his waist and gazed up with him.

He wrapped his arm around her shoulder with a sigh. His longing to be a vicar and have his own parsonage had not come to fruition. But what had come was something that filled his heart with joy and peace.

Chapter 28

August, in the year of our Lord 1666

FIRE, SCREAMING, BURNING! Her nightmare woke Brianna in a sweat.

"Are you alright?" Arwen asked, waking and sitting up with her.

"I had a dream so real I felt like I was there. I don't know if it is a premonition or just a nightmare, but so intense did the images appear that I will not rest until I beseech Dafydd to write his daughter to come home."

"We will go at first light. Now come here and let me hold you." Brianna moved into his arms and the two lay down to wait until the sun rose.

"But I can't write," said Dafydd, and how would such a missive reach her anyway?

"I will write it for you, only tell me what to say. I have fetched paper and ink with us. As for delivery, I have called already upon Stan who is, this very day, taking his fleeces to Hereford. From there he will beseech someone to carry it to Gloucestershire, and from there we are told the post is carried weekly to the capital."

"You have it all planned!" Dafydd chuckled, "I should have known!"

They sat at the table and Brianna took out of her basket, the miniature writing table that Mrs. Tanner had given her as a wedding present.

"What shall we say?" asked Dafydd.

"Is there some name that only you called her, so she will know this has indeed come from you? Or maybe there is a childhood story she was fond of hearing that we could mention?"

"I used to call her Beca, my little buttercup."

"Wonderful, that is how we shall start."

Soon a letter of urgent intent had been compiled. Short, but loving and urging Beca and her family to return post-haste to Trapp as a great family need had arisen.

"It is best we don't say you are summoning her on the back of my bad dream!" Brianna concluded.

Brianna had started the letter with… In the year of Lord 1666, in the month of August, I Dafydd Davies do beseech my daughter, Becca my little buttercup, to come home.

October, in the year of our Lord 1666

Brianna had the impression that someone was watching her; it sent tingles down her back. She moved around the yard as if not bothered by anything, then when a glimpse of something caught in the corner of her eye she spun around.

"Whoever you are – come out now! My husband is close by and if I scream he will come running."

"It is only I," came a voice across the way. Then the shadow from behind the tree moved and into her vision stepped Zendaya.

258

"Zendaya," she cried with honest surprise.

He approached her slowly, and the smile of welcome on her face faded as she took in his ragged appearance.

"O, Zendaya, what wars have you been in?"

"None I wish to retell."

"Come, come on in and let me put some meat back on those bones."

"Brianna?"

"Yes?"

"I am not alone."

"You have a friend with you? Well, call them forward; if they are a friend of yours they too are welcome here."

Zendaya turned and waved at the trees. Very slowly, a woman stepped out from the shade but she did not move forward.

"Come on inside, I have food just waiting to be eaten, you are welcome to share it with us."

Hesitantly, the heavily pregnant woman came forward.

Brianna was struck by her beauty. Her ebony skin was a much paler shade than Zendaya's, but her eyes were the exact same velvety-brown. Whereas Zendaya had skin pockmarked from illness, hers with as smooth as silk. Besides her large bump, she was as tall and as skinny as the field's rake.

"Welcome," said Brianna when the stranger drew up to them. Zendaya took her hand in his.

"Let us go inside," said Brianna.

She cupped her hands over her mouth and called out to her husband who was in the field next to the farmhouse. "Supper," she cried in a mighty loud voice, then turned to grin at Zendaya.

Zendaya, however, was backing away.

"O no 'tis nothing to fear, my husband is a good man, he will welcome you the same as I."

As if to prove the point, Arwen came striding into the yard just then. He came straight to them with a smile on his face. When he reached them he offered his hand.

Zendaya took it and they shook as good acquaintances.

Brianna had been working hard all day in the vegetable patch and hadn't planned a cooked meal, so their repast was simple bread, cheese and a jug of milk.

Though their meal was modest, Zendaya did show satisfaction and gratification to reflect a kingly feast.

"It seems you have a tale to tell," said Arwen when they had finished. "Let us gather around the fire-side and sit in comfort."

Once they were settled, Brianna asked, "Pray tell, how did you get to be in such a pitiful state Zendaya?"

"When I left you, I went in the direction I thought was for London. Upon the way I was set upon by men who were bounty hunters. Ngod has put a bounty on the heads of any surviving slaves who did not automatically return to him. There were three of them, but somehow luck was with me and I felled them all. Amara here had already been caught by them and was tied and bound to a wagon. I did what I could, so I bound them and freed her, and then we ran.

"We ran and hid for many months but we needed somewhere to live and so I joined some travelers who put on shows. They put me to fighting when they realized my strength, if I won the fight I was paid, if I lost I was punished. I soon became a constant winner. Unfortunately, news of me spread and Mr. Ngod came for us.

"We've been running ever since. Then I remembered the cave and knew it would be a good place to hide. We have been there a long time, but now the baby comes and I must provide something better. I have been watching you for a while before I gathered the courage to come and seek help from you."

"Of course we will help you, won't we Arwen?" Brianna placed a hand on Arwen's arm, he laid his hand over it.

"Yes of course. Even as you have been telling us what happened to you my mind has been building a plan. There is an almost derelict cottage on the edge of my land. The roof has partially collapsed and needs new thatch and the building only has two rooms. The walls will need new dabbing and the floor replacing, but we can work on these things. I will have to pay for a thatcher but the rest we can do ourselves. In exchange for your home I would like you to work on the farm with me. I cannot pay until the next spring fair when I will sell my old sheep, but you will be welcome to join us at our table every day. What say you?"

"You will teach me to farm?"

"I will. I have many ideas for expansion but my dreams are too large for one man, together we could make them work. Will you accept?"

Zendaya looked at Amara and quickly explained all that had been said, as her English was still limited. She had spoken to him in Swahili and when she finished she turned and nodded and smiled her thanks. It was understood by all that they accepted.

A new family had arrived in Trapp.

As new family arrived at the Evans farm, old family arrived at the Beavin farm.

"Tad?"

It took a moment to register that someone had arrived in the yard outside the house.

"Tad?"

It sounded like… but no, it couldn't be!

"Tad, are you here?"

"O my Lord!" cried Dafydd and went charging as fast as his wobbly legs would take him to open the door.

He rushed outside. "Beca, O my Beca!"

She flew into his arms, his eyes too blurry to take in her thin appearance.

"O Beca, my buttercup, my buttercup!" He wept tears of joy and she did the same.

"It's been too long," he said when he eventually pushed her off him so he could look at her properly. "But I don't mind that, 'tis glad I am to see you one last time before I die. O 'tis mighty glad I am!"

"Now Tad, don't be speaking like that!"

"Tis only the truth, but you are right. Now is a time to celebrate not lament. Let me greet my grandchildren."

Beca introduced the children from eldest to youngest and then let Dafydd's gaze eventually fall upon the man who had taken his daughter so far away.

Aled was never well-built, but now he appeared so thin as to make Dafydd suck in his breath. He kept his thoughts in his head however, as he shook hands with his son-in-law.

"Welcome home," he said, hoping to impart the sincere truth of his words by the warmth of his tone and the shake of his hand.

That they had come on foot and had hardly a bag between them spoke volumes to their situation and Dafydd's heart cracked for sorrow. "Come, come inside. Are you hungry? I've plenty."

The children all piped up that 'yes, they were hungry' and Dafydd ushered them all inside.

When they had finished eating and the children had fallen asleep from exhaustion in front of the fireplace, Dafydd turned to Aled. "Tell me son."

Aled took a deep breath and then poured out what had happened to them over the last year. First, Aled had lost his job when the plague closed most of London and the tavern he worked for closed. They had spent a time getting by, by standing in line at the food wagons and just getting enough to live on. When Dafydd's missive had arrived they went to the tailor's shop, for they knew he was a learned man, and asked him to read it to them. They'd wanted to come immediately, but with the plague getting passage out of London was too hard and cost money they didn't have. And then, like a miracle, the Jewish tailor offered a ride out under his bales of cloth. The guard at the tollgate was his grandson no less, and he had waved them through after pretending to search the cart.

"We had only been out of London for one day when we got news that the city was on fire!" Beca burst in.

"When we reached a high point, we turned and could see behind us a red flickering light reaching into the sky. A family, who overtook us with their horse and cart, stopped a moment and told us that a fire had broken out in Pudding Lane and the city was all in flames," said Aled.

"Pudding Lane Tad, that was but one street over from ours. Just imagine, if your letter hadn't come, and us so urgent to return to you, then we would have been there as the flames jumped from house to house!"

Dafydd made the sign of the cross over his face. "Blessed be the Lord."

"Amen," said both Aled and Beca together with much emphasis.

The next day, washed, fed and having slept well for the first time in a year, the newly arrived Beavin family accompanied Dafydd over to the Evans farm.

Dafydd threw his arms around Brianna as soon as he saw her. "Bless you child," he said wiping away a stray tear.

"Whatever for?" asked Brianna, "And who have we here, Dafydd don't tell me this is your family?"

"It is, it is," he declared with breathless enthusiasm. "Come all the way from London on foot, and all due to your missive!"

Greetings were exchanged and then Arwen and Brianna ushered everyone inside.

They spent the next few hours exchanging tales and putting together a meal with much merriment. The children at first were a little in awe of the two tall people from Africa, but when Zendaya showed them how to make reed whistles they soon forgot their shyness.

"It seems it was good we did not make it to London," said Zendaya.

"Indeed," agreed everyone.

Amara said something to Zendaya in Swahili and then waited for him to translate. "My wife says that God must not like the people of London very much." He looked a little uncomfortable at the comment, not wanting to offend anyone.

"I think you are right," Brianna said to Amara.   Zendaya translated.

"It is that flippant king with his immoral ways," said Arwen.

"I don't think," said Dafydd, "that if these things were the punishment of God, and I am not saying they are, but if they were... then I should think it is not the sin of one man that has brought these things about, but the sin of every one of us who falls short of His Glory.   For who is to say the king's sin is any greater than ours?   And talking of sin, gluttony is calling, for I would surely like a second piece of that heavenly gooseberry pie please Brianna."

Chapter 29

March, in the year of our Lord 1667

THE CHAPEL BELL RANG its dulcet tones heralding bad news. Arwen dropped his fork and ran to the chicken coop, where Brianna was mucking out.

She wiped her brow when she spotted him racing across the yard, when she deciphered his worried expression she dropped her bucket and came out to meet him.

"What can it mean?" she asked.

"Bar Sundays and weddings, the only other time it rings is to announce someone has left us."

"Left us?"

"Passed on."

"O…"

"I won't bother hitching up the cart if you don't mind; we'll ride old Nellie together."

"That's fine, just let me rinse my face."

A few minutes later, Brianna sat behind Arwen and wrapped her arms tightly about his waist.

They didn't make it to the village, for half the village was already upon the road and heading towards Dafydd's farm. Arwen couldn't see her face pale but he felt her body stiffen, holding the reins in his right hand, he used his left to grasp her hand.

The farmyard was full of people going in and out of the farmhouse. Solemn faces nodded at their friends and family and people spoke with low voices. Slipping off the horse, Brianna's legs nearly gave way beneath her. She wobbled and placed a hand upon Arwen's leg.

He jumped down beside her and flung the reins over the fence, before wrapping his arm around her shoulder. Together they entered the house where the windows had been covered over and the light around flowed from a few candle-lanterns. Her eyes searched for Dafydd but not finding him, her eyes fell upon his daughter. Beca's face displayed her sorrow, and blotches of red revealed she had been crying hard.

"Brianna!" she called when she spotted the new arrivals. She rushed to her and threw her arms around her. "O child of God, how blessed I am that you came into my father's life." She sobbed and would not let go.

"Is he… is he…"

Over Beca's shaking head her eyes caught the stare of Aled. "Peacefully, in his sleep last night."

"O…" a wail for forming, like a wave, building and building until the pressure was so great. Brianna began to shake, her head wobbling as if it might fall off.

"Beca… if you will?" Arwen gently pried Beca off Brianna and pulled his wife onto his chest. He wrapped his arms around her body, engulfing her in his love. She wailed into his chest, and he tenderly maneuvered her through the house and into the yard. She was unaware that they were moving; lost in her sorrow she drowned in the dark. He led her to the stone bench near the apple orchard. He sat down and pulled her onto his knee as if she were no more than a child. She kept her head on his chest and sobbed her grief upon him.

Silently, and without Brianna's notice, Agatha did sit on the bench next to them and waited for Brianna's grief to subside.

Eventually, when her sobs were no more than shuddering breaths, Agatha placed a hand on Brianna's shoulder. "Arwen, would you mind leaving us for a short time?"

"I think I should stay," he said, tightening his arms around his beloved wife.

"It's alright Arwen, I will be fine. Go and pay your respects, I shall join you presently."

"Are you sure?"

"Yes, indeed." Brianna slipped off his knee so he could stand. When she sat down again, Agatha grabbed both her hands within her own.

"Your grief is great because your acquaintance with Dafydd was short, a mere two years. You didn't have time to tell him everything you wanted, and to share all the events you wanted to share with him. You feel deprived."

Brianna couldn't answer for that is exactly how she felt. *Life isn't fair*, she thought, but couldn't bring herself to say it aloud.

Agatha placed a hand over Brianna's stomach, which now slightly showed a curved bump.

"This is our cycle, our eternal giving and taking, our beginning and our ending, to live, to grow in love and to die. If you could look at life from beginning to end in one image, you would see clearly the only thing that matters are the connections we make and the love we share. There is no life without love and no purpose to living without connections.

"Chin up my sweet-pea, Dafydd was delighted to connect with you in the last part of his life. You became one last connection that would mean the world to him. He loved you as a daughter, and this I know for he told me oft. You brightened his last days and restored the joy of living within him."

She wanted to respond, she really did, but the lump in her throat was too painful.

"You have had far too few connections to absorb this loss in grace and celebration of his life. Worry not though, for your spiritual links are growing every day. You will be fine; we are standing beside you now."

At last she could speak, "Thank you, from the bottom of my heart, thank you." She stood and brushed down her skirts, an action not needed but used to take a moment for control of her emotions.

"We are not designed by God to live apart from one another. Have you noticed how one ember from the fire once removed from the rest burns out? That is us, child. We are made for fellowship, both with God and with man. I don't pretend to understand why God should have set you and your mother apart like He did, but I trust His reasons. But what I do understand is your nomadic days are over, you are home at last."

Agatha embraced Brianna and then left in a flurry to help the grieving household in offering refreshments to everyone.

Brianna placed both her hands on her stomach and thanked God that the child growing inside her would be raised by a very large family. Her eyes caught Arwen's whose face was questioning. In response she smiled and walked towards him. It was time to say her farewells to a man she thanked God she had met and loved.

There was no doubt that she had lost much in her life so far, not least her extraordinary miraculous faith. But as clear as day she now saw how much she had been given. Agatha was right, she would say goodbye to Dafydd with joy in her heart, for not only had she received Dafydd's love but she would meet him again one day in Heaven, of that she was sure.

Two days later, at Dafydd's funeral, his coffin was carried with tears. The vicar spoke of him with great fondness, and nearly choked on the blessing, but managed it just. "The Lord bless you and watch over you. The Lord make His face shine upon you, and be gracious to you." After the ending "Amens" the people threw dirt in the grave, hugged one another and then made their way to the Cennen-on-the-Brook Tavern. Dafydd's expressed wishes being that once the dirt had been scattered no one was to cry, they were instead to partake in much ale and dancing, where he had promised to show up and join in!

The farmers and village folk recalled every tiny aspect of his life, and discussed it with much laughing and joke telling. He was well-known and much-loved and would be dearly missed. Everyone celebrated his life as they bid farewell in their own way to one of the cornerstones of Trapp.

September, in the year of our Lord 1667

The crooked lane meandered through fields and small copses, and with gentle slope did lead Brianna down to what had become her favorite spot in all the world – the pond in the valley where the Nightjars sang.

The sun was only just creeping up over the tor and its flickering light danced upon the vale like dancing fireflies. The dew of Heaven's blessing dripped droplets of moisture onto rich green leaves. Petals opened to embrace the gift of light, and grasshoppers chirruped amongst the tall grasses. Into this beautiful piece of Eden arose to flight a myriad of Nightjars. Their wings caused a whoosh as they rose and flew away, embarking upon their long journey.

She had been just in time to bid them farewell. "Don't stay away too long," she called as she watched them fade from sight.

After dropping her blanket over the bench that Arwen had made for her, Brianna sat down and prayed. Her heart overflowed. When she reached 'amen' she burst into song to continue her praise. So lost was she in her adoration that she was unaware that Arwen had approached and was standing not far away.

Her ballad so sweet and fair did charm the birds from the trees to come to the grass and hop around her feet, as she reclined with stately grace. Her hallelujahs rose and fell with strings that pulled upon his heart and called him to tears, though he knew not why.

And in her arms their newborn gurgled merrily as if joining in. Brianna gently brushed her thumb over the babe's cheeks and smiled down upon the angelic little face of Esther, their gift from God.

Chapter 30

ONCE UPON A TIME, there lived a woman who understood the Word of God. Believed in it so much in fact, that she could say to a mountain 'move' and it would be so. Yet there came a day when she saw her faith as keeping her from being normal. So in her endeavor to fit in she cast her faith aside, needing to be acceptable to man and desiring to live in comfort.

The seed of faith held within Brianna's heart was half-empty. It left her with a continued yearning to be complete, the absence of completion – a constant reminder of the distance between herself and God.

The seed of faith held within Brianna's heart was half-full. It flooded her with peace and contented joy. Gratitude for God's mercy and graciousness sometimes overwhelmed her, driving her to her knees in prayer as tears rolled unchecked down her cheeks.

October, in the year of our Lord 1679

As she stood on the porch steps of their homestead, and watched her children and husband gather in the last of autumn's crops, her spirit sang with indescribable joy. For God is good... all the time.

She had learned to accept the new her, where the *'eternal-dilemma of choice'* had taken precedence in her life. Now, instead of 'doing' she was found on her knees 'asking.' No longer could she command a broken bone to heal, or a disease to leave, for now her mind was in two halves. One side understood who she was in Christ and therefore the power that creates worlds was at her fingertips. Yet the other side, in equal measure, focused on her failings, her unworthiness to be a daughter of the King of Creation. That split mind was what prevented her from going down a different path, a different calling. Instead, she had settled on a road of debate, a way that kept her from the full promises that Jesus had given to His disciples, and from comprehending the extraordinary truth – that God had made man in His image, put His Holy Spirit within them and waits upon them reflecting His Glory. But… her heart still sang with joy, for she knew she loved Jesus and that He loved her. That He not only forgave her shortcomings but remembered them no more.

Brianna had chosen the path that millions would follow. A safe place of worshipping God and being pleasing in His sight, yet never quite reaching full knowledge that would bring Jesus a little closer to non-believers.

For that is what miracles are all about. Not to bring comfort to a few, but to bring salvation to many.

This woman of diminished faith, her husband and their children had become beacons of light in a darkened world. People traveled from far and wide to visit their humble home, partake of bread, and listen to their faith-filled teachings of God's Holy Bible. For the family didn't believe the Word had been given as stories and fables, but as daily instructions on how to live their lives, then and always. Sharing their faith became their life's mission. And God used what they had, and blessed their measure of faith. They prayed that God would guide their steps, put order among their thoughts, be instrumental with every decision they made, bless the works of their hands and keep them far from evil. Because they started the dawning of each new day with these prayers, they lived their lives in abundant joy and peace, for they knew the Lord their God was in control.

Earlier on that year, Benedict Everleigh had brought his wife and children to visit. He shared with them how the Lord was using his tavern turned coaching house to bless many a traveler and how they poured their profits into helping the poor – especially widows. Brianna had basked in the love that radiated from the once witch hunter, and marveled that miracles took all shapes.

Every now and then, Brianna would catch sight of a white wolf standing on the tor of Cennen Castle, watching over them and all the valleys. She knew He vigilantly guarded over everything they did… and ensured they lived… happily ever after.

Thank you for reading.

If you enjoyed Brianna's story could I please encourage you to leave me a review? Without reviews a book never succeeds, and I would really appreciate your endorsement and support. Many thanks.

If you would like to receive updates by receiving my email newsletter, please sign up at https://sendfox.com/tntraynor

In my newsletter will be updates about my books, book competitions, a book review from me and eBooks that are on offer or free by other authors. The newsletter is only quarterly, so only 4 a year ☺ no spam or sharing of details.

COURAGE

Courage is the ability to do something that frightens you
– bravery, to have strength in the face of pain or grief.

Here are the conclusions to the books in this series.

GRACE

Grace had to find the courage to carry on, even when she'd lost
everyone dear to her. One day she picked up the courage to
embark on a new life. Little did she know that God was waiting
for her in Mombasa. Giving herself the mission of helping the
people of Kenya as much as she could, gave God an opening to
come back into her life and reclaim his 'lost' daughter. What
she would never know is that, Mr. and Mrs. Reynolds (the
people who employed her as a governess) prayed for Grace
every Sunday, without fail, up until when they died from old
age. Those faithful prayers, combined with the years of daily
praying by her father, had surrounded her with a strong tower.

FAITH

Disgraced and shamed, Faith thought life was nothing but
hardship and sorrow. She had a disability and started life with a
spirit of rejection, for the world was cruel to those who weren't
normal. One day she summoned the courage to fight for her
happiness, and she embarked on a journey that was nearly
disastrous. What she didn't know at that time was that her
mother (a new convert) had been on her knees daily for her
daughter. On the power of prayer, angels had been sent from
Heaven to keep her safe when she got lost and wandered off the
path in the storm. Also, hidden in the background was
Margaret, (the mother of Harrison, the cad who had 'ruined'
her). From the moment she found out what her son had done,

275

she had lifted Faith up to God in continued prayers, for mother and child's safety and for the forgiveness of her son's actions.

CHARITY

Leaving one life, to start another, takes enormous courage. Charity had been stumbling through life unsure of her purpose. One day she takes courage in her hands and asks her husband for a divorce. Leaving financial security and comforts, and respectability, takes every ounce of her courage. Her Nan had prayed before sleep every night of Charity's life, beseeching the Lord to bless and keep Charity safe, and to surround her with love. Those prayers were eventually answered when Charity digs deep and pulls up the courage to face change.

HOPE

The courage to carry on living, when everything is so hard, is probably the most difficult courage to find. But Hope found it, buried deep within her. She decided to live and to forgive, but more, she took strength from rising every morning and being grateful for another day. Something she never thought she would do. She also took the risk of loving again, and said yes when Ted asked her to marry him. It took every bit of courage she could muster to take that risk. From the first day that John had met her, he had prayed for Hope to be happy. United with Charlotte in Heaven, the two of them continued to surround Hope with prayers of blessing and peace. They were answered, and Hope and Ted added three more souls to the world. Hope sought out her mother and attempted reconciliation. Unfortunately, some people never soften, even in old age, but Hope was joyously reunited with her sister Sally, who came to live in the happy home of Hope and Ted until she married at the ripe old age of thirty.

BRIANNA

O Lord! The courage this woman needed was tremendous. When she rejected God, she instantly knew she had made a mistake, but it was too late. She was removed from the path she had been on, and placed on another. She thought she needed courage to hide from the witch hunters, but that stark fear was nothing compared to the loss she felt after her tussle with God. She needed courage to face her fear, and courage to take on the Black Wolf. She needed courage to trust Arwen again, and courage to change the course of her life. She needed courage to live what everyone perceives a 'normal' life, for her heart had once had a calling that was now lost. What she would need in the years to come would be the courage to allow her children to grow and take their own path.

COURAGE

Courage comes in all shapes and sizes, but I believe great courage is found through prayer. God sees us, hears us and His gifts of peace and hope encourage us.

Author Information

If you'd like to know more about my books please check out my web.

http://www.tntraynor.uk

You can also find me on Facebook.

https://www.facebook.com/groups/292316321513651

Or Twitter: @tracy_traynor

If you enjoyed this book you might also enjoy one of my other books:

Women of Courage Series

https://www.amazon.com/Women-Courage-4-Book/dp/B091TTXQ6V

MULTI AWARD WINNING SERIES
WOMEN OF COURAGE

| Inspired by the life of Moira Smith 1912 - 1985 | Inspired by the Welsh Revival 1904 - 1905 | A 2020 Love Story | A story of hope 1958 |

Standalone Stories with a theme of courage and love

Young Adult Fantasy, Born to Be, series

https://www.amazon.com/dp/B01C1UDQKC

AMAZON FANTASY #1 BESTSELLER
BORN TO BE

BOOK 4 COMING SOON!

Glossary

All Bible Passages taken from the King James Version

1)   Psalm 23:4

2)   Hebrews 13:5

3)   John 14:8-9

4)   John 14:10-11

5)   Ephesians 6:10-20

6)   Acts: 6:32-34

7)   John 8:7

8)   Matthew 5:39

9)   Job 42:15

10)   I John 4:4

11)   I John 1:9

12)   I Corinthians 2:11

13)   Exodus 20:13

14)   John 3:16

15)   Matthew 5:11

16)   Matthew 12:25

Printed in Great Britain
by Amazon

25645281R00158